Melody squirmed with humiliation every time she remembered Jason's laughter.

The big dope! He could have refused to believe she was Cheyenne's sexy new deejay without laughing in her face. She stalked over to study herself in the mirror.

Her figure was all right, but it sure wasn't voluptuous. Her jeans were more comfortable looking than sexy. Her sweater looked neat, but, well, on the prim side. The only thing even vaguely eye-catching about her appearance was the acid-green color of her socks, and she wore those for warmth, not to make a fashion statement.

Dammit, she looked exactly like what she was—a short, skinny, dark-haired, quiet schoolteacher who wore glasses. But inside her short, unspectacular body was a tall buxom redhead screaming to get out! In her heart and mind, she felt like one hell of a warm, loving, sexy woman. Why couldn't anyone else see that in her? Why couldn't Jason?

Dear Reader,

Each and every month, to meet your sophisticated standards, to satisfy your taste for substantial, memorable, emotion-packed stories of life and love, of dreams and possibilities, Silhouette brings you six extremely **Special Editions**.

Now these exclusive editions are wearing a brand-new wrapper, a more sophisticated look—our way of marking Silhouette **Special Edition**'s continually renewed commitment to bring you the very best, the brightest and the most up-to-date in romance writing.

Reach for all six freshly packaged Silhouette **Special Editions** each month—the insides are every bit as delicious as the outsides—and savor a bounty of meaty, soul-satisfying romantic novels by authors who are already your favorites and those who are about to become so.

And don't forget the two Silhouette *Classics* at your bookseller's every month—the most beloved Silhouette **Special Editions** and Silhouette *Intimate Moments* of yesteryear, reissued by popular demand.

Today's bestsellers, tomorrow's *Classics*—that's Silhouette **Special Edition**. And now, we're looking more special than ever!

From all the authors and editors of Silhouette **Special Edition**,

Warmest wishes,

Leslie Kazanjian
Senior Editor

MYRNA TEMTE

Wendy Wyoming

Silhouette Special Edition
Published by Silhouette Books New York
America's Publisher of Contemporary Romance

To Tom, my husband and very best friend,
who has brought more joy into my life
than I ever dreamed possible.

My special thanks to my brother-in-law, John Temte, and his friend Lisa, who spent an evening reacquainting me with Cheyenne's night life;

And to Kathie Gier of station KEZJ in Twin Falls, Idaho, for her information about the radio business;

And to Richard Boswell, D.V.M., at the Green Acres Pet Complex in Twin Falls, for answering my many questions about equine diseases.

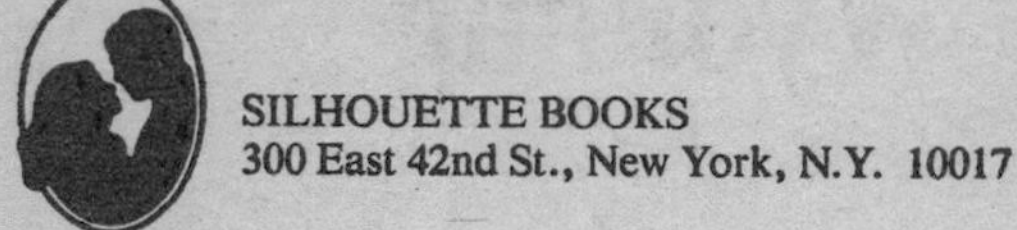

SILHOUETTE BOOKS
300 East 42nd St., New York, N.Y. 10017

ISBN: 0-373-09483-3

First Silhouette Books printing October 1988

Printed in the U.S.A.

MYRNA TEMTE

grew up in Montana and attended college in Wyoming, where she met and married her husband, and, coincidentally, where her first Silhouette novel is set. Marriage didn't necessarily mean settling down for the Temtes—they have lived in six different states, including Washington, where they currently reside. Moving so much is difficult, the author says, but it is also wonderful stimulation for a writer.

Though always a "readaholic," Ms. Temte never dreamed of becoming an author. But while spending time at home to care for her first child, she began to seek an outlet from the never-ending duties of housekeeping and child rearing. She started reading romances and soon became hooked, both as a reader and writer.

Now Myrna Temte appreciates the best of all possible worlds—a loving family and a challenging career that lets her set her own hours and turn her imagination loose.

The *Wyoming Star* challenges area readers to guess:
WHO *IS* KBOY'S WENDY WYOMING?

Wendy Wyoming is the sweetest little gal west of the Mississippi. Only a blonde could sound that good, so I say she's gotta be Suzy Jackson, the weather lady on Channel 4. If I'm right, tell her there's a lonely old bachelor who's

Pining in Pine Bluffs

Wendy Wyoming is really Tilly the Tassel Tosser down at Al's Green Door. Of course, I'd never visit a place like that myself because my wife would kill me, and I'm

Bashful in Buffalo Ridge

I can't believe a decent newspaper like the *Wyoming Star* could stoop so low! The Wendy Wyoming show is scandalous if not downright pornographic, and you are supporting it with this ridiculous contest. The only reason I'd want to know who she is, is to see that she's run out of town!

Burning Mad in Burns

I think Dr. Mary Shelton in the psych department over at the community college is Wendy Wyoming. She's warm and funny, and you can tell her anything and she understands how you feel—just like Wendy. She makes me glad to be a woman.

Admiring Alice

I know who Wendy Wyoming is, but I don't want to say because she might get in trouble, and I like her a lot. When *you* find out who she is, would you ask her if she'd go out with a ninth grader?

Curious at Carey Jr. High

Chapter One

"Hey, all you cowpokes out there! It's time to kick off your boots and spurs, snuggle up by the fire with your favorite lady and get ready for an evening of sweet country music here on Cheyenne's most popular FM station, KBOY."

Jason Wakefield stared at the radio, his attention captured by the sound of a voice he'd never heard before.

"I'm Wendy Wyoming, filling in for Greg Parker, who got snowed in over at the University of Wyoming in Laramie tonight."

Wendy Wyoming? Who the heck was Wendy Wyoming? Jason wondered, turning his attention back to the pot of canned chili he was heating up for his supper.

"The storm—or should I say blizzard—is expected to last through the night." Her voice dropped to a low, husky, almost purring pitch that sent a shiver of awareness up Jason's spine. "Brrr! I can almost hear that wind howling from right here in the control booth. I hope you're not all alone tonight. But if you are alone, pardner, remember that doesn't mean you have to be lonely. Stay tuned and let Wendy Wyoming keep you company."

Jason wiped his forehead with the back of his hand. That voice! That incredibly sexy voice! When she'd breathed out "pardner" like that and said being alone didn't mean you had to be lonely, he'd felt as though she were talking directly to him. He'd been trying to convince himself of that same message only an hour ago.

"Now, since we're all stuck inside for a while, we might as well get comfortable and enjoy it," the new deejay continued. "Why don't you make some popcorn, dig out that good book you bought three months ago and haven't had time to read or get some paper and a pen and write to that old friend you forgot to send a Christmas card to this year, and I'll play an old romantic tune from Kenny Rogers to...get us in the mood."

Jason grinned at Wendy's advice. She made it sound so cozy, popcorn sales were bound to go up, and there were probably people digging through bookcases and looking for stationery all over town. He looked down at the pot of chili and sighed. It would sure taste a lot better if he had someone like Wendy here to eat it with him. They'd talk and laugh, maybe play cards or Scrabble, and then...

He shut his eyes, imagining her reclining on a king-size bed. She'd have to have a luscious body to go with that voice, so he envisioned her full, gorgeous breasts peeping through a black negligee and her long, glorious legs stretched out in invitation. And she'd have long, shining red hair that fanned out across the pillows—

An acrid smell rose from the pot, yanking Jason back to the reality of his kitchen. Shoving the pan aside, he glared at the scorched mess and wondered what had happened to the spoon. He poured the chili into a bowl, cursing when the lost spoon plopped out of the pan, splattering both him and the counter with beans and sauce.

Something like this always happened to him whenever he tried to cook for himself at his apartment in town! Carolyn Peters, his foreman's wife, usually cooked for him out at the ranch, and he got spoiled. Well, he'd better get used to it. He'd be stuck in Cheyenne for at least a couple of months after the legislative session started on Monday morning.

He finished wiping up the mess just as Kenny Rogers stopped singing. Jason held his breath, then sighed when Wendy's sultry voice washed over him again like warm, dark honey.

"Wasn't that just about the best make-out music you've heard lately? Whew! I wish I had a big old handsome cowboy here to keep me company tonight. Maybe a blond one. Yup, I'm definitely in the mood for a blond. Of course, he'd have to be a gentleman, and he'd have to love me for my mind and all that... But for now let's keep the music playing. Now, ladies, wait'll you hear what I've got coming up for you next. Listen to Alabama's latest release and see if it won't... warm you up."

Chuckling admiringly, Jason ran his fingers through his own blond hair and wished he could oblige the little lady. But it wasn't what Wendy said, it was more the way she said it that was getting to him. He suspected she was getting to every other male between the ages of ten and ninety-five in the listening audience, as well. He wouldn't mind meeting Wendy Wyoming.

She sounded sexy as all get-out. That alone was enough to get his attention, but there was something else in her voice that attracted him, as well. Warmth, sincerity, empathy—he wasn't sure what to call it, exactly. But she sounded as if she were the kind of woman who really could keep a man company on a cold winter's night, who would give a man a hot supper and a backrub after a hard day's work, who would listen to his hopes and dreams and have dreams of her own to share.

Maybe he'd give his old buddy David Hunter a call. David managed KBOY for his father's company, Hunter Communications. David could introduce him to Wendy. But would he do it without hassling him? Jason shook his head. Nope. Ever since David had announced his engagement two months ago he'd been driving Jason berserk, trying to play matchmaker.

But there was sombody else who was sure to know Wendy—David's litle sister, Melody. Jason grinned at the thought of Mel. She was a sweet little gal. Before he and David had gone to college, she'd been like a little sister to him. They weren't all that close now, but they were still good enough friends that he figured she'd tell him what he wanted to know. He grabbed the phone and dialed her number. After six rings, he gave up and sat down to eat his chili.

Mel was probably out on a date or over at her parents' house. If he didn't reach her on the phone tonight, he'd pay her a little visit tomorrow after the snowplows had cleared the streets. In the meantime, he'd spend the evening with a good book, a fire in the fireplace . . . and Wendy Wyoming.

"All right! I'm coming!" Melody Hunter hollered at whoever was beating down her door at the ungodly hour of . . . She squinted at the clock, yawning while her eyes focused enough for her to see that both hands were pointing straight up. Good grief, she never slept until noon!

As she grabbed her glasses from the nightstand, the hammering started again. She threw back the blankets, poked her feet into a pair of slippers and pulled on a warm peach-colored bathrobe before hurrying to the front door, muttering, "I'm coming, I'm coming!" After running a hand through her sleep-tousled curls, she yanked open the door and shivered when a blast of arctic air hit her.

A deep voice boomed from somewhere in the stratosphere. "Hi, Squirt! Where were you last night?"

Melody tipped her head back to an uncomfortable but all-too-familiar angle and felt her heart break into an all-too-familiar tap dance at the sight of Jason Wakefield's smiling hazel eyes. They looked more brown than green this morning, probably because he was wearing a dark brown suede jacket and his favorite beige Stetson, she thought absently. When another shiver racked her body, Melody stepped back.

"Come on in, Jason, before I freeze to death."

She studied him as he entered, wondering what had prompted this unexpected visit. Then, looking down at herself, she grimaced. Jason Wakefield was just a friend, but she'd rather have greeted him wearing something a little more dignified than her robe and her pink bunny slippers! Ah, well, it was nice to see him under any circumstances, and she'd come a long way in learning to handle her old crush on him.

The accelerated heartbeat whenever she first saw him didn't count. After all, who could resist his tall, hard-muscled body, his heart-stopping smile framed by a neatly clipped mustache, his gorgeous, intelligent eyes or his thick, shaggy hair which practically begged for a little attention? No woman in Cheyenne—probably no woman in the whole state of Wyoming—could look at Jason Wakefield and not feel a throb or two.

"Got any coffee, Mel?"

Stifling another yawn, Melody shook her head. "Not yet. You woke me up."

Chuckling at her admission, Jason reached out and gently ruffled her already tangled curls. "What? Little Mary Sunshine? The disgustingly chipper morning person slept this late?"

Melody grinned at his teasing reminder of the days when Jason had boarded with the Hunter family because his father's ranch had been too far from town for him to live at home and participate in after-school athletics. He'd become an extra big brother to Melody, fair game for her gleeful enjoyment of being the only person in the entire household who woke up with a smile.

"Give me your coat, and I'll start the coffee," she offered.

Jason handed her his hat, unbuttoned his coat and shrugged it off while Melody watched, fascinated in spite of herself by the play of muscles across his massive chest and shoulders. Years of football and basketball practice and the hard physical labor of working a ranch had kept him extremely fit. His forest-green sweater, tucked into a brand-new pair of jeans, immediately brought out the green tones in his eyes. She didn't realize she was staring until he snapped his fingers in front of her face.

"Mel? Are you in there? I think I'd better make the coffee."

His last statement spurred her to action. Heading for the kitchen, she replied, "No thanks, Jason. I want to wake up, not go into orbit."

"My coffee's not that bad!"

"Not if you want to grow hair on your chest."

Jason chuckled at her remark, and Melody smiled as she switched on the coffee maker. "Have a chair, Jason. I'll get dressed while this is brewing and be right back. Help yourself when it's ready."

"Thanks."

She returned a few minutes later, feeling more confident dressed in jeans and a sweater and with her teeth brushed, her hair combed and a touch of makeup on her face. Jason was seated at her kitchen table, flipping through a *Newsweek* she'd left on the sofa. When she headed for the coffee maker he abandoned the magazine, turned his chair around and straddled it. Stretching his long legs out in front of him, he folded his arms across the back of the chair.

"So what were you up to last night?" he asked. "I tried calling a couple of times, but you weren't home."

Melody shrugged. "Nothing exciting. I was over at one of the stations doing some work for David and got snowed in. He brought me home on the snowmobile about five o'clock this morning."

"Which station?"

Melody glanced over her shoulder at Jason, then filled two stoneware mugs with coffee because he hadn't helped himself. "KBOY."

"Hey, that's great!" Jason left the chair and walked over, leaning one hip against the counter.

Frowning slightly, Melody asked, "What's so great about it?"

Jason sidled closer and bent down, looking deep into her puzzled brown eyes. He put on his most charming smile, the one guaranteed to turn a woman's will to mush, and said, "I was listening to KBOY last night. I want to meet Wendy Wyoming, Mel."

Melody blinked, gulped and slowly shook her head. Then, hiding a smile, she said, "I can't let you, Jason."

His eyebrows shot up in surprise. He straightened away from the counter, ran one hand through his hair and folded his arms across his chest. Melody thought he looked like an affronted Goliath, glowering down at her mere five-foot-two frame from his lofty six-foot-five height.

"Why not?" he demanded.

Sighing, Melody turned back to the coffeemaker. "Last night half the disc jockeys had the flu and a couple of others were snowed out of town. Mike Harrison's wife went into labor, and David had already promised Steve Harmon the night off to go to his daughter's wedding. Wendy Wyoming only did the show as a favor to the family. David promised to keep her identity a secret."

"And I'm not part of the family?" Jason asked stiffly.

Melody looked back at him, startled at the determination she saw in the green depths of his eyes. What in the world was going on here? Jason wouldn't get seriously hung up on any woman, certainly not on an airhead like Wendy Wyoming!

"I didn't mean it that way, Jason!"

His expression softened. A wry smile spread across his lips as he relaxed back against the counter. Brushing the backs of his knuckles across her cheek, he said, "I know you didn't, Mel. You wouldn't hurt Attila the Hun if you could help it."

He moved closer to her then, wrapping his long arm around her waist and pulling her close against his side for a friendly hug, coaxing. "Aw, come on, Squirt! Tell me where I can find Wendy Wyoming."

She smiled up at him, though inwardly she wanted to choke him. His nearness and his joking flirtation were stirring up all kinds of emotions in her, emotions she'd learned were damnably futile. Of course, she couldn't really blame Jason for what he was doing to her.

He didn't know his casual touch burned through her clothing, igniting her skin with excitement. He'd have been shocked to find out that the woodsy scent of his after-shave made her long to turn into his arms and nuzzle against his muscular chest. He'd have been appalled if he'd known that his sexy smile and deep voice made her want to tear off his clothes, throw him down on her kitchen floor and have her way with him.

She shook her head at him, and his smile became positively wicked. "Besides, Melody, *you* didn't promise to keep her identity a secret. *David* did."

Chuckling, Melody handed one of the steaming mugs to Jason, then led the way to the table and seated herself. When he joined her and proceeded to dump three spoonfuls of sugar into his cup, she shuddered.

"Yuck! How can you do that to good coffee?"

"Don't change the subject."

"I can't tell you, Jason."

"You mean you won't."

Melody rolled her eyes at the ceiling. He was understandably curious, and a curious Jason Wakefield was a relentless Jason Wakefield. He was so used to getting whatever he wanted, he would tease her and coax her and drive her bananas because he thought his charm was irresistible to women. Unfortunately for Jason, she could and would resist him!

Looking over at his handsome though somewhat craggy features, and the knowing, confident look in his eyes, she groaned silently. He was so darn appealing, it wasn't going to be easy. Keeping her tone light, she said, "You're right. I won't tell you."

"Why not? You know you can trust me," he coaxed, leaning closer until her field of vision was limited to his face—the face that had starred in some of her most erotic adolescent fantasies. Her ears tingled at the husky caress in his deep voice when he said, "I'd tell you, Melody."

Melody grumbled, "You just want to meet her so you can hit on her."

His grin spread from one ear to the other as he admitted unrepentantly, "Yup."

She couldn't help laughing. "You big dope! For all you know, Wendy Wyoming is five-foot-four, weighs three hundred pounds and eats garlic sandwiches!"

"No way! She's gorgeous. I can tell."

"Jason, trust me. She's not your type at all."

"How do you know what my type is?"

"Judging from your track record," Melody shot him an exasperated glare as she ticked off the attributes on her fingers, "your type is between five-eight and five-ten, she has enough red hair to start her own wig factory, she has, uh, a generous bosom and an IQ somewhere between that of a good horse and a turnip."

How do I know? she continued silently, still glaring at him. *I know, Jason old pal, because your type of woman is everything I'm not and never will be!*

Jason had the grace to flush slightly, but his grin remained devilish. "What's wrong with that?"

Melody held out her hands, palms up, in a plea for understanding. "Jason, Wendy Wyoming isn't anything like that. She's not beautiful, and she's not really what you'd call sexy."

"I still want to meet her," he insisted.

"Okay, Jason. I'll give you a little hint."

He groaned and covered his face with his hands. "Not one of your hints! I never guess your dumb hints!"

"It's a hint or nothing, Wakefield."

Spreading his fingers, he peeked out, then groaned at the mulish set to her chin, the smug grin on her face. "Okay, give me the hint."

"You already know her."

His big hands crashed to the table. Leaning forward, he gave her a long, suspicious look. "I do?"

Melody laughed at his expression. "Yup. You've known her quite a while, Jason."

"Oh, Lord," he muttered. "And that's all you're gonna tell me?"

"Yup."

"Darn you, Melody! You're driving me nuts just for the hell of it, but you don't understand how important Wendy Wyoming is to me."

Melody's brow wrinkled in confusion. Jason really sounded angry! But he'd teased her so often in the past, he should be able to take it when she teased him back for once. He was usually a good sport. She cleared her throat, upset by his fierce scowl.

"Why is she so important to you, Jason?"

Propping his elbows on the table, he rested his chin on laced fingers. His eyes took on a wistful expression, changing from a lively green to an odd, brownish-gold color. He looked right at her, but Melody knew he wasn't really seeing her. She felt the fine hairs on the back of her neck rise. Finally, in a deep, gritty tone, he answered.

"I'm not sure I can explain it. I love her voice. You know how she sounds like she's part kitten and part tigress?" Melody nodded. "I think it's that mixture of innocence and seduction that really gets me. I don't care what she looks like, Mel. There's one hell of a warm, loving, sexy woman inside her. If I could meet her and she was anything at all the way her voice sounds, I'd probably marry her."

Melody gasped. "Marry her?"

Jason gave her a sheepish smile and shrugged. "Being a bachelor isn't all it's cracked up to be sometimes."

Stunned by his revelation, Melody flopped back in her chair. She'd met Jason when she was ten years old. That was sixteen years ago, for heaven's sake! She'd known he had his vulnerabilities as anyone else did, of course, but she'd never seen him openly display them before.

Jason had always struck her as the most self-contained, independent person she'd ever met. As a state senator, prominent rancher and sought-after bachelor, he led an extremely active social life, and she'd never known him to need anyone. But was it possible that Jason was lonely?

Reaching out to touch his hand, Melody said softly, "But you've always seemed content with your life."

"Maybe I'm jealous of David and Liz," he answered, turning his hand over to clasp hers. "Did you know they're planning to start a family as soon as they're married?"

She nodded. Jason shrugged and looked away as if he felt embarrassed, but not before she caught a flash of yearning in his eyes. Melody felt something wrap around her heart and give it a hard squeeze.

"I never knew you wanted children, Jason. Whenever you talk about kids you call them rug rats and curtain climbers."

"I've always wanted a family. But I haven't met a woman yet I wanted to spend the rest of my life with. Most women don't really see me. They see the Wakefield name and assets. And of course—" he puffed out his chest and preened, as if he were admiring himself in the mirror "—there's always my gorgeous bod. They just can't keep their hands off me!"

Melody chuckled at his foolishness and elbowed him in the ribs to deflate his chest—if not his ego. "It might help if you dated somebody with a higher IQ and a smaller bust measurement," she said, tipping her head to one side for a better view of his reaction.

Roaring with laughter, Jason gently cuffed her chin with his big fist. "You could be right, Mel."

"I know I'm right. The women you go out with aren't much deeper than a mud puddle. You deserve better."

Jason shook his head, but there was a thoughtful light in his eyes that made Melody hope he would think about what she'd said. If she couldn't have Jason—and she'd accepted that long ago—she didn't want some gold digger or social climber to marry him. He did deserve better.

"Then I think you should tell me who Wendy Wyoming is," he said, a triumphant smirk turning up the corners of his mustache.

She sighed and sipped her coffee, wondering what in the world she should do. She'd fallen passionately in love with Jason the day he'd moved into the Hunter home, a tall, golden young god in her ten-year-old eyes. Tagging along with David and Jason whenever they would allow it, she'd listened, practically writhing with jealousy, as Jason had raved over one gorgeous girl after another. She'd cried herself to sleep for months when he'd started dating one tall, stacked redhead after another.

As the years had passed, Melody had told herself that what she felt for Jason was only an adolescent crush, and she had always been careful to hide her feelings from him and the rest of her family. But though Jason had invariably treated her as a sister, her attraction to him hadn't gone away. She'd even broken off her own engagement three years ago because she'd finally admitted, deep down inside, that she still loved Jason more than she loved her fiancé.

But she was over that now—or at least she tried to be over it. Besides, Jason would always see her as a sister, and he was too darn fickle for a lasting relationship. She wanted, needed, to fall in love with someone else and have her own family.

A wistful little voice inside her head piped up, *But he said he'd marry Wendy Wyoming if she was anything like she sounded.* Melody silently told the little voice to shut up.

"Please, Mel. Tell me." He leaned forward, his shoulders tensed, an eager, expectant light in his eyes.

She looked up at him, still hesitating. After all he'd said, it would sound as though she were proposing to him if she blurted out the truth. And when he knew the truth he might get mad at her for letting him pour his heart out to her. But he would give her no peace until she told him something. Maybe she ought to test the waters a bit first. Faking a nonchalant shrug and a sassy grin, she said,

"Maybe I'm Wendy Wyoming, Jason."

Chapter Two

Jason stared at her for a long, breathless moment. Then his shoulders drooped, and he sagged back against his chair. He threw back his head, clutching his belly as a shout of laughter erupted from him. Melody felt as if he'd kicked her in the face with one of his gigantic cowboy boots, but years of practice at concealing her emotions kept her eyes dry and a tentative smile on her lips.

"Oh, Mel," he gasped, pointing a long finger at her. "That's rich! You really had me going that time."

Though she felt a small, tender piece of her soul shriveling—along with the final shreds of her girlish hopes and dreams regarding Jason Wakefield—Melody kept smiling at him. If this was his reaction, thank God he thought she was joking! But as his laughter went on and on and he wiped tears of mirth from his eyes, a hot kernel of fury ignited in her heart.

Just who the hell did he think he was, laughing at the idea of her being Wendy Wyoming? Granted, she wasn't Playboy bunny or Miss America material, but she wasn't exactly repulsive, either! Vic Grant, her ex-fiancé, certainly hadn't thought so, and neither had any of the other guys she'd dated!

By the time Jason stopped laughing, Melody vowed she would get him for it if it was the last thing she ever did. Her resolve didn't even flicker when he scooted his chair closer, laid his arm across her shoulders and gave her his most persuasive smile.

"Okay, Mel. That was a great joke. Now tell me the truth. Who is Wendy Wyoming?"

"I've told you all I'm going to tell you, Jason. Now why don't you drop the subject?"

He crossed his arms over his chest. "I can't do that. I know it sounds kinky to get hung up on a woman's voice, but I have to meet her."

"Well, how do you think it makes me feel to know you see me as a blabbermouth?"

"I don't see you as a blabbermouth—"

Melody shoved back her chair and stood, ignoring the harsh grating sound it made as it scraped across the linoleum. Planting her feet wide apart and yanking off her glasses before propping her hands on her hips, she turned on him.

"Yes, you do! You still call me 'Squirt' and treat me like I'm ten years old. In case you hadn't noticed, I'm all grown up now, and I've learned how to keep secrets."

"You're overreacting," Jason muttered, noticing with a sense of shock that Melody was absolutely right. He'd never seen her quite like this before—standing over him, enraged, her dark eyes flashing with the heat of her emotions, her small breasts heaving. By golly, Mel looked—well, downright sexy!

"I am not! You think if you pester me long enough I'll give in and tell you. You wouldn't do that to any other woman my age."

"That's because you're the only woman I consider my friend!"

"Friends don't badger one another."

Jason looked away, mentally backing off from the intensity of the argument. He couldn't remember when he'd ever felt so uncomfortable. He didn't know how to handle this strange new Melody. Oh, she'd been madder than hell at him before, but this time seemed different. He had a sinking feeling in his gut that if he didn't give up trying to find out about Wendy Wyoming, he damn well might lose Melody's friendship! The idea made him feel sick. But all this fuss only made him more determined to solve the mystery. Finally he looked at her again, saying quietly, "I can't help feeling curious about her, Mel. Something about her really hit me hard. I'm sorry I upset you, but I'm not giving up. I can't."

Melody shut her eyes and took a deep breath. Maybe she *was* overreacting. Jason hadn't meant to hurt her feelings. He simply viewed her as an asexual being, the way most brothers viewed their younger sisters. But dammit, he *wasn't* her brother! His laughter had hurt! Still, she didn't want to destroy their friendship. Shaking her head, she said, "I'm sorry I yelled at you."

She smiled at him then, and Jason felt warmed by the simple gesture, as if the sun had come out from behind a cloud. Looking up at her, he found himself swallowing hard. Why, Mel really was a lovely woman!

Why hadn't he ever noticed how pretty her dark eyes were before? Or how soft her skin looked? Or that she had breasts? And—oh God, what was he thinking? Mel was his little sister! Well, not exactly, but he felt like an incestuous pervert, sitting here and looking her over as a potential bed partner. And dammit, that was exactly what he'd been doing!

He forced a smile onto his face and stood beside his chair, feeling better to be looking down at her again. She felt more like a little sister when the top of her head barely grazed his armpit. He reached out to ruffle her hair the way he always did, then dropped his hand back to his side. He didn't want her to think he was treating her like a ten-year-old again.

"Want some more coffee?" Melody asked in an attempt to regain a friendlier atmosphere.

What he really wanted was a hug, just to know everything was all right between them again. But after his lecherous thoughts about Melody a minute ago, he didn't dare ask for one.

"No, I'd better get back to my apartment. I've got some papers to read before the session starts tomorrow morning."

"That reminds me. Will you come talk to my kids about the legislature while you're in town? We're starting the unit on state government next week."

"I'll call you when I've got my calendar handy, and we'll set a time," he answered, practically fleeing to the living room for his coat and hat. Mel was looking more appealing by the second, and he'd better get the heck out of her apartment.

She followed him to the front door. "Thanks. They always enjoy listening to you."

Jason turned to face her, wondering if he dared give her his customary goodbye hug and kiss. He offered his hand for a handshake instead. "Friends again, Mel?"

Ignoring his hand, she wrapped her arms around his waist beneath his jacket, giving him a warm hug. "Of course we are!"

He hugged her tightly in return, then quickly moved away when his body began heating in a familiar but unexpected way as he felt her soft frame press against his bigger, harder one. A moment later he was out the door, sucking the frigid January air deep into his lungs. What the hell was the matter with him? Spying Melody's snow shovel, he grabbed it and hurried down the front steps to dig her car out of the snow. Under the cirumstances, he felt it was the least he could do for her.

Melody retreated to the picture window in the living room to watch Jason leave. The snowdrifts in front of the apartment covered the bumpers of her aging blue Mustang. The scrawny, naked trees in the empty schoolyard across the street jerked and danced in the relentless gales that made Cheyenne one of the windiest cities in the country. Then Jason strode into view.

Bless his heart, he didn't have to dig her car out! She was used to fending for herself, but that didn't mean she couldn't appreciate having a big strong man shovel snow for her.

Jason glanced up and waved when he spotted her watching him through the window. Melody waved back, mouthing a thank-you. He shrugged, as if to say, "No big deal," then turned and quickly finished the job. Then he was gone, his Blazer trailing a white cloud of snow and steaming exhaust in its wake.

Melody waited until he was out of sight before walking back to the kitchen to rinse out the coffee mugs and get ready for an afternoon of grading exams. But the activity didn't distract her as she'd hoped it would. Her thoughts stubbornly returned to Jason and to Wendy Wyoming.

Even though he'd obviously felt remorse for making her angry, she still writhed with humiliation every time she remembered his laughter. The big dope! He could have refused to believe her without laughing in her face.

Tossing her grade book and papers aside, Melody stalked over to study herself in the mirror hanging on the back of her bedroom door. Much as she hated to admit it, maybe Jason had had good reason.

Her face was more cute than beautiful. Her figure was all right, but it sure wasn't voluptuous. Her jeans were clean and fairly new, but more comfortable-looking than sexy. Her pale pink sweater, worn over a long-sleeved white blouse, looked neat but, well, on the prim side. The only thing even vaguely eye-catching about her appearance was the acid-green color of her socks, and she wore them because they were warm, not because she wanted to make a fashion statement.

Maybe if she grew her hair out and wore more dramatic makeup, and bought some new clothes that weren't practical for once... Nah! Then she'd look like a little girl trying to play dress-up.

Dammit, she looked exactly like what she was—a short, skinny, dark-haired, quiet schoolteacher who was only mildly pretty and wore glasses. But inside her short, unspectacular body was a tall, buxom redhead screaming to get out! In her heart and mind she *felt* like one hell of a warm, loving, sexy woman. Why couldn't anyone else see that in her? Why couldn't Jason?

Sighing, Melody returned to her fourth period class's test papers, determined to concentrate this time. David had really scraped the bottom of the barrel when he'd shoved her into the control booth. She'd never get another chance to be Wendy Wyoming again anyway. She'd probably never get any revenge on Jason, either. But if the opportunity ever presented itself...

A week later, Melody was sitting in the same spot, grading another stack of papers, when again she heard pounding on her front door. "Before I pay another penny in rent, that landlord is going to fix the doorbell," she muttered as she hurried to see who her impatient caller could be. After opening the door, she jumped back as her brother rushed past, the distinctive smell of hot pizza trailing behind him.

"Come on in, David!" she called to his retreating back, then followed him into the kitchen.

"Thanks, Mel, I will!" he called back, grinning mischievously at her over his shoulder.

He looked so pleased with himself as he dropped the enormous cardboard box on the kitchen table, then plunked down a six-pack of Budweiser stashed under one arm and a brown paper sack clutched against his side with the other arm, that she couldn't help returning his grin. Holding out her hands to take the coat and hat he was rapidly shedding, she asked, "What on earth are you up to?"

David clutched his chest. "Mel! Can't a guy bring his own sister a Sunday-afternoon snack without being accused of being up to something?"

After observing the ingratiating smile on his handsome face, she laughed, then rescued her grade book and papers from the mess he was efficiently spreading over the table. "Not in your case, David."

He sidled next to her and put a beefy arm around her shoulders. "Well, there is a little favor I'd like you to do for me, sis."

Looking up into his dark eyes, eyes so like her own, she wondered how the three Hunter siblings could have come from the same set of parents. Though his hair was also close to the same color as hers, David's features were classically handsome. He was nearly as tall as Jason, and he had an outgoing personality that made him the life of any party. And their older sister Barbara was even more outgoing and attractive than David.

Melody loved her brother and sister, and she'd quit trying to compete with them long ago. They were out of her league—as was Jason. Still, sometimes she couldn't help wishing she could be a bit more like Barbara or David or Jason.

Heaving a silent sigh of resignation, she asked her brother, "What is it this time?"

"Sit down and have some pizza first," he insisted, opening the box and seating her with enough charm to raise her suspicions.

"Out with it, David."

"Now, don't go all schoolteacherish on me, Mel."

"David!"

"All right!" He reached across the box and grabbed the sack, then pulled out a thick stack of envelopes held together by a rubber band. Tossing them in front of Melody, he said, "Open them. They're yours."

While David tore into the pizza, Melody cautiously picked up the envelopes and turned them over, gasping when she saw that the top one was addressed to Wendy Wyoming. She glanced at David, and her heart beat faster when he waved a hand at her and mumbled around a mouthful of pizza, "Read 'em. Fan mail."

Unable to resist, she removed the rubber band, opened the first letter and began to read. Her face grew hot at the suggestions the writer—obviously a man—made in his hastily scrawled paragraph. She didn't know if what he was hoping for was anatomically possible, but it certainly sounded interesting! The next letter was more tactful, but equally suggestive.

By the time Melody had finished the last letter, she was giggling and flustered, but also proud that she'd inspired so many fan letters. When she looked back at David, his expression reminded her of that of a pudgy cat belching canary feathers.

"We've been getting at least five letters and ten phone calls a day at KBOY since you did your show, Mel. And every one of those people wants to know when Wendy Wyoming will be back on the air. Want to take another crack at it?"

Returning his wicked grin, she reached for a slice of pizza. Noting that it was her favorite, Canadian bacon with mushrooms and green peppers, she realized that David must really want her to do this. And she wanted to do it more than he would ever have guessed. All week long, at the oddest, most inconvenient times, she'd found herself inventing outrageous new things for Wendy Wyoming to say. But first she'd let him lay all his cards on the table. It paid to be cautious when dealing with David.

"Maybe," she answered noncommittally.

"You little snot," he chuckled. "You're gonna make me go through a whole sales pitch, aren't you?"

"Of course. And be sure to include how you're going to keep my identity a secret," she instructed before taking a bite of the pizza.

"Aw, sis," he protested. "Do you have any idea how hard that'll be?"

She laid the slice of pizza on a paper napkin and gave her brother a no-nonsense look. "I teach junior high kids, David. Kids in the throes of puberty. I could never face a room full of their weird, raging libidos again if they found out I was Wendy Wyoming. And if their parents and the school board and the principal found out, I could lose my job!"

"So what? Then you can come to work for Dad and me full-time. You'll make more money, and you told me not long ago you've been feeling restless."

"I wasn't planning on leaving the profession with a scandal on my record, David," she answered dryly. "I was thinking about going back to school for my master's degree in counseling, and I sent off for an application for a teaching job in Denver. But I haven't decided what I want to do yet."

He leaned forward, bracing his elbows on the table. "I think you're being paranoid. Since your family owns the station and you help out with the books and writing ads, you have every reason to visit whenever you want. And the way you look and act, nobody will suspect a thing."

She snorted at him. "Thanks a whole chunk, David! But Cheyenne's not that big. Somebody will find out if we're not careful."

He cupped his chin in one hand, his eyes narrowed thoughtfully. "Well, I guess you could tape the shows in advance so you won't have to be at the station while you're on the air."

"And I could use the old control booth in the basement. Nobody ever goes down there anymore."

"Yeah, and I could have the music director work out the playlists and give them to me, and have another deejay around to play your tapes and cut in if there's any hot news breaking."

David reached over and gently tweaked the tip of Melody's nose. "I've gotta admit, you really surprised me, sis. I never would have discouraged you from majoring in broadcasting if I'd known you could pack such a wallop on the air. Dad wouldn't have, either. Now I'm glad you took all those classes just to spite us."

Melody scowled at him. Her self-esteem had suffered a severe blow when her father and brother had told her she didn't have the right personality to become a disc jockey and join the family business. Though she knew they both wanted only the best for her, their assessment of her abilities had made her feel even more like the odd one out in the Hunter family than she usually did.

Her father was Cheyenne's media mogul, her mother a successful syndicated columnist. Her sister Barbara was climbing the ranks of reporters for a major television network, and David had enjoyed an exciting career as a disc jockey in Denver before coming home to manage the family radio station. Melody's teaching career seemed awfully mundane compared to everyone else's fame and achievement. She was the quiet one, the short one, the untalented one. But now, maybe, some of that was going to change. She punched her brother on the arm and said, "Don't remind me."

David chuckled. Then his eyes lighted up as he asked, "Did you know Jason is already your biggest fan?"

Melody nodded. "He came over here last Sunday asking me about Wendy Wyoming."

"You must not have told him anything!" David hooted with laughter. "Oh, I love this! Jase thinks Wendy's another one of his redheads, and he's been going nuts all week trying to make me tell him who she is!"

Melody turned her head away until she'd controlled her reaction. There was no sense in letting David in on everything. Her eyes gleaming with conspiratorial glee, she faced him again, suggesting, "I don't think you should tell him anything, either. It'll be a good lesson for him if and when he does find out I'm Wendy."

"Oh, don't worry. I'm enjoying this too much to tell him. He wouldn't believe me if I did."

Melody nearly choked at David's reply, but managed to recover before he noticed. Deciding the conversation had gone on long enough, she started clearing the table. David took the hint and went in search of his hat and coat. She walked him to the door, agreeing to stop by KBOY after school the next day, then went back into the kitchen.

Her mind raced as she wiped off the table and spread out her schoolwork again. Her life was going to change! Maybe she'd go to Denver and have a complete make-over to celebrate. She was sick to death of being so prim and boring that nobody would ever guess or believe she could be Wendy Wyoming.

That thought brought an image of Jason to mind, and a new, determined glint entered her eyes. This would be the perfect time to shake up his perception of her. He was sure to find her out eventually. But before he did he was going to see a new and exciting and, yes, sexy Mel, or her name wasn't Melody Jane Hunter!

By the time she was through with Jason, he'd regret laughing at her. And in the meantime she'd enjoy tormenting him just a little bit. He would never fall in love with her, but dammit, at least he could see her as a woman!

She hugged herself, as if by doing so she could contain her excitement at the prospect of being Wendy Wyoming again, then forced her attention back to correcting papers. Since she was going to be taking on a new part-time job, she'd better work ahead on her lesson plans. Then she could make some other plans for Wendy Wyoming. And for Jason.

Chapter Three

"Hello, pardners. This is KBOY, Cheyenne. I'm Wendy Wyoming, here to bring you some good country music to warm your hearts on this cold, cold January night. Thanks to all your kind calls and letters, I'll be coming your way every Monday, Wednesday and Friday night. Let's get this party rolling with Reba McIntyre's new single."

Melody turned up the volume, then slid a couple of cartridges into the tape deck to run commercials when the song finished playing. After consulting the playlist the station's music director had compiled, she cued the next record on the second turntable. Keeping a close watch on the clock, she sat back with a sigh of satisfaction.

It had been a long time since she'd taken broadcasting classes at the University of Wyoming, but after a little after-hours coaching from David she felt reasonably competent in the control booth. Thank heaven she was working with tape instead of doing a live show this time. It was far less nerve-racking knowing she could erase her major bloopers before they went out over the air waves.

She punched the red button on the tape deck to start a commercial for a local car dealership and glanced over the rest of her program materials. David had done a good job of stocking the old control booth for her. She started the next commercial, then closed her eyes as she psyched herself up to talk again.

"I want to say thank you to all the ladies out there who heard my first broadcast and wrote to me here at KBOY. But to you men who sent me letters, well, I just don't know what to say!"

Melody chuckled deep in her throat, knowing the sound would come across as a husky purr over the air. "Some of you guys have the wrong idea about me. I'm really a nice girl, fellas! Oh, I like men as much as the next gal, but I'm no party animal. Nosiree. I'm a one-man woman, fellas. I believe in love, honor and cherish and till death do us part. When I meet that one special man I'm lookin' for, well, he won't have to worry about my being true. And I'm tellin' you, I'd better not have to worry about him strayin', either. Why rip each other apart with a bunch of silly shenanigans like that and waste time you could have spent lovin'? Now, just to make sure you get your minds on more... spiritual things, I'm gonna play you a gospel tune from the Oak Ridge Boys."

She switched off the mike, grinning at her own audacity. That one ought to drive Jason bonkers! She hadn't seen him since that bizarre Sunday afternoon two weeks ago, but David had told her Jason hadn't given up his search for Wendy Wyoming. Though she'd had plenty of time to cool off, Melody's wounded pride still demanded revenge.

It was one thing for a man not to see you as a desirable woman. It was something else entirely for him to laugh hysterically at the very idea that you might be one! And it was high time Jason discovered a woman didn't need to look like Raquel Welch to be sexy. If their friendship couldn't survive what she had planned for Jason, it wasn't worth continuing anyway. And maybe by the time he realized she really *was* Wendy Wyoming she would finally have him out of her system for good.

As she fell into the rhythm of her program, Melody gradually relaxed, enjoying herself more and more. Each time she spoke she incorporated as much seduction in her voice as she could without being tacky. Though he would never know it, in her mind, every line she uttered was directed at Jason. If she only had the nerve to talk to him this brazenly face-to-face, he'd never see her as a sister again!

Feeling extremely bold by the end of the four-hour stint, she sent Jason a final zinger. She played George Strait's recording of "The Chair," a story song about a man picking up a woman in a bar, then said, "What a line that guy has! Now, gals, you need to watch out, 'cause there's a man right here in Cheyenne who's every bit as smooth and dangerous as George Strait. I can't say his name on the air, but can you believe it? He's one of our very own state senators! That about wraps up our time together for tonight. This is Wendy Wyoming, reminding you to stay warm, be kind and gentle with each other, and I'll be back to spend another evening keeping you company on Wednesday. Good night, all."

After taking off her headphones, Melody rubbed her hands together gleefully, then rewound the tape she'd just finished and shut down the control room. David had told her Jason knew Wendy Wyoming would be on the air again tonight. He couldn't help but guess she'd been referring to him in that last speech. He had promised to come and talk to her classes on Wednesday morning, and she couldn't wait to see him. Whoever said that revenge was sweet was absolutely right!

After checking in at the junior high office on Wednesday morning, Jason started off in search of Melody's classroom. The hallways had the midwinter grubbiness he remembered from his own schooldays—black scuff marks on the tile floor, a notebook-paper airplane smashed against a trash barrel, the fringe of an orange scarf sticking out of a hastily slammed locker door.

But the noises coming from the rooms he passed were the sounds of learning—desktops banging, chalk skating across a blackboard, a teacher making an assignment, followed by the obligatory moans and groans of her students. When he turned into the final corridor, Jason heard laughter coming from Melody's room.

"Do another one, Miss Hunter!"

"Okay. Let me think for a minute."

Intrigued, Jason stopped just outside the classroom, hoping to find out what was going on before he entered. He could see Mel standing at the front of the room. To his surprise, she squared her shoulders, stuck out her chest, put a pruney expression on her face and spoke in an impeccable British accent.

"I'm a world leader. I'm called a conservative. My country is having difficulties with its economy—"

"I know! It's old what's-her-face!"

Shaking her head at a boy in the front row, Melody answered, "Come on, Eric. 'Old what's-her-face' is not an appropriate answer. But you're right that it's a woman."

A girlish voice chimed in. "It's Margaret Thatcher!"

Melody grinned. "That's right, Amy. But who is Margaret Thatcher?"

"The prime minister of Great Britain."

"Good answer."

"Do another one, Miss Hunter. Please?"

To Jason's delight, Melody continued doing impressions, including one of the president and one of the governor of Wyoming that had him doubled over with laughter out in the hallway. When he'd finally composed himself again, he knocked on the door and stepped into the room. A smile lighted Melody's face when she saw him, and Jason felt his heart give a funny little lurch.

A moment ago she'd looked like his kid sister Mel, clowning around. But now, walking toward him, wearing a slim-fitting bright red dress accented by chunky gold jewelry and delicate black high heels, her hair a little tousled but shining with deep auburn highlights he'd never noticed before, Melody became the desirable woman he had first noticed in her apartment two weeks ago.

He shut his eyes, hoping she'd look more like a kid sister again when he opened them. It didn't work. Damn! He had purposely avoided her, assuring himself that what he'd felt for Mel in her apartment was only a temporary aberration that would go away if he ignored it. When the hell had she changed from a pigtailed, scabby-kneed tomboy into this self-confident, attractive woman? Now he needed to meet Wendy Wyoming just to get his mind off Mel!

"Senator Wakefield, we're glad you could come," Meldoy said, escorting him to the podium at the front of the room.

Looking out at the rows of curious young faces, Jason wished he'd written out a speech. He usually got along fine without notes, but at the moment his mind was blank, only capable, it seemed, of absorbing how pretty Melody looked in red, the sweet fragrance of her perfume, the enthusiasm and zest for life in her voice. Suddenly she finished her introduction, walked gracefully to the back of the room and perched on top of a desk.

Jason gulped, then tugged at his tie, which suddenly felt too tight. He took a deep breath, noticing at least half the boys in the class gazing back at Melody like a bunch of lovesick puppies. Well, it looked as if he were not the only one attracted to Miss Hunter. The thought made him smile. Leaning forward, he rested one forearm on the podium and asked, "Okay, what do you want to know about the legislature?"

As Jason started talking, Melody smoothed her dress down over her knees and settled into a more comfortable position. He was doing a great job of involving the kids in the discussion, but then she'd known he would. Of course, by tomorrow, only the boys would remember one word he had said. The girls were too busy salivating over the gorgeous hunk at the podium and passing notes about him to listen much.

Melody sympathized with her girls. Jason's blatant masculinity affected most grown women. But these poor babies were all suffering the raging hormones of adolescence. Who could blame them for reacting to his physical magnetism rather than listening to his insights on the issues before the legislature?

He glanced back at her and smiled, and she wondered if he'd noticed her new dress or the rinse in her hair. Probably not. Ah, well, she felt terrific, so it wasn't a total loss.

For the rest of the day, Jason carried on like a veteran teacher. Melody enjoyed his company but concluded from his brotherly behavior by the end of her last class that he hadn't noticed the changes in her appearance. Well, what had she expected? That he'd take one look at her and declare his undying love? Hah! Maybe she should give up this insane idea...

The bell interrupted Melody's thoughts, and she called out a reminder of the next day's assignment to her stampeding students. She walked to the front of the room to erase the board, not even trying to talk to Jason until the cacophony of yelling and laughing and banging lockers died down.

Groaning, Jason stretched his arms over his head. "I don't know how you do this all day every day, Squirt. Lord, but my feet hurt!"

"You get used to it after a while."

"Melody... Oh, excuse me! I didn't know you had company."

Melody winced at the sound of that voice, though she knew she should have expected it. Debbie Adams taught seventh-grade social studies down the hall and often dropped in for an after-school chat. Melody liked Debbie well enough, but today she'd hoped to have a little time alone with Jason after the kids left. Besides, Debbie was single, and except for the fact that she was an extremely intelligent woman she was Jason's type with a capital *T*.

Jason's eyes roved over the redhead's gorgeous curves, and his mouth automatically stretched into his best lady killer smile. He lowered his arms and extended a big, work-roughened hand toward Debbie before Melody could even finish an introduction.

"Debbie, this is Jason Wakefield. Jason, this is Debbie Adams, a fellow teacher."

Melody stifled a sigh as Jason took Debbie's hand and held it far longer than necessary. As she maintained sizzling eye contact with Jason, Debbie didn't appear to mind. They both mouthed the usual platitudes of strangers meeting for the first time, ignoring Melody's existence as if she were merely an extra desk.

Packing her satchel with the books and papers she needed to prepare for the next day, Melody muttered, "Just like a couple of Pavlov's dogs."

"Did you say something, Melody?" Debbie asked, her eyes not leaving Jason's face for a second.

Her smile feeling as artificial as a pair of stick-on fingernails, Melody answered, "No, just talking to myself. I'm ready to leave now."

"Why don't we go out for a drink?" Jason suggested, smoothly taking Debbie's arm as if she were a fragile knickknack instead of a strapping five-foot-nine-inch amazon.

Ignored by the other two, Melody followed them down the corridor to the teachers' lounge to collect her coat and snow boots. Jason helped Debbie put on her coat while Melody struggled into hers alone. As they left the building, she veered away from Jason and Debbie and walked to her Mustang.

"Aren't you coming along?" Jason called in surprise across the parking lot when he realized she was no longer with them.

"No, thanks," she answered. "I've got some errands to run. Thanks for spending the day with my kids."

"I enjoyed it. See you later, Mel."

Inside the privacy of her car, Melody mimicked him nastily. "See you later, Mel!" Darn Jason's hide! He treated her like excess baggage and then expected her to go with them for a drink? Putting her aging car into gear with more roughness than usual, she drove away from the school.

The worst part was, Melody didn't think Jason was honestly interested in Debbie. He never would have invited Melody along in the first place if he was. He just had a knee-jerk response to any tall, shapely woman with red hair. There must be a command in his brain that read Tall, Gorgeous Redhead: Turn on Charm. The big dope! Wendy Wyoming would get him for this.

Melody turned onto Lincolnway, fuming as she maneuvered through the busy late-afternoon traffic. She barely missed smacking the bumper of a black Volkswagen beetle when she whipped into the parking lot at KBOY, earning an indignant honk from its driver. Parking as unobtrusively as possible, she turned off the ignition, then sucked in deep, cleansing breaths to calm herself.

To heck with Jason and his redheads! It was time for another Wendy Wyoming show, and Melody Jane Hunter was going to enjoy herself. Hugging her coat tightly against the biting wind, she hurried into the building.

Four hours later, Melody left the studio feeling exhausted but elated. It had been easier to slip into her Wendy Wyoming personality this time, and the show had gone extremely well. There had even been a few more fan letters for her in the control booth from Monday night's show.

The wind had miraculously died down for the night, and the stars looked close enough to touch. She took a moment to breathe in the clean, cold air, enjoying the outdoors after the claustrophobia of her hours in the windowless basement control booth. She jumped when a voice called to her from the back row of cars in the parking lot.

"Hey, Mel!"

She heard a car door open, then saw Jason waving to her, illuminated in the darkness by the dome light in his Blazer. Her boots crunched across the frozen pavement, stopping beside the wagon. He shut the door again, then rolled down the window.

"What are you doing out here in the dark, Jason?"

"Waiting for Wendy Wyoming," he replied, flashing a devilish white smile. "And wouldn't you know, the heater on this buggy isn't working."

"Why don't you go inside where it's warm?" she asked.

"I don't want David to see me, and his car's right over there," he explained, gesturing to his right with his thumb. "I'll tell ya, Mel, your brother's a real turkey about Wendy."

"How long have you been sitting here?" Melody asked, repressing a wicked grin of her own.

"About twenty-five minutes, but her show starts in half an hour, so I figure she oughtta be along any minute now. Want to point her out to me just in case I miss her?"

Melody shook her head. "No. I wouldn't want to cramp your style. I've got to get home and work on my lesson plans. Be seeing you, Jason."

As she started off toward her own car, Jason called after her, "What are you doing here so late, Mel?"

"Just a little work for David."

She giggled like a goofy seventh-grader all the way home. Poor Jason. The big idiot would freeze his tush off, waiting in a snowy parking lot in the dark for a woman who wasn't coming! She'd have given almost anything to see his face when Wendy Wyoming came on the air tonight!

Once inside her apartment, Melody changed into a comfortable pair of jeans and a fuzzy blue sweatshirt, then fixed herself a pot of coffee and a piece of peanut-butter toast for supper before spreading out her lesson plans and books on the kitchen table. She turned on her radio for company, laughing out loud when Wendy Wyoming opened her show with a cheery "Is it cold enough out there for you, pardners?"

Twenty minutes later, she nearly suffered heart failure when a furious banging started on her front door. The minute she unlocked it, Jason stormed inside, raging.

"I oughtta spank your butt, Melody Jane!"

"Hello, Jason," she replied, struggling to hold back the laughter bubbling up inside her.

He flung his Stetson onto her sofa, then shed his sheepskin-lined jacket and tossed it beside his hat. Turning back to face Melody, Jason planted his hands on his hips and stood there, scowling down at her. She swallowed, taking in the bright pink color of his nose and earlobes, the frost on his mustache, the anger in his eyes.

"You knew, didn't you?" he demanded, his voice low and gritty.

"Knew what?" she asked, keeping an innocent expression plastered on her face.

"That Wendy Wyoming wasn't coming. That she tapes her shows in advance!"

"Now that you mention it . . ." She couldn't hold it back any longer. It started out as a snicker, then progressed to a giggle, then to a full-fledged belly laugh.

Jason shook his head at her in disgust, but before long one corner of his mouth twitched and turned up. He had to admit it, the little stinker had really put one over on him this time. A moment later he was laughing along with her.

When the laughter faded, they stood there in her small living room, grinning at each other. Melody's cheeks were flushed, her eyes shining. Jason laid his hand on her shoulder, nudging her toward the kitchen.

"The least you can do is make me a cup of coffee, Squirt."

When she moved forward to comply, he grabbed the back of her neck, chuckling when she yelped and jumped out of reach, yelling, "Geez, your hands are like ice!"

"And it's all your fault, Mel."

"I'm sorry, Jason."

"You are not, but I'll forgive you this time. Just remember, it may not be today and it may not be tomorrow, but one of these days, Melody Jane, I'll get even."

As they entered the kitchen, Melody moved to turn off the radio, but Jason said, "Don't, Mel. I want to hear her."

She shrugged, then filled a mug with coffee for him and carried it over to the table. He sat down in front of the mug, wrapped his cold hands around it and eyed the mess on the table.

"What's all this stuff?"

"Lesson plans."

His sandy eyebrows drew together. "But there's at least fifteen stacks here, and you only have five classes."

"Not all of my kids do the same thing every day, Jason. Some of them have special needs, and I have to work out different ways to give them the material we're working on."

"What do you mean?"

"Some of them can't read well enough to learn much from the textbook, so I read the chapters out loud for them on tape and try to find filmstrips and movies to help them out. And some of them are such good students they get bored if I don't find extra projects for them to work on."

"Do all teachers go to so much trouble these days? Mine sure didn't when I was in school."

"Most try to, but a lot of them have families and can't put in so much time. But I enjoy it, Jason."

"Well, I'm impressed, Mel. I could tell the kids were really happy being in your classes. What were those impressions you were doing when I got there this morning?"

To his delight, she flushed. "You heard that?"

"Yup. I got there just as you were doing Margaret Thatcher. I really cracked up over your renditions of the president and the governor."

She wrinkled her nose at him. "That's my version of current events. If I do one they can't guess, it drives them crazy, and they watch the news every night until they get it."

He laughed, then sipped his coffee, studying Melody over the rim of the mug. Now she looked like his pal Mel again, but she also seemed more mature somehow, more womanly. That fuzzy sweatshirt made her look as soft and cuddly as a teddy bear, and yet there was a new self-confidence about her that erased the girlish image he'd always had of her. He wondered what it would feel like to kiss those soft, smiling lips of hers, and how she'd react if he did.

He shifted on his chair, leaning closer to her. He caught a whiff of a light floral fragrance and noticed again the new auburn highlights in her glossy hair. The only thing that stopped him from reaching out to touch her curls was the sound of Wendy Wyoming's voice purring from the radio.

"And now I have, next on the air, a hot group I've come to love. Lordy, don't I wish they were right here in my studio! Folks, I give you Exile!"

Jason shook his head as if to clear it, then sat back in his chair, sternly reminding himself that Wendy Wyoming was his kind of woman. Melody was too young and innocent for him. And yet there was something new about her that called out to the male in him. Aw, hell, he'd better make tracks before he did something really stupid.

But before he could push his chair back she was on her feet, bringing him more coffee and asking him about his ranch and how his stock was getting along with all the snow they'd been having and making him feel so comfortable he couldn't force himself to move. Suddenly he realized that this was what was missing from his busy life—having someone to come home to at night and talk to and share the events of the day with. Someone who cared about him.

Feeling as if some unseen force were directing him, he reached over and picked up her small hand, holding it in a warm grasp. When she looked up at him, her lips parted in a little smile, his heart flipped over. He tried to speak but had to clear his throat and try again.

"You looked mighty pretty in that red dress you had on today. Is it new?"

She tipped her head to one side, smiling up at him with a suspicious glint in her dark eyes and an unmistakable blush high on her cheeks. "Yes, it's new."

He lifted his free hand and wrapped a dark, shiny curl around his index finger, enjoying the soft, silky texture of it. She batted his hand away from her hair, and her blush deepened. Jason chuckled.

"And what have you done to your hair, Mel? I like that reddish color."

Melody tried to pull her hand away, but Jason clapped his free hand over it and enclosed it between both of his own. She huffed at him. "What's with you, Wakefield? If I didn't know better, I'd think you were flirting with me."

"And from the way you're blushing and getting all flustered, Hunter, I'd think you liked it. If I didn't know better, of course, I might even think you were sweet on me."

Her dark eyes widened and her blush intensified, and then, to Jason's chagrin, she burst out laughing! He released her hand, propping one elbow on the table and drumming on the Formica top with the long, blunt-tipped fingers of his other hand. Well, he thought wryly, now I know how she'd react if I kissed her! But as her laughter continued he felt a hot flush creep up the back of his neck.

When she finally stopped, he demanded, "What's so damn funny about that?"

"Oh, Jason, I'm sorry," she murmured, gazing deep into his eyes, as if she were looking for something.

"Don't you even like me?" he asked more quietly.

"Of course I do! It's just that, well..."

"Well what?"

"You're not really my type," she answered, then started laughing all over again.

Affronted, Jason stared at her, trying to remember what the guys Mel usually dated looked like. They were all shorter than he was, of course, but then he was taller than most other men. But now that he thought about it, Mel generally went out with dark-haired men, men who were more settled than he was—predictable men, like accountants and lawyers and other teachers. Hating himself for asking, but needing to know, he said,

"Why not?"

"Well," she said more seriously as she wiped her eyes with her fingertips, "Jason, I guess I'd have to say you're too fickle. I mean, I love you as a friend and think you're an extremely attractive man, but I wouldn't want to really fall in love with you."

And if she repeated that statement a few million more times, Melody thought wryly, she just might be able to convince herself that she really believed it. But at least it helped her keep her feelings for Jason in perspective.

"I'm not fickle! I just haven't fallen in love myself yet. The women I date know the score."

"I know they do, but that's just it. You go out with so many women, I don't know how you keep their names straight. And take today, for instance. You've been dying to meet Wendy Wyoming, and you said you didn't care what she looked like. But the minute you laid eyes on Debbie Adams this afternoon you forgot all about Wendy and asked Debbie out."

"I expected you to come along, Mel. It wasn't really a date, for cryin' out loud!"

"And play kid sister, tagging along while you two made gaga eyes at each other? No thanks."

He grinned. "Why, Melody Jane, you sound jealous."

Laughing, she punched him on the arm. "How do you carry that enormous ego around with you?"

"It's a rough job, but somebody's gotta do it, Squirt," he answered, hoping she couldn't tell how deflated his ego actually felt at the moment. Pushing back his chair, he climbed to his feet. "I'd better be headin' home and let you finish your schoolwork."

Following him into the living room, she asked, "Did Mom call you about Friday night?"

Shaking his head, he shrugged into his coat. "No. What's going on?"

"Barbara's visiting for a couple of days. We're having a family dinner to welcome her home. You're invited, of course."

"Sounds great. It'll be nice to see your big sis again. I'll pick you up."

"I'd like that. Is six-thirty too early for you?"

"That's fine," he answered, turning back to face her at the front door.

He held out his arms to her for his goodbye hug and kiss. She moved into his embrace willingly, lifting her cheek to him as she put her arms around his waist. He sucked in a silent breath at the sensations caused by her warm, soft body pressed closely against him. She felt so damn . . . right!

He bent down and brushed his lips against her smooth, warm skin. She gave him a hug, then started to pull away. But suddenly he couldn't let her go—not yet. Tightening one arm around her, he raised his other hand and tipped up her chin, aligning her mouth with his. Through slitted eyelids, he watched confusion and what might have been wariness enter her eyes. She started to speak, but he covered her lips with his own before any sound came out.

Melody stiffened at first, but after a moment she relaxed against him. He watched her eyelids slowly close, then shut his own eyes and gave himself up to simply feeling. Not wanting to scare or upset her, he controlled an urge to plunge his tongue deep inside her mouth and settled for a gentle, tentative touching of lips to lips, savoring the warmth and closeness, the soft, heartfelt sigh she breathed against his mouth.

He felt light-headed when he raised his head, and his heartbeat kicked into overdrive when he saw the sweet, bemused expression in her dark eyes as she gazed up at him. Smiling, he dropped another quick kiss on the tip of her nose and whispered. "Night, Mel." She was still standing there, trembling fingers touching her lips, when he let himself out.

Elation filled him as he climbed into his Blazer and let the engine warm up for a few minutes. Mel had let him kiss her! Shoot, she'd done more than that—she'd responded to him and enjoyed it as much as he had. But as he drove through the dark, snowy streets of Cheyenne on the way to his apartment, her words came back to haunt him.

"*... You're too fickle ... I wouldn't want to really fall in love with you.*"

So what the hell was he doing? Why was he so happy she'd responded to him despite what she'd said? And why had he felt so insulted to hear he wasn't really her type? She wasn't really his type, either. Dammit, she was his friend! Why was he messing around with a good friendship, one he valued a helluva lot?

Cursing at his own idiotic confusion, he snapped on the radio just in time to hear Wendy Wyoming sighing, "I have to say, most people like spring or summer, but I think winter's the best time of the year. And that last song makes me think of snuggling up by the fire with a special man and passing on a little . . . love."

He groaned at the way she exhaled that last word and the way his body reacted to it. Or was he really reacting to the feelings still surging through him from kissing Melody? Dammit all. Now he *had* to meet Wendy Wyoming. He absolutely *had* to!

Chapter Four

Attending a Hunter family dinner was a lot like trying to eat on the floor of the U.S. Senate when a major tax revision was under consideration, Melody mused, glancing around the table. Her father, Michael Hunter, threw out a comment about the upcoming election, then sat back in his chair at the head of the table, smiling while his wife, David, Barbara and Jason debated the merits of one of the candidates as if they could sway the entire electorate by the logic of their arguments.

Melody sighed, rolled her eyes and almost started giggling when she caught Barbara's longtime lover, Alan Jordan, who was always included in family gatherings as Jason was, make the same face.

Losing interest in the conversation, Melody observed the members of her family in turn. At fifty-six, her father was losing his dark hair or, as he put it, growing a heck of a lot more forehead. He was also beginning to develop a slight paunch. But in Melody's eyes he was still the same handsome, stubborn, energetic man she'd adored since childhood.

On his right, Barbara held court, gesturing gracefully with her hands to emphasize a point she was making, then smoothing down the sides of the chin-length honey-blond hair she'd inherited from her mother. The animation in her vivid green eyes, her chic navy designer pantsuit and its hot pink blouse and matching accessories, her erect posture, all demanded and received the attention she obviously felt was her due.

Sitting at Barbara's right, Alan smiled at Melody and winked before turning back to listen to Barbara again. Melody wondered for the umpteenth time why a man as handsome and talented as Alan Jordan remained devoted to her sister when Barbara continually insisted she wasn't ready to settle down and marry him yet.

In Melody's opinion, Barbara treated Alan abominably. Over the years he had built a successful medical practice and become influential in community affairs. He also had a warm sense of humor that attracted female attention the way pollen attracts bees. And yet Barbara breezed in and out of Cheyenne three or four times a year, taking it for granted that Alan would be there waiting for her.

Melody skipped over Jason. He'd dominated her thoughts too darn much since Wednesday night. Besides, looking at her mother was much less disturbing. Karen Hunter was an older, softer replica of Barbara. Streaks of grey peppered her hair now and, at fifty-four, a few lines creased her fair skin, but Melody sincerely hoped she would age as beautifully as her mother had.

Though Melody couldn't see David's fiancée, Liz Erickson, very well since she was sitting on the same side of the table as Melody and David, it was easy to conjure up a mental picture of her. Melody had more in common with Liz than with any of the other people present. Liz was only five-foot-five, had short black hair and was quiet and unassuming, although she could be assertive when she wanted to. She raised Appaloosa horses with her family and usually dressed like a cowgirl, but tonight she wore a pretty lavender skirt and sweater.

Melody's survey of the dinner guests was interrupted when her mother sighed and started to get up. "It looks like it's time to face the dishes."

"Sit still, Mom. I'll take care of it," Melody offered quickly, glad of an excuse to leave the table. Since her political views tended to be more liberal than the rest of the family's, she rarely entered into their debates.

"This is just like old times, having you all here for dinner," Michael Hunter declared, patting his stomach with both hands.

Melody paused in the midst of clearing away her father's dessert plate and dropped an affectionate kiss on his cheek before teasing, "You sound like an old mother hen, happy to have all her chicks home, Dad."

"Darn right," her father answered, aiming a swat at her backside. When she easily dodged it, picked up Barbara's plate and moved on to pick up Alan's, Michael asked his elder daughter, "How long can you stay this time?"

"Just for the weekend," Barbara answered. "I have to be in Washington by Monday afternoon to get ready for the president's press conference."

David leaned forward, staring across the table at his sister. "Whoa! Did you say the *president's* press conference?"

Barbara shrugged nonchalantly but couldn't entirely suppress an excited smile. "Just got the promotion last week."

Alan's right shoulder knocked against Melody's arm as he whipped around to stare at Barbara. Melody juggled her load of dirty dishes, heard him gasp, then saw his naturally fair complexion pale even more before flushing a dull, angry red that clashed with his coppery hair.

Pandemonium erupted as the rest of the family clustered around Barbara, offering kisses and hugs of congratulation. A pang of jealousy ripped through Melody as she hugged her sister, but she pushed it aside. Jealousy was a self-destructive emotion, and she'd experienced the feeling enough to ignore it most of the time. After all, Barbara couldn't help being so successful.

When the commotion died down, Melody looked at Alan. His normal color had returned, but his frozen expression worried her. Frowning at her sister's insensitivity, Melody unobtrusively slipped into the kitchen.

Barbara should have told Alan her news in private, she thought as she started loading the dishwasher. Barbara might be gorgeous and talented, but she wasn't always very bright when it came to handling personal relationships. It wasn't her way to consider anyone else's feelings. Melody didn't think her sister intended to be cruel. She was just self-absorbed and loved the spotlight and was . . . well, Barbara. A moment later, Alan joined Melody at the sink.

She worked silently, sympathizing with his unspoken shock and hurt. He handed her the dinner plates, then turned away, clutching the rim of the sink so tightly that she feared his fingers would break. He shuddered with a deep, wrenching sigh. Melody wiped her hands on a dishtowel, then gently touched Alan's shoulder.

"It's hopeless. She doesn't even confide in me anymore," he murmured.

Melody nodded but didn't speak. After a moment, he continued.

"When she first left, it was all right because I had medical school ahead of me and a practice to start. I wanted her to be happy. But I thought eventually she'd realize she belonged in Wyoming with me."

"You could always move back east to be with her, Alan," Melody suggested.

He shook his head, then gave her a sad smile. "I've thought about it, but I love Wyoming. And the way she bounces around with her job, we wouldn't have much of a marriage. Besides, her life is so exciting now, I don't have much to offer her. I've just been clinging to an impossible dream."

"Those are the hardest ones to give up," Melody said quietly, knowing only too well what it felt like to try to compete with the glamour surrounding her sister.

"How would you know?"

"I loved somebody with that kind of a life for a long time." She glanced away and sighed. "But he was way out of my league."

Shaking his head, Alan reached out to lift her chin with his index finger and looked deep into her eyes. "I can't imagine anyone being out of your league. You're a special woman, Melody. If I had any brains at all, I'd forget Barbara and fall in love with you. Are you over this guy now?"

She shrugged. "Probably as much as I ever will be."

Alan leaned down and placed a gentle, friendly kiss on Melody's lips. Jason, who had been listening for the last several minutes from the doorway, immediately cleared his throat and entered the room.

"Are you guys about finished? The others want to go out dancing."

Alan dropped his hand from Melody's chin as if she'd suddenly become radioactive and stepped back. Melody shot Jason a quick frown, then nodded.

"Let me wash up the rest of the pans first. It'll only take a minute."

"I'll, uh, go back to the dining room," Alan said. He hesitated, then added, "Thanks for listening, Melody."

"Anytime, Alan."

Melody turned back to the sink. Jason fished a clean dishtowel out of the appropriate drawer and silently held out his left hand for the first pot. Busy with her writing career, Karen Hunter had long ago trained all her "kids" in the art of kitchen duty.

"Making time with Alan?" Jason asked in a deceptively neutral tone.

"He just needed a sympathetic ear."

"And everyone knows how sympathetic you are."

Melody looked at him over the tops of her glasses, wondering why she'd detected a trace of sarcasm in Jason's voice. "I don't mind. Why should you?"

"I don't, but I wouldn't give old Alan too much sympathy. He's been a fool to put up with the situation all these years. He should have found someone else a long time ago."

Melody slapped another pan into Jason's waiting hands frowning thoughtfully. "People can't just decide who they're going to love, Jason. Sometimes emotions exist whether we want them to or not."

Jason paused in the middle of drying the pan while he considered Melody's statement. "Like your feelings for the guy you think was out of your league?"

Melody stiffened. "Yeah, Mr. Nosey Parker. Something like that."

"Who was he, Mel? That jerk you were engaged to? I saw him at the capitol last week, by the way."

She glanced up at him, wishing she had the nerve to tell him. Wendy Wyoming would. But Melody shook her head and murmured, "Never mind, Jason."

"I'll punch his lights out for you if you want me to."

Melody chuckled at the mental picture of Jason punching himself in the nose for her. "That's not necessary, but thanks for the offer."

Jason grinned back at her. "Anytime, Mel Just say the word."

David stuck his head through the doorway then, complaining, "Can't you guys speed it up? We're all ready to go."

"You go on ahead. We'll have to take two cars anyway," Jason answered. He glanced over his shoulder to make certain they were alone again, then said quietly, "Alan was right about one thing, Melody."

"What's that?"

"This guy you loved wasn't out of your league. Nobody is. You were just too damn good for him."

She handed him the last pot and pulled out the drain basket before smiling up at him. "Thanks, Jason."

He ruffled her hair, then stepped back and snapped the dishtowel at her. "Come on, Squirt. Let's go boogie."

Twenty minutes later Melody was admiring Jason's broad back as he led the way into the bar of the Roadway Inn, one of Cheyenne's popular watering holes for singles. Just inside the door he paused for a moment, to let their eyes adjust to the darkness of the bar after the bright lighting in the motel lobby. Then he reached behind him, took her hand and pulled her up beside him to point out the table across the room the others had staked out. She nodded her understanding, sure that her voice would never carry over the music blasting from the bandstand. When Jason started shouldering his way through the crowd, she followed, clinging tightly to his hand.

Melody didn't like bars much, and particularly not crowded, crazy ones like the Roadway. With her petite stature and youthful appearance, she always got carded and had to put up with the inevitable teasing that went along with it. But it had become something of a tradition for the six of them to celebrate Barbara's homecomings, so she had felt compelled to go along tonight.

As usual, Jason was greeted on all sides as they moved toward their table. By the time they got settled in, greeted the other members of the group and ordered drinks, Melody felt overwhelmed by the smoke, the noise and the endless stream of people approaching their table to greet Barbara and laugh and swap stories with David and Jason.

Melody would happily have spent the evening people-watching from the safety of her seat at the table. But when the band started playing "Sometimes a Bad Girl, Sometimes a Lady," Jason grabbed her hand and hustled her onto the crowded dance floor.

During an evening out with the gang, Jason usually danced with her two or three times while he scanned the crowd for a more suitable playmate. Melody looked up, caught him winking at someone behind her and clenched her teeth in irritation.

Perhaps it was sibling rivalry rearing its ugly head at having the ever-popular Barbara home again. It might be that tall, buxom redhead inside her challenging the boundaries, as she seemed to be doing more often now that Melody was playing Wendy Wyoming on a regular basis. Or maybe it was simply wounded feminine vanity at being treated as a warm-up act—again.

Whatever the reason, Melody felt a sudden consuming desire to command Jason's complete attention, at least for a little while. But how to go about capturing his attention without doing something outrageous, such as kicking him in the shins, for instance? What would Wendy Wyoming do?

Normally, Melody simply moved to the rhythm of the music and left the fancy stuff to Jason. But Wendy would... A secretive smile curved Melody's mouth. She closed her eyes for a moment, concentrating on bringing out her alter ego, much as she did in KBOY's control booth. She couldn't use Wendy's voice without giving her secret away, but she could use Wendy's personality.

The next time Jason twirled her away, she threw back her shoulders, allowing her hips more freedom and encouraging the slit up the right side of her skirt to fall open. When he pulled her back to him again, she unbuttoned the top two buttons at her neckline and fanned herself with one hand to indicate that she felt too warm when he raised an eyebrow at her. Sheer feminine instinct prompted her to raise her left hand, fluff out the curls at the back of her neck and send him a naughty, mysterious smile.

To Melody's gratification, Jason's eyes remained glued to her every movement for the rest of the song. When the band moved into what they called "belly-rubbin' music," she turned smoothly into Jason's arms before he could even think about suggesting they go back to the table or change partners. She felt his chest heave out a deep sigh, then smiled wickedly and laid her head against the front of his shirt when he gathered her close and began to shuffle slowly around the dance floor.

Willing his body to relax as Melody snuggled against him, Jason closed his eyes for an instant and wondered what the hell had come over her. When had she learned to dance like that? She hadn't done anything all that unusual; he'd seen plenty of more suggestive moves before. But the subtle sensuality she emitted was affecting him more than if she'd started to shimmy or take off her clothes. Had she always been this appealing, this desirable?

Lately it seemed that Mel had turned into a chameleon on him. Tonight at the Hunter house, among the extroverted, dominating personalities of the other members of her family, she'd almost faded into the background. He hadn't even noticed what she'd been wearing then. She'd just been quiet little Mel who took over household chores without complaint and nurtured anyone who needed her.

But here on the dance floor, Melody had transformed into a beguiling, sexy woman. He couldn't take his eyes off her slim body, enhanced by her royal-blue dress with the slit up the right side, which showed an alarming amount of shapely thigh whenever he twirled her.

Why was it suddenly impossible to remember that she'd been a sister for him for nearly half his life? Tonight she felt like a lovable kitten in his arms, one he wanted to stroke and pet and hold even closer. And for the first time he noticed other men eyeing her speculatively, and he wanted to button her dress up to her chin and go find a safety pin for that slit in her skirt!

At that moment she raised her head from his chest, tilted her chin up and bestowed a smile of such warmth and invitation on him that his breath caught in his chest. Her soft red lips enticed him, the sparkle in her eyes pulled him down, and the sweet fragrance of her perfume enveloped him as he bent closer. He felt his groin tighten. The urge to kiss her was compelling enough to make him forget that they were not alone.

Then someone bumped into him from behind and the spell was broken. Jason jerked his head up and glanced around, hoping nobody else had noticed what he'd been about to do. He felt his neck flush when he received several sly grins and a surprised glare from David Hunter, who was dancing nearby with Liz.

Melody cuddled closer, the little wretch. The feel of her soft breasts rubbing against him just above his belt buckle shot hot sparks of arousal through him. He gulped, then tried to subtly ease her away from him, but she wrapped her arms tightly around his waist and didn't budge. Sweat broke out on his forehead, and he knew he had to get away from Mel and stay away.

Luckily, the song finally ended and the band announced they'd be taking a short break. Jason grabbed Melody's hand and nudged her along in front of him. Back at the table, he gulped down the rest of his drink and scanned the room for another woman, any other woman, to get his mind off Melody.

Debbie Adams gave him a coy smile from a table in the next row. Without excusing himself, Jason bolted out of his chair and was across the narrow aisle in seconds flat.

"What's with him?" Liz asked.

Craning his neck to have a look, David grinned when he located a woman smiling with open admiration at Jason. "Looks like he spotted a redhead."

"Is he *still* doing that?" Barbara asked.

"Of course," Melody answered wryly.

Barbara shook her head as she turned to Melody. "I must have been imagining how chummy you two looked out there on the dance floor, then."

Struggling to keep a satisfied smirk off her face, Melody shrugged. Let everyone else think what they wanted. *She* knew she'd gotten to Jason out there. And for now that was enough.

Jason walked by with a glowing Debbie Adams on his arm. Melody acknowledged them both with a smiling nod, then turned to converse with David's fiancée.

Liz inclined her head in the direction Jason and Debbie had headed before asking, "Doesn't it bother you when he takes off with other women?"

"Why should it? We're not really out on a date," Melody replied.

Liz grimaced. "I guess what bothers me is that he and David are so much alike. I'm afraid David will miss having his stable of women if Jason doesn't settle down soon."

"I heard that," David protested, "and you don't have a thing to worry about."

Liz smiled at him before turning back to Melody, anxiety evident in her smoky gray eyes. The band started playing again, forcing them to lean closer together in order to be heard.

"I know David hates it when I act jealous," Liz confided, "but sometimes I can't help myself." She glanced pointedly around the room. "And places like this—this meat market, give me the creeps. Some of these women ought to buy hunting licenses."

Liz turned to talk to David then, and Melody sat back and watched the crowd, chuckling when a blonde at another table snatched her date's hat off his head, held it up in front of their faces to create an illusion of privacy and gave him a sizzling kiss that everyone could see, Stetson or no Stetson.

Jason strolled by again a few minutes later, this time with a woman whose name Melody vaguely remembered was Erica. Erica's left arm was wrapped around Jason's waist, while his right hand rested on the curve of her hip. Melody sighed unconsciously, then jerked her eyes away from the striking couple when Liz tapped her hand.

Eyeing Melody thoughtfully, Liz said, "Sometimes I get the impression you feel more for Jason than friendship."

"It wouldn't do me much good if I did," Melody answered calmly.

"Maybe you're in love with him and don't even know it," Liz suggested, a hopeful note in her voice.

Melody shook her head and smiled. Liz opened her mouth as if she wanted to say something more, but David was standing beside her chair, obviously ready to dance again. Taking the hand he extended to her, she stood, calling over her shoulder as they left, "We'll talk more later, Melody."

Melody waved in acknowledgement, then settled back in relief when Barbara and Alan also left the table. Liz had been getting just a little too close for comfort. She liked Liz and hoped her brother would be smart enough to hang on to her, but David's history of fidelity wasn't much better than Jason's.

Melody admired Liz's courage in loving David, and applauded her insistence on a long engagement, despite his pleas to move up the wedding date. Liz was intelligent and perceptive. Thank goodness she was wrong about Melody's feelings for Jason.

What Melody felt for Jason, especially when confronted with him pursuing a string of women, couldn't be love. She wouldn't deny a strong physical attraction to him, of course. But as she watched him waltzing slinky Erica around the dance floor, Melody didn't feel the gut-wrenching jealousy she had suffered several years ago, only a kind of sad resignation. And a fierce, growing determination to teach him a lesson.

A shadow fell across the table then, and a low voice from her past spoke close to her ear, "Hello, Melody."

Her eyes widened in surprised for a moment as she looked up into the warm brown eyes of her ex-fiancé, Vic Grant. "Vic! I heard you were back in town, but I— It's been a long time."

"Too long, Melody," he answered with a smile.

"Are you still living in Los Angeles?"

"Dance with me and I'll tell you all about it," he invited, inclining his head toward the dance floor.

Melody studied him warily for a moment, remembering how hurt and angry he'd been when she'd broken their engagement. Though convinced of the rightness of her decision, she had been hurt, as well. He looked good to her now, with a California tan, a conservative sport coat and a new self-confidence in his bearing, and she was curious about his life since she'd last seen him. But she didn't want to give him any encouragement about resuming their old relationship.

Smiling, Vic held up his palms. "I know I acted like a jerk when I left, but don't worry about the past, Melody. All I want is a friend."

Reading the sincerity in his eyes, she felt a flash of affection for Vic. They'd always been good friends. It was only when they'd become lovers that she'd realized she couldn't commit herself to him for the rest of her life.

Smiling, she answered, "Sounds good to me," and followed him onto the dance floor. They danced together for the rest of the set. Melody was pleased to learn that Vic had moved back to Cheyenne for good because he'd become tired of L.A.'s rat race and because his parents needed more assistance now that his father's health was failing.

They spent the next hour and a half talking and dancing, but by midnight Melody's feet ached and her eyelids drooped. Her students were always a handful on Friday afternoons, and she'd worked late the night before taping her Wendy Wyoming show so she could be free for the family dinner tonight. She covered a yawn with her palm and sat up straighter.

Jason and the others would want to stay until the place closed, then go out for breakfast. She didn't want to spoil anyone's fun, but she wondered how she'd survive another two hours. Vic caught her stifling a second yawn and offered to drive her home.

"Thanks. I'd appreciate that," she said. "Just let me tell Jason I'm leaving."

She found him five minutes later, sitting at a table in the rear of the bar with Erica on one side of him and Debbie Adams on the other. He excused himself when he saw Melody, then approached her with a grumpy scowl on his face.

"Sorry to interrupt," she said quickly. "I just wanted to let you know I'm going home. Vic Grant's offered me a ride."

Jason's body stiffened. He craned his neck until he located Grant gathering up Melody's coat and purse at the other table. He'd spent a miserable evening avoiding Melody and had been painfuly aware of her dancing with Vic for the last two hours. He'd finally admitted to himself not five minutes ago that he felt jealous as hell—an alien, almost frightening experience for him.

He resented feeling possessive about any woman, but it seemed even worse that Melody should be the one to make him feel that way. He didn't like it, didn't understand it, but he couldn't ignore it. When he'd seen Alan kiss her in the kitchen, an alarm had gone off inside him like a smoke detector's shrill warning. And when he'd first realized that the man she was dancing with was her ex-fiancé he'd been haunted by the need to know the identity of the man Melody had told Alan she had loved. Was it Vic Grant? For the rest of the evening he'd practically ignored Debbie and Erica and had put away Scotch as if there were no such thing as a hangover.

He had to find out if what he thought he was feeling for Melody was real. He'd have to handle her carefully. He respected and liked Mel too much to risk hurting her. But he needed some time alone with her now, and he'd be damned if he'd let that weasel Grant worm his way back into her life.

Taking her arm in a less-than-gentle grip, he announced, "I'll take you home."

Melody argued, "Don't be silly, Jason. There's no reason for you to cut your evening short."

He stopped and glared down at her. His jaw clenched for a moment before he said in a no-nonsense tone, "I brought you here, Melody Jane Hunter. And I'll take you home."

She opened her mouth to protest, but Jason pulled her along with such determination that her only choices were to follow or to allow herself to be dragged. When they reached the table, Jason informed the others of their plans, removed Melody's coat and purse from a startled Vic's hands, then hustled Melody outside before she could protest.

He unlocked the Blazer before curtly asking, "How much hooch did you have in there?"

"One drink. I switched to Coke after that."

"Good. You drive. I've had too much."

Melody's eyebrows rose in surprise. He didn't look or act as if he'd had too much to drink. But he wasn't exactly behaving normally, either. He handed her the keys and opened the door for her, then hurried around to the other side of the vehicle.

Pulling his Stetson low over his eyes, he slouched down in the seat, and seemed exasperated as Melody struggled to reach the gas pedal and brake. Ignoring his irritating behavior, she moved the bench seat forward, turned on the ignition and backed out of the parking space.

Melody's temper simmered during the ride to his apartment. Finally, when she could stand the hostile silence no longer, she demanded, "What's the matter with you, Jason?"

"Nothing."

"Don't give me that. Why are you so mad at me? David's usually the one who gets all brotherly and protective. And it's not like we were out on a real date, for heaven's sake."

"Maybe *I* felt brotherly and protective. I haven't forgotten how much Grant hurt you."

She glared at him across the darkened car. "Read my lips, Jason. You are *not* my brother!"

"Watch the road, Squirt."

"I don't understand your attitude," she complained.

He shrugged and remained silent until Melody parked in front of his apartment complex. She slammed the gearshift into neutral and left the engine idling, then shot him an exasperated, expectant look that clearly said, "Well, hurry up and get out so I can go home." He reached over, shut off the ignition and pocketed the keys.

"Jason—" she began impatiently.

"Wait a minute. There's, uh, something I want to talk to you about."

Sighing, she rubbed her forehead. "I don't think that's such a good idea right now. I'm tired, and you're crabby and..."

"Please, Mel. It won't take long."

"Oh, all right."

"Uh, could we go inside so I can unkink my legs?"

She couldn't help grinning at his request. Now that he mentioned it, he did look pretty uncomfortable. Once inside his second-floor apartment, Melody refused his offer to take her coat, since she didn't intend to stay long. Jason left his coat on, as well. Melody settled into one corner of the big sofa in Jason's living room. He took the other corner and turned to face her.

The serious, hesitant look in his eyes made Melody feel irritated and anxious. Whatever Jason wanted to discuss was clearly important to him, but she suspected he was about to give her a brotherly lecture. And if he did, she just might belt him a good one.

The silence stretched out between them until Melody finally asked, "What's on your mind, Jason?"

"Well, uh . . ." He squirmed in his seat for a moment before looking directly into her eyes. "First I want to say I'm sorry if I embarrassed you tonight. And I know I'm not your brother."

"But . . ." she prompted when he looked away.

His voice softened to a low rumble. "But what if we *were* out on a real date tonight?"

Melody's heart skipped a beat. Was he saying what she thought he was saying? "Don't be silly, Jason. We're just friends."

"Maybe we could be more than friends."

Now it was Melody's turn to look away. A giddy excitement flooded her, followed by a tidal wave of confusion. This was what she wanted, what she'd hoped for and dreamed of for years. Wasn't it? Words rushed out of her mouth before she could stop them.

"I don't understand. You know I'm not your type—"

Jason tossed his hat onto the end table and ran frustrated fingers through his hair. "Dammit, Mel, will you stop telling me what my type is?"

"Well, you always go for the same kind of woman. You had two of them swarming all over you tonight. And then, of course, there's Wendy Wyoming. You sat out in a cold car for over an hour hoping to get a glimpse of her."

He chuckled, then said with a devilish smile, "Why, Mel, you *are* jealous!"

"I am not!"

He held up one hand to silence the anger in her voice and said softly, "Look, I didn't enjoy being with those women tonight. The whole crowd seemed kind of, well... shallow. Maybe I want to follow your advice about dating a woman with a bigger IQ and—"

"Never mind the rest. I get the picture," she replied tartly. "I get to be your guinea pig."

"I wouldn't quite put it like that, Mel. I, uh..." He looked away again for a moment, then turned back and gazed deeply into her eyes. "Shoot, I don't know why it's so hard for me to say this to you."

She leaned forward, surprised at his open vulnerability, wanting to help and encourage him. "Go on."

Giving her a nervous smile, he took a deep breath and said in a rush, "The fact is, I've always thought of you as my little sister. But lately you don't seem like a sister. I don't know why, but all of a sudden I'm, well... Dammit, Mel, I'm attracted to you!"

A lump formed in her throat, making speech difficult. Her confusion mushroomed. She should have been deliriously happy to hear Jason say he was attracted to her. But now that he'd actually said it, she felt more scared than happy. The wise thing to do would be to back off and see if they couldn't regain their old, comfortable friendship.

But tonight on the dance floor she'd had a glimpse of what it was to have Jason's full attention. It was exciting and wonderful. If he meant what she thought he did, how could she refuse an opportunity to get closer to him? But he could hurt her so deeply....

When she didn't answer, Jason gulped and rushed on. "Look, I know you said I'm not your type, but haven't you felt something, too?"

Touched by his uncertainty, she nodded slowly, admitting, "Yes, Jason. I've felt something."

He let out a relieved sigh, then laughed out loud. "Thank God for that! You wouldn't believe how weird this has been for me. I felt like a real lech.'' He scooted closer, taking her hand and clasping it between his hard palms. ''Will you go out with me, Melody?''

''I don't know,'' she said, her voice wobbling. ''Dating each other could wreck our friendship.''

''It wouldn't have to. We'll take things real slow.... Say, maybe start out with just a movie and a drink,'' he coaxed. He raised his left hand and gently stroked her cheek.

She shut her eyes and felt a lump harden like concrete in her throat. Until this moment she'd felt relatively safe playing her little game with Wendy Wyoming and Jason. She'd been able to maintain a realistic perception of him and accept the knowledge that she could never have him. She'd told herself she was only trying to make him see her as a woman. But if she spent time with him in a dating atmosphere, could she continue to control her feelings for him? Not likely.

''I wouldn't hurt you for anything, Mel.''

She gulped when she opened her eyes and found him close enough to kiss, his expression earnest and intense. No, he wouldn't hurt her intentionally. But did she have the nerve to take a chance on falling in love with him again? From somewhere deep inside, Melody heard Wendy Wyoming's sultry voice demanding, ''Go for it, you wimp!''

Jason smiled at her then, a sincere, boyish, almost pleading smile, and she was lost. She felt her lips curve up at the corners as she slowly nodded her head. Jason let out a whoop and enveloped her in a bear hug.

Then his mouth found hers, and Melody pushed doubt aside and gave herself up to the magic of his kiss. His lips were warm and firm, his mustache soft and tickly. She raised her hands and stroked his cheeks, feeling the raspy evening stubble against her palms.

She moaned when his tongue parted her lips, sweeping into her mouth and gently exploring. When she inhaled, she caught the scent of his after-shave and a smoky reminder of the Roadway Inn. He moved her arms up to his neck and pushed her back into the soft cushions, molding their torsos together. She clung to him, reveling in the pressure of his muscular chest against her breasts, the warm nip of his lips down the length of her neck and the soft, springy texture of his hair as she ran her fingers through it.

Jason groaned—she thought in pleasure and frustration—as she felt his big hands caressing the length of her spine through her winter coat. She sighed in empathy. Her hands itched to touch his warm, hard flesh but encountered the cool, slick material of his down jacket instead.

They were both breathing heavily by the time Jason eased away. He rested his forehead against hers, then let out a deep, rumbing chuckle that sounded like pure contentment. Melody smiled in response, glowing inside and out when he pushed her head against his shoulder and simply held her.

"You pack a heck of a punch for such a little gal."

"I know."

He chuckled again, then sighed. "I don't know if you've changed or if I've changed, but I think this could be dynamite for both of us, Mel."

"Mm-hmmm." She closed her eyes and snuggled closer.

"You falling asleep on me?"

She tipped her head back to look up at him. "Never. But it's getting awfully late."

He gave her one more squeeze before disentangling himself and pulling her gently to her feet. "Come on, then. Let's get you home."

Melody didn't want to leave, and from the heated look in Jason's eyes she knew he didn't want her to leave, either. But she wasn't ready to spend the night with him, and that was what would happen if she didn't go now. Jason looked deeply into her eyes for a moment, then nodded and, tucking her against his side, walked her back out to the Blazer.

He opened the door for her and handed her the keys before pulling her into his arms for one last lusty kiss. Drawing back to study the sweet, bemused expression on her face, he laughed out loud when he saw that the lenses of her glasses had steamed up in the frigid air.

"Maybe I'd better drive you home after all."

Melody shook her head as if to clear it, then turned and climbed up into the vehicle. "I'll be fine, and so will your beloved Blazer," she assured him.

He closed the door and rapped on the window. When Melody rolled it down, he asked, "How about seeing that movie tomorrow night?"

"All right. Good night, Jason."

"It won't be a good night at all, Mel," he answered in a grim tone belied by the wicked twinkle in his eyes. "I'll have to take a cold shower now."

"Oh, you," she scolded, fighting down a blush as she started the engine. Having Jason treat her as a woman was going to take some getting used to.

"I'll come over around six-thirty, and we'll choose one."

"See you then," she answered before starting the engine.

Melody drove home and got ready for bed as if she were on automatic pilot. But when she crawled between the cold sheets and pulled the blankets up, the pleasant numbness wore off and confusion returned. She'd wanted to teach him a lesson, but she had an uncomfortable premonition that Jason could easily become the teacher instead. Was she already in over her head?

"Stop that, Melody," she ordered herself, scooting back into a sitting position, her arms wrapped around her knees.

"You agreed to go out with Jason, and you're not, absolutely *not* going to let anything spoil it."

She must have something going for her, she mused, leaning back against her pillow. All in all, it had been quite an evening. Alan Jordan had come to her with his troubles, had told her she was special and had hinted that he could be interested in her if things were different. She'd had a good time with Vic, something she wouldn't have believed possible only this morning.

But the real highlight of the evening had been hearing Jason admit he was attracted to her and ask her for a date. He'd held her and kissed her in a way she'd only been able to dream about for years. Maybe she was a fool to get involved with him, but she didn't care if she was.

Chuckling in delight, she grabbed the extra pillow and hugged it before murmuring, "Yeah, Mel, you did all right tonight."

Still hugging the pillow, she slid down in the bed, rolled onto her side and willed her body to relax. Morning and the inevitable doubts and jitters would come soon enough. But for now she was determined to fall asleep and relive in her dreams those ecstatic moments in Jason's arms.

Chapter Five

Melody spent the next morning cleaning her apartment and catching up on her laundry. But she ran out of work by eleven-thirty and found herself pacing the small living room, brooding about Jason. Fifteen minutes later, when Barbara arrived unexpectedly, Melody was so relieved to have a distraction that she practically yanked her sister inside.

As she shed her coat and gloves, Barbara looked around and nodded her approval. "No matter where you live, Melody, you always make a home."

Surprised by the wistful note in Barbara's voice, Melody shot her a sharp glance. She noted that for the first time in years, her gorgeous older sister looked less than camera-ready. There were dark circles under Barbara's eyes, her hair lacked its normal sheen and bounce and her shoulders slumped ever so slightly. Though her oversize sweater and gray wool slacks were fashionable, Barbara's usual panache was missing somehow.

Melody rarely felt close to Barbara. In fact, she'd often envied Barbara and felt intimidated by her. But they were sisters, after all, and Melody loved her despite their uneasy relationship. If Barbara needed an ear—and she looked as if she did—Melody would provide it. Melody ushered her into the kitchen, indicated a seat at the table and started heating a kettle of water on the stove.

Barbara exhaled a sigh when Melody served her a mug of herbal tea. After seating herself, Melody asked quietly, "Is something wrong, Barbara?"

"Nothing much." Barbara sipped from her cup, then sighed again, staring off into space. "Last night Alan told me flat out that as far as he's concerned our relationship is over."

Melody winced inwardly at the cool, hard tone of her sister's voice. Barbara thrust her chin out at a defiant angle and smiled, but beneath that smile Melody detected real pain. "I'm sorry if you're hurting," she said quietly.

"Hurting?" Barbara's voice rose on the last syllable. "God, Melody, I feel like he's ripped out my heart and stomped on it!"

More than a little shocked by the intensity of her sister's statement, Melody stared at her. Barbara had always been affectionate toward Alan, but nothing in her past behavior had indicated that she felt any grand passion for him. Melody shifted uncomfortably before her sister's outraged glare but said firmly, "Barbara, be reasonable. Surely you knew Alan wouldn't wait forever. He's got a life, too, and he gets really lonely sometimes."

Barbara's glare faded. She looked away them, her voice softening slightly, "I thought he'd give me plenty of warning when he got fed up and we could work something out. But he wouldn't discuss it at all last night. Has he found someone else?"

"Not that I know of. I think it was the way you announced your promotion that set him off. He was hurt you hadn't confided in him first." They remained silent for a moment. Then Melody continued, "Frankly, I'm surprised at your reaction. Your career has really taken off now. I thought you wanted that. And you must meet lots of interesting men through your work."

"I do want it. It's the most exciting thing that's ever happened to me. There's a great big world out there, and I need to explore it," Barbara answered. "And I do meet lots of men, but I'm never in one place long enough to get seriously involved."

She set down her cup before looking away again. "My career is hectic and exciting, but it's lonely for me, too, sometimes. And as long as I had Alan I didn't have to worry about growing old alone or listen to my biological clock ticking away."

Melody spoke hesitantly at first. "Barbara, think about what you just said. You've been using Alan like a security blanket. Do you really think that's fair to him?"

"No. I know it's not," she replied, weariness evident now in her tone, "but I never thought I'd have to choose between Alan and my career. He's been a big part of my life for a long time, and I don't know if I can give him up. But then, he may not give me any choice."

Melody had no answer to that. It was a revelation to learn that Barbara, who had always seemed totally confident, sure of what she wanted and able to get it, could feel pain and loneliness and insecurity. It made her seem more human, more approachable, more like Melody. Did David and Jason feel those emotions, too?

Barbara was seven years older than Melody; David and Jason were five years older. When she'd been growing up, they had always already passed beyond whatever stage of development she was suffering through as a timid little girl or troubled teenager. In her eyes, they had been popular and perfect. They hadn't been plagued with zits or shyness. They had been invulnerable. But maybe she'd been too young, too involved with her own worries and problems, to notice theirs.

Now that Melody thought about it, while Barbara, David and Jason all had dynamic, exciting careers, their personal lives weren't any more settled than hers. And they all came to her for emotional support from time to time.

Finally Barbara smiled more naturally and said, "I know I haven't been much of a sister to you, but I appreciate your listening to me."

Melody smiled back, feeling closer to her sister than she had in years. "Let's go out to lunch. It'll make you feel better, and I could use some advice about clothes and makeup."

Barbara's eyes lighted up at the mention of two of her favorite topics, and within minutes they were on their way to the Owl Inn. Once they were seated in a private booth and served steaming bowls of clam chowder, Barbara put a determinedly cheerful expression on her face. "Did you say something about wanting my advice?" she asked.

"I've been trying to change my image lately. I want to look more...oh, I don't know, I guess 'sophisticated' is what I'm aiming for," Melody answered.

Barbara's eyes narrowed as she studied her little sister thoughtfully. "I noticed the dress you were wearing last night was more daring than what you usually wear. And that rinse on your hair looks good. Any special reason you're doing this?"

Melody nodded hesitantly, unsure of how much she wanted to tell her sister. It was ironic, really, that while so many people came to her for sympathy she rarely shared her own problems with anyone else. But because Barbara knew all the people involved and would be leaving Cheyenne soon anyway, she was the perfect confidante.

After glancing over both shoulders and all around the room and finding the restaurant reassuringly empty, Melody quickly filled Barbara in on her new job as Wendy Wyoming, Jason's reaction to her confession and everything else that had happened in the past few weeks.

Barbara listened intently, her green eyes reflecting her amazement, her amusement and her sympathy for Melody's feelings about the situation. When Melody finally ran out of words, Barbara leaned forward and enthusiastically began offering suggestions for Melody's new image.

"First, we'll have your color analysis done. No, with your hair and eyes I'm positive you're a winter. We'll just hit the mall. I think I know a couple of styles that would look great on you. Have you thought about getting contacts?"

Melody scowled. "I've already had an appointment with the optometrist, but he doesn't recommend them for me because of my astigmatism."

Barbara tipped her head to one side, studied Melody's face, then pronounced, "No problem. We'll just have to find some frames that emphasize your eyes more. Then we'll go back to your apartment and play beauty shop. I've learned a few tricks from all the makeup people and hairstylists over the years."

"Oh, I don't know if this is worth so much trouble," Melody said with a sigh.

"Why not? I've always thought you and Jason would be perfect for each other."

Melody's eyes widened. "You really thought that? I always thought *you'd* be more his type."

Barbara chuckled. "No way. Jason and I are too much alike. We're both restless and get into trouble looking for excitement. He needs somebody practical and steady, somebody who can see the real Jason—like you—and I need . . . well, never mind what I need."

Melody hesitated before asking, "Do you think Jason could ever settle down with one woman?"

"Of course he could," Barbara assured her confidently. "He just needs to grow up a little. And from what you've told me, I think he's ready to do that."

Muttering, "I hope you're right," Melody climbed out of the booth and shrugged into her coat. Barbara followed suit, then put her arm around Melody's shoulders and gave her a quick hug.

"Come on, kid. Let's shop till we drop. We'll knock Jason's socks off when he sees you tonight."

Four and a half hours later, Melody stepped out of the shower, feeling about ready to drop. Accompanying Barbara on a shopping spree had a lot in common with attending boot camp, she thought wryly. She was now the owner of three new outfits, new glasses, two new pairs of spiky high heels and a ton of accessories she never would have thought of buying for herself.

"Hurry up, Melody," Barbara called through the bathroom door. "It's almost five o'clock, and we still have to do your hair and makeup."

By the time Barbara had finished working on her, Melody barely recognized her own reflection in the mirror. With its natural curliness subdued, her hair looked sleek and chic. Her eyes looked big and mysterious and sparkled with excitement. And with blush added in just the right places, her face looked longer and more elegant.

Before Melody could say a word, Barbara was hustling her into the bedroom, cutting off the tags on Melody's new hot-pink sweater dress and fussing around her like a mother of the bride. Melody was touched by her sister's concern, especially since an occasional touch of sadness in Barbara's eyes revealed that she still hadn't resolved her own feelings about Alan.

Finally Barbara pronounced her ready, wished her luck and returned to the Hunter house. Melody waved her sister off, eyeing the clock with grave misgivings. Jason wouldn't arrive for another thirty minutes. The apartment was horribly silent without her sister's encouraging chatter.

She'd kept so busy all day, she hadn't had time to get nervous. But now, alone in her quiet living room, she felt a herd of frantic butterflies galloping around in her stomach, and her mouth suddenly went dry. She closed her eyes for a moment, then turned on the TV, kicked off her high heels and settled on the sofa to wait, telling herself sternly that the evening would be fun—after waiting all these years to go out on a real date with Jason, it just had to be!

David Hunter answered his front door with a towel around his waist and one side of his face slathered with shaving cream. Jason grinned at him and stepped inside.

"Gettin' ready for a date?"

David shut the door, gestured to Jason to follow him and hurried off to the bathroom, calling over his shoulder, "Yeah. Liz and I are having dinner with her folks tonight. I'm going to be late if I don't put a rush on it."

Jason hung his coat and hat on a rack beside the door before strolling back to join David. He leaned against the bathroom door casing, chuckling at the faces David made getting at the whiskers on his chin.

David caught sight of him in the mirror and asked, "What's up? You look like you're ready for a hot date yourself."

Jason nodded. "That's what I came to talk to you about."

"Oh yeah?" David asked, pausing to shoot Jason a devilish grin. "Want my advice on how to handle her?"

"No. I wanted to tell you who I was going out with." Jason crossed his arms over his chest.

Jason's guarded expression and defensive stance turned David's attention away from his shaving. He finished hurriedly and then asked, "What's the big deal?"

"Mel's my date tonight," Jason answered evenly.

"Melody? As in my kid sister?"

Jason nodded. "I thought you should hear it from me. You gave me a hell of a funny look last night when I was dancing with her."

David's eyes narrowed as he thought back to the previous evening. Then he pointed a finger at Jason. "Yeah, I remember. You looked about ready to kiss her right there on the dance floor—"

"I was. I don't know if I can explain it to you, but I've been attracted to her for quite a while now."

"But you went off with that teacher friend of Mel's, and then later you were with Erica," David argued.

Jason sighed and raised his hands. "I was trying to get my mind off your sister, Dave. But it didn't work. So when I took her home I asked her out, and she accepted."

David shouldered his way past Jason, entered the bedroom and started yanking clothes out of his dresser and closet. He dressed with quick, agitated movements, then marched back to face Jason again, his face flushed, his eyes dark with concern.

"What do you want from her, Jase?"

Jason gave a small shrug, confusion evident in his expression. "I don't know for sure. I've always loved Mel like a sister, but lately I—"

"Well get one thing straight, pal," David answered, poking a hard finger into Jason's chest. "Keep your hands off her until you *do* know for sure. Melody trusts and admires you. You could probably get her into bed without much trouble, but if you don't love her she could really be hurt. Bad."

"Do you think I don't know that? Hell, I've been trying to forget about her for weeks, but I can't. Believe me, Dave, I don't want to see her hurt any more than you do."

David's glare faltered, then faded away, but his voice remained grim. "All right. I believe you. But dammit, Jase, be careful with Mel. She's such a warmhearted, loving little soul, I'll really be ticked off at you if she does get hurt."

Jason nodded his understanding before asking plaintively, "But what if she hurts me?"

David raised his eyebrows, then clapped Jason on the back sympathetically. "Sounds like you've got it bad."

"Maybe," Jason answered, looking away. "I've never been in love, so I don't know what it feels like. And your kid sister's got me wondering if I know her at all."

Laughing, David led his old friend over to the bed and pushed him down into a sitting position. Then he walked to the closet and pulled out his shoes. Sitting down beside Jason, he said, "When I first met Liz, I didn't think much about her. I mean, she was nice and all, and kind of pretty, but she wasn't really like the babes you and I chased, so I didn't pay much attention to her."

Jason leaned back on one elbow, prompting David when he started staring off into thin air with a silly smile on his face. "So what made you notice her?"

"I finally asked her to dance one night when she was out at the Roadway with a bunch of her friends, and she turned me down cold. When I asked her why, she told me flat out that she didn't dance with little boys."

Jason threw back his head and howled with laughter at the indignant expression on David's face. David scowled at him for a moment before asking impatiently, "You want to hear this or not?"

"Go on. I'll shut up," Jason answered, struggling for a sober expression. If David only knew he was laughing because he remembered how much Melody's telling him he wasn't her type had wounded his own ego.

"Well, to make a long story short, every time I ran into her after that I made it a point to sit down and visit with her. Finally I was able to convince her I wasn't such a bad guy after all."

"But how did you know you loved her?" Jason asked. "It sounds to me like you were just responding to a challenge."

"That took some time," David admitted. "I didn't stop seeing other women for quite a while, and I felt confused a lot, but I guess I realized she was the one I really enjoyed being with. I thought about her all the time and found myself calling her just to talk and always looking forward to seeing her. I felt... at peace when I was with her."

"Doesn't sound very passionate," Jason observed dryly.

David turned on him, his eyes rolling in exasperation. "A lot you know! I don't usually talk about my sex life, but you of all people need to hear this, Jase. When I make love with Liz, she's so unselfish that I want to be unselfish, too, and it's just plain dynamite. But it only happens because we care so much about each other."

David looked away then, but not before Jason caught a bleak look in his eyes. He waited, knowing David would tell him what was wrong if he felt like it. A moment later, David continued, his voice heavy with regret. "But you know something? Even after I've asked her to marry me and walked a straight line for months, Liz still doesn't really trust me."

"Do you blame her?" Jason asked quietly.

Shrugging, David left the bed and started combing his hair in front of the mirror hanging over the dresser. "I didn't at first, because, well, I did sow quite a few wild oats in this town. But dammit, Jase, every time another woman even says hello to me, Liz gets all uptight and gets this look in her eyes like she's wondering if I slept with this one, too. It's getting damned old."

"Maybe she just needs a little more time. Or maybe you need to spend more time alone with her where you won't run into so many of your old flames," Jason suggested.

"Maybe," David conceded, laying down the comb. When he reached for the bottle of cologne, he caught Jason's grin in the mirror. "I wouldn't smirk like that if I were you, old buddy. If you do get serious about Mel, you just might run into the same problem."

"You're probably right," Jason answered, standing when David finished preening in front of the mirror and looked ready to leave.

As they shrugged into their coats at the front door, David warned, "Have a good time with Mel, but keep your hands to yourself."

Jason headed toward his Blazer, which he'd picked up from Melody's that afternoon. "Right. See you later, Dave," he called over his shoulder.

When the doorbell, which she'd successfully prodded her landlord into fixing, finally rang, Melody sucked in a deep breath, crammed her feet back into her shoes and scurried to the bedroom for one last reassuring look in the mirror. The bell sounded again, and she straightened her shoulders and forced herself to walk back through the living room as if she had all the time in the world.

Jason stepped inside, wearing his sheepskin-lined coat over a forest-green ski sweater and brown cords. He bent to kiss Melody's cheek before stepping back to study her from head to toe. A surprised expression stole over his face. Melody pulled herself up straight, wishing she felt as sophisticated as Barbara had made her look.

A slow, sexy smile spread across Jason's mouth. He twirled the index finger of his right hand in the air, indicating that he wanted her to turn around for him. Feeling awkward as a newborn colt, Melody complied, smiling in spite of her jittery nerves at his low wolf whistle.

When she faced him again, he said quietly, "Mel, you look gorgeous."

She turned her head in a regal gesture she'd seen Barbara use effectively on occasion but found she couldn't manage a properly haughty expression. Laughing softly, she looked up into his eyes and felt warmed by the sincere admiration she saw there. "Thanks, Jason."

Then that crazy fluttery sensation rose up from the pit of her stomach again, and she looked away. Silently chiding herself for being such a nervous Nellie, she retrieved the newspaper's entertainment section from the coffee table. Jason followed her to the sofa, tugging at the neckline of his sweater as if he were wearing a shirt and tie.

Seated a foot apart, they were both exceedingly polite, each insisting that they go to the movie the other most wanted to see. Since they'd haggled like fishwives over such decisions in the past, Melody found the whole situation bizarre. It would have been funny if she hadn't felt so blasted awkward. And though Jason appeared relaxed, she noticed he was checking his watch more frequently than necessary, and he hadn't cracked one joke or teased her since he'd arrived.

When they finally settled on a musical comedy that had received good reviews, Melody put on her coat and collected her purse. As they drove to the Cole Shopping Center she hoped fervently that the atmosphere between them would improve once they got to the theater. But everything felt out of sync, as though neither could believe they were really out on a date but both were trying hard to go through the motions anyway.

They'd taken Jason's Blazer. Used to being treated as a pal, Melody opened her own door and stepped out onto the pavement before Jason could get around the vehicle to help her. Though he didn't say anything, she could tell by his startled expression that his regular dates expected such service from him. She felt like kicking herself.

And when Jason took her hand and headed for the theater, he walked with his normal long-legged stride, forgetting that she was wearing three-inch heels rather than the more casual shoes she usually favored. He didn't realize what he'd done until they entered the lobby and he noticed that she was flushed and out of breath from trotting to keep up.

Their conversation while they waited for the movie to start sounded strained and trite to Melody. She couldn't remember ever acting so tongue-tied around him before, and Jason heaved an obvious sigh of relief when the lights finally went out. Then the real torture began.

Melody didn't think much about it when Jason put his arm around the back of her seat. A big man like Jason had a hard time getting comfortable in the small theater chairs. But when he started caressing her shoulder and upper arm, as he probably did with his regular dates, she completely lost track of what was happening on the screen and broke out in goose bumps.

Oh, this whole idea is ridiculous, she thought, crossing her legs and then uncrossing them again. Before, whenever Jason had touched her, she'd usually been more turned on than she'd wanted to admit. But it had felt natural and right for him to touch her that way. And the times when he'd kissed her recently had been so spontaneous that she'd enjoyed every single second of contact.

But now, ever aware that they were out on a real date—God, she was beginning to hate that phrase—she was hypersensitive to everything he did, worried that he'd be disappointed somehow, afraid she'd do something so stupid she'd be humiliated for life. Their actions toward each other seemed . . . premeditated.

Melody squirmed beside him, and Jason hastily removed his arm. The evening was off to a lousy start, but he wasn't sure what he could do to improve it. They were both nervous as hell, and this wasn't helping anything. How could he help Melody relax when he couldn't forget David's grim warnings about his behavior?

He glanced down at her, marveling at her changed appearance. Gussied up as she was now, she could give Erica or Debbie a real run for their money. But now that he thought about it, he wasn't sure he liked all the changes.

Oh, he couldn't fault her subtle makeup or sleek new hairdo and glasses, and he loved the way her dress clung to her curves. It touched him that she'd gone to so much trouble to look so beautiful for him. But he kind of missed the old Mel—the one he'd always felt so comfortable with. His friend.

When the movie ended and they were back in his Blazer, Jason decided to see if he couldn't at least try to salvage what was left of the evening. He turned on the radio to fill in any awkward silences and drove west on Pershing Boulevard until he reached the entrance to I-25. Heading north, he followed the highway to the Horse Creek overpass and turned into the driveway of the Little Bear Inn.

This time, Melody waited with mounting anxiety and depression while he came around to the passenger side to open the door for her. She appreciated Jason's choosing a quiet spot for a drink, but her stomach was still churning, and her palms were sweaty. She hadn't been this gauche and, well, downright uncool on her first date in junior high!

After helping her out of the Blazer, Jason put his arm around Melody, hugging her close against his side while he locked up. But instead of moving off toward the building he leaned back against the door and turned her to face him, lacing his fingers across the small of her back. Giving her a wry, lopsided grin, he asked,

"Are we having fun yet, Mel?"

"I don't think so," she answered miserably, bowing her head in mortification. Then she whispered, "I'm sorry, Jason."

"You're sorry?" He snorted in self-derision. "Shoot, it's not your fault. I haven't felt this nervous since the first time I tried to kiss Sally Terkovich in the sixth grade. You do strange things to me, Melody Jane."

She looked up at him, her eyes wide with surprise. "I make you nervous?"

"Hell, yes. I really wanted this to be a special evening, but I guess I've been trying too hard and made a mess of things. I forgot you're my friend first and my date second."

Melody chuckled, put her arms around his waist and rested her forehead against his chest as the tension drained away. Jason gave her a warm squeeze, and suddenly touching him and having him touch her felt right again. Smiling impishly at him, she said, "I must have forgotten that, too. This has been the weirdest date I've ever been on."

Laughing, he kissed the tip of her nose, then turned her against his side again. Matching his stride to her shorter one this time, he escorted her into the restaurant. And once they were settled at an intimate booth in the lounge, they did begin to have fun.

There were six other couples in the dimly lighted bar. Though a small combo played country music from the bandstand, it was still fairly quiet, and the atmosphere invited conversation. They talked about Jason's ranch and his work in the legislature, about Melody's students, about mutual friends, about everything and nothing, but at last they were talking and enjoying each other's company.

Then, after setting down his glass of Scotch, Jason propped his elbows on the table and studied Melody for a moment before saying, "You know, I realized last night that back when you and Grant called off your wedding I was so wrapped up in my own life I didn't pay much attention to what was happening with you. I still don't know why you didn't marry him. Will you tell me about it?"

Melody gave him a regretful smile and a shrug. "There's not much to tell. Vic's a wonderful man in a lot of ways, but I just didn't love him enough. He deserved more than I could ever give him."

"Who decided that?"

"I did."

"Then why were you so hurt? I had the impression Grant called it off, because you dragged around like a sad little ghost for a long time after he left town."

She winced at his accurate description of that bleak time in her life. "Vic wouldn't accept my decision. He accused me of wanting a fantasy marriage and being immature, and a few other things that cut pretty deep. But he only did it because he was hurting so much." She looked up at Jason then, a shadow of pain in her eyes as she continued. "Maybe I did expect too much. But I couldn't give up wanting a marriage like my parents have, and something was missing between Vic and me."

Jason leaned forward and clasped her hand in a firm, comforting grip. "What was missing, Mel?"

She considered his question for a long time, so long that he thought she wouldn't answer him. Then a dreamy, faraway expression entered her eyes, and a subtle yet sensual smile graced her lips.

Finally she said softly, "It was . . . well, I'd have to say it was real passion that was missing. You know how when we were kids every once in a while we'd catch my folks making out like a couple of teenagers on the couch or in the pantry or the laundry room?"

Jason's low, delighted chuckle and nod encouraged her to go on. "Well, I still catch them doing that sometimes when I drop in unexpectedly. I just couldn't picture Vic and I doing that after we'd been married for twenty years. That's not the only thing or even the most important thing I want out of a marriage, but I think it would get awfully dull after a while without it."

"You made the right decision, Mel," Jason assured her quietly, squeezing her hand when she looked away as though she felt embarrassed by what she'd said. "What else do you want in a marriage?"

"An equal partnership, companionship, the ability to laugh and cry with each other, children, freedom to pursue my career," she answered. Then she gave him a cheeky grin. "I don't ask for much."

Jason chuckled. "You're not asking for too much, honey. I think most people want that kind of marriage. I know I do."

Melody sipped her rum and Coke, then nearly choked on it when Jason's expression became more serious and he said thoughtfully, "That's why I got so interested in Wendy Wyoming. She sounds like she knows a lot about relationships like your folks have. That first time I heard her, I pictured a real sexy woman, I admit, but I also saw a woman who would make a real home. *And* I saw an independent woman, who would stand up for herself and keep a man on his toes. I like that."

He looked directly into her eyes then and said, "In fact, some of the things I like about her are things I like about you too, Mel. Especially your straightforwardness and your sense of humor."

"Do you still want to meet her?" Melody asked faintly.

"Aw, I don't know. I wouldn't mind meeting her just to see what she really looks like, but she's becoming more of a fantasy to me." He gave Melody a lazy, lusty smile that made her feel hot all over before adding, "I'm more interested in somebody else now."

She arched an eyebrow at him and unconsciously sent him back a smile that had the same effect on him. "Oh yeah?"

"Yeah."

"Who?"

"Dance with me and maybe you'll figure it out."

Melody accompanied him onto the tiny dance floor and moved eagerly into his arms. Another couple was dancing, but as Jason led her to the slow, romantic strains of a Don Williams ballad, all awareness of other people faded away. She heard only the soft music, the strong, steady thump of Jasons heart beneath her ear and the beat of her own pulse picking up speed. She felt only the fuzzy texture of his sweater against her cheek, the ridge of his belt buckle against her midriff and, gradually, the insistent press of his arousal against her abdomen.

They danced through three more songs. Melody's feet might have touched the floor, but she couldn't have sworn to it. She closed her eyes and inhaled deeply the combination of scents that would always be Jason to her—his soap, his tangy cologne, his clothes, which always brought to mind the image of line-dried laundry.

Practically hypnotized by the warmth and strength of his embrace, she shivered when one of his hands moved slowly up and down her spine, stopping to caress and define her shoulder blades before sensitizing the nape of her neck with delicate circular strokes. He tugged gently on the curls at the back of her head, coaxing her to look up at him. She sighed and snuggled closer instead, unwilling to let anything disturb the moment.

"Mel."

"Hmm?"

"The music stopped."

She pulled back slightly, blinking owlishly up at him until her eyes focused on his. She swallowed at the emotions she found there—admiration, tenderness, desire. He smiled, then said in a husky tone, "Let's get out of here."

Melody nodded her agreement, unable to speak over the sudden tightness in her throat and chest. They were quiet again in the car during the drive back to her apartment, but this silence was charged with anticipation and excitement and contained none of the agonizing discomfort they'd suffered earlier in the evening.

Jason parked in front of the white frame house that held Melody's apartment, helped her out of the Blazer and accompanied her inside without waiting for an invitation. Melody kicked off her high heels by the door and wriggled her toes into the carpet with relief.

As they hung up their coats, she asked, "Want some coffee?"

Shaking his head and grinning wickedly, he advanced one step, then two. "Nope."

Though she knew exactly what he did want and knew she wanted it, too, Melody instinctively backed away. Jason lunged without warning, scooping her up high in his arms and chuckling at her startled shriek. Her arms wrapped around his neck automatically. In three long strides he reached the big overstuffed chair in her living room, lowered himself into it, then allowed her to slide down his chest and into his lap.

Their mouths met before her bottom reached his thighs. Jason nibbled gently at her lips for a moment, enticing a response. Melody smiled at the soft tickles from his mustache, parting her lips willingly when she felt the first tentative probing of his tongue. She reveled in the harsh groan he exhaled when she met him with her own tongue, hesitantly at first, then with growing confidence.

He tasted of Scotch, a drink she'd never liked before. But on Jason it tasted better than rum, headier than champagne and more intoxicating than anything.

His hands were still cold from being outdoors, but they felt like fire as they roamed over her neck and stroked behind her ears. She slid her hands into his hair, combing through the thick, glossy strands with spread fingers. His mouth shifted, peppering her cheeks, temples and eyelids with sweet kisses, then jumped down her chin before trailing the length of her neck. She moaned and arched her head back, giving him greater access.

Fingers trembling, Jason unfastened the buttons at the neck of her sweater dress and dropped hot, moist kisses along her collarbone while he reverently traced the swelling contours of her breasts. Melody sighed out his name, reeling with pleasure she ached to give back to him. But the next instant he tore his mouth away, clenched his hands into fists at her hips and leaned his head back against the chair, leaving her bewildered and uncertain. Had she done something wrong?

"Damn. I promised David," he muttered, the uneven rasp of his breathing punctuating his statement.

She reached up and traced his mustache with shaky fingertips, asking quietly, "Promised David what?"

"And I promised you, too," he continued as if he hadn't heard her, smiling in spite of his frustration at the tickling sensation when her fingers moved on to glide across his mouth.

"Promised what, Jason?" she repeated, reaching up to kiss his chin.

He gazed down at her, his eyes burning with intensity. "I promised to keep my hands off you, but what I really want to do is haul you off to the bedroom and make love to you all night long."

She laid her hands on his shoulders, unable to resist the temptation to dig the tips of her fingers into his sweater and feel the solid muscles beneath. Then she looked him straight in the eye and said in a hoarse purr, "David ought to mind his own business. What if that's what I want, too?"

His arms wrapped around her convulsively, crushing her against his chest. "Mel, don't say that," he groaned. "I'm havin' a hard enough time controlling myself as it is. We're not ready for it yet, honey."

She wrinkled her nose at him but relaxed against his chest and sat very still while he took several deep breaths. Dammit, she *did* want him to make love to her—every part of her ached for it. But he was right. Their bodies were ready to make love, but their new relationship was still fragile.

When his breathing steadied and she couldn't feel his heartbeat slamming against his chest any longer, she climbed off his lap. He followed her out of the chair and walked silently over to the closet to retrieve his coat and Stetson. With one hand on the front doorknob, he turned to face her.

"I've gotta make a run out to the ranch to check on things tomorrow. Want to come along?"

"Sure. I haven't been out there in years. But I've got report cards due next week, so I couldn't stay late," she answered.

"I'll pick you up at nine and have you home by three at the latest." Seeing her warm smile, he let go of the doorknob, reached out and pulled her against him for a quick hug. "It turned out to be a pretty good first date after all."

Hugging him back, she said, "Yes, I guess it did at that."

He leaned down to quickly kiss her forehead, her cheek and then, much more thoroughly, her mouth, before murmuring, "Night, Mel. See you tomorrow."

Her husky "Night, Jason" echoed in his ears as he drove back to his apartment. Something about the way her voice had sounded niggled in his mind like an itch he couldn't reach to scratch. When the idea hit him, he slammed on the brakes, sending the Blazer fishtailing down the icy street.

After bringing the vehicle back under control and pulling over to the curb, he checked the rearview mirror and glanced out the windshield and the side windows, heaving a sheepish sigh of relief that there weren't any other cars in sight. Then the thought came rushing back. Mel had sounded a helluva lot like Wendy Wyoming!

His first instinct was denial. It was only a fluke or a trick of his imagination. She'd been as aroused by that last kiss as he had. Shoot, his own voice had been pretty ragged when he'd said good-night.

But as he thought back over the evening, he remembered another husky purr that sounded like Wendy—when she'd asked him, "What if that's what I want, too?" He drummed his fingers on the steering wheel, searching his memory for other clues. They weren't hard to find.

Melody had gotten that funny look on her face out at Little Bear when he'd said something about Wendy. She had a broadcaster's license, and she'd been out at KBOY that night he'd waited in the parking lot hoping to see Wendy. Hell, the day after Wendy made her first broadcast, she'd practically *told* him she was Wendy!

He shook his head, uncertain whether he wanted to be right or not. Mel had acted as if she were pulling his leg when she'd said maybe she was Wendy. All the other evidence was pretty circumstantial. And though he'd seen a sexier side to Mel's personality than he'd ever dreamed existed, he still couldn't quite picture her as the lusty, uninhibited Wendy Wyoming.

Shaking his head, he signaled, then pulled out into the street. Mel as Wendy Wyoming? On the surface, it seemed ridiculous. But he'd already learned she was a lot more complicated than he'd once thought. Maybe it wasn't such a ridiculous idea after all.

He was tempted to drive right back to her apartment and ask her point-blank. One of Mel's more endearing traits was that she was a lousy liar. But he wasn't about to do anything to upset the delicate new balance in their relationship. He wasn't intrigued enough with Wendy Wyoming to risk having Melody refuse to date him again. He'd just have to watch her more closely from now on. If she was Wendy, she'd give herself away sooner or later.

Chapter Six

Melody flung back the covers and bounced out of bed when her clock radio blasted out an Alabama record at 8:50 the next morning. She squinted at the digital clock, then gasped, grabbed for her glasses and took another look. Rats! She had thought she'd set the alarm for 7:50 so she could get ready for Jason without hurrying.

Oh, well, she thought as she rushed into the bathroom. She'd been on such a natural high after Jason had left last night, it was a miracle she'd remembered to set an alarm at all. After a quick shower, she dressed in jeans, knee socks, a white turtleneck and a bulky purple sweater before hurrying through her morning hair-and-makeup ritual.

After tugging on knee-length snow boots, she dug a lavender ski jacket out of the closet by the front door, then stood on tiptoe and groped along the front edge of the shelf for the matching hat and gloves without success. Grumbling about the inconvenience of being short, she dragged a kitchen chair through the living room. She climbed it and poked her head back into the closet just as the doorbell rang.

"Come on in, Jason, it's open!" Melody hollered, and went right on sorting through the jumbled contents of the closet shelf. Pitching over her shoulder scarves, an umbrella and other assorted items she'd tossed up there at one time or another, she heard the front door open and shut, followed by muffled footsteps, then Jason's low chuckle.

"Gettin' a head start on your spring-cleanin', Mel?" he drawled close to her left ear.

She wrinkled her nose at him, noting briefly the cocky angle of his Stetson and the teasing glint in his eyes before turning back to her quest. Finally she spotted the hat and gloves, way in the back behind a stack of paperback books she'd meant to take to a used bookstore.

With a triumphant "Got 'em!" she turned around to find Jason's hands on her waist. Expecting him to help her down, Melody put her hands on his shoulders for balance and leaned forward. But Jason slid his arms around her instead and, crushing her breasts against his coat, gave her a kiss that curled her toes inside her boots.

Melody kissed him back, enjoying the heat of his lips beneath his frosty mustache, the scent of soap and after-shave and the outdoors that clung to him, the taste of toothpaste as their tongues met. And in that moment she knew she still loved Jason Wakefield. She always had. And she always would. She sighed when he pulled back, blinking to clear her vision until she realized he'd smudged her glasses with his nose.

"Hey, this is nice," he murmured.

"What's nice?"

"Having you at eye level for a change."

"Mmm."

He kissed her again briefly, then lifted her to the floor. "Ready to go now?"

"In a minute. Just let me clean up this mess."

While Jason carried the chair back to the kitchen, Melody picked up the junk she'd dumped on the floor and lobbed it item by item back onto the closet shelf with expert aim. She put on her coat, tugged the hat over her hair, then hurried past Jason into the kitchen to wash off her glasses. He laughed at her explanation of why she needed to clean them and hustled her out to the Blazer.

He picked up doughnuts and coffee on the way out of town, and Melody sat back to enjoy the forty-five-mile ride and breakfast. Since the highway crews had plowed and sanded the interstate, it was a smooth, quick trip heading west on I-80 until Jason turned north at the Harriman exit. From there he had to drive more slowly over a snow-packed gravel road.

Melody made a face at the enormous gravel pit marring the landscape of Harriman, which brought on a good-natured argument with Jason about several environmental protection bills before the legislature. After that they argued about a proposed lottery for Wyoming and the possibility of cutting the State Department of Education's budget.

Finally Jason complained, "Geez, Mel, you're rougher than the most demanding constituent I've got! Why don't you ever go after your dad and David at the family dinners?"

"And let all you nasty old conservatives gang up on me? Besides, my father and brother aren't in a position to change things. You are," she retorted. She bit her lip, then asked, "Do you mind discussing issues with me?"

"Heck, no. You really know how to keep me on my toes. And—" he shot her a considering glance "—you've given me some things to chew on. Even you soft-hearted liberals have a good point to make now and then."

She huffed at him, looked out the window to hide her smile and got caught up in the scenery. Snow piled in drifts against the fences lining the road, then spread over the plains like miles of seven-minute frosting. Clusters of Hereford cattle, scrubby pines, and boulders—some stacked up as if a giant child had tired of playing with his blocks and wandered off in search of other entertainment—provided intermittent breaks in the white blanket.

It was a familiar sight in Wyoming, but one that never failed to move Melody. And from the contented smile on Jason's face as he turned into the lane leading to the Lazy W, she knew he felt the same way. After parking in front of the sprawling brick ranch house, Jason stepped out into the snow, pausing for a moment to look over his home.

Melody, too, stood breathing in the cold clean air and admiring the land and the house. When she heard Jason mutter a curse, she turned in surprise. Following his line of sight, she noted a green pickup parked in front of the barn.

Walking around the front of the Blazer to stand beside him, she asked, "What is it, Jason?"

"That's the vet's truck."

She tipped her head to one side, watching him and wondering at his worried frown and the tension immobilizing his body. Surely having the vet out was a common occurrence on a ranch the size of the Lazy W. "Shouldn't we go find out what he's doing here, then?"

He shook his head, as if negating some thought he didn't want to consider, then looked down at her. "It'll be cold in the barn. Maybe you should go on up to the house."

"Don't be silly. I'm bundled up, and I'd love to see the animals."

She reached for his hand, and after a second's hesitation he wrapped his long fingers around her gloved hand in a grip that was almost painful and set off at a resolute pace. Melody hustled to keep up, glad of the shelter his big body provided from the biting, gusty wind. Jason paused inside the barn door, then let out a sigh that sounded as if it had come up from the toes of his boots.

Two men, one tall and rangy, the other shorter and stocky, stood deep in conversation in front of a stall on the right. They turned at the sound of the door closing. The stocky man raised a hand in greeting and jerked his head to indicate he wanted to talk to Jason.

Muttering, "Damn. I knew it," Jason dropped Melody's hand and hurried over to the others. Melody followed, but since she didn't want to disturb the men's discussion she stood off to one side by the stall.

An awful wheezing sound came from a horse standing in the wooden box, as if every exhaled breath were pure torture. Its head was down, and Melody couldn't see if it was a male or a female, but she could tell from its distinctive sorrel coloring that it had once been a beautiful animal. She reached over the stall and gently patted its withers, feeling sympathy for any creature in such misery.

She heard snatches of the men's conversation then and turned to watch them for a moment. The short stocky man laid a hand on Jason's shoulder, saying quietly but firmly, "Doc won't say it, Jason, but I will. It's time to put her down. Her wind is broken, and she ain't gonna get any better."

Jason shrugged off the man's hand. Even from where she stood, Melody could see the fire in his eyes. "Forget it, Harlan. The weather's calmed down enough that we can get her out in the fresh air more, and the atropine will help, won't it, Doc?"

The veterinarian shifted his weight to the other foot and rested his hands on his hips, nodding. "It'll help some. And we can try changing her feed again. But alveolar emphysema is a progressive disease. She'll get better for a while, and then worse again."

Jason looked over his shoulder at the horse and gulped, and Melody wondered if it was a trick of the lighting or if she really saw a sheen of moisture in his eyes. Then his eyes fell on her as he turned back to the men again, and she felt like crying herself at the bleakness in his gaze.

Leaving the men for a moment, Jason walked over to her. His voice as grim as his expression, he said, "I'm sorry, but this'll take a while. Why don't you go up to the house and relax? Make yourself at home, and I'll be there as soon as I can."

"All right," she answered, wishing she understood more of what was going on and why this horse was so special to him when he had so many others. But obviously this was not the time for questions.

Jason turned back to the veterinarian, and Melody gave the horse one last pat and left the barn. A red Subaru wagon roared up the drive and rolled to a stop in front of the house as she reached the walkway. A hefty, smiling woman with a head of graying auburn hair waved, then got out and walked around to open the rear door.

She pulled out a laundry basket and slung a handful of shirts on hangers over an index finger, pausing to shut the rear door with her ample bottom before bustling up to meet Melody. Melody couldn't help smiling at the woman's cheery "Hi there! Can I help you?"

Melody shook her head and held out her arms for the basket. "No, but it looks like you could use a hand. I'm Melody Hunter. Jason invited me out for a visit."

The woman surrendered the basket, her smile widening. "You're that rascal David's sister?" At Melody's nod, she introduced herself. "I'm Carolyn Peters. My husband Harlan is the foreman here." She held the shirts up a little higher. "Jason usually does his own laundry, but I help him out when the legislature's workin'. Where is Jason, by the way?"

"In the barn. There's a sick horse out there. I think your husband's there, too, but we didn't get around to introducing ourselves."

The merry light faded from Carolyn's blue eyes. She shot a worried glance toward the barn before hurrying ahead of Melody up the walk and opening the door for her. She kicked off her snow boots on the mat inside the front door, then disappeared down a long hallway Melody guessed must lead to Jason's bedroom. She returned a moment later without the shirts, took the basket from Melody and disappeared back down the hallway again.

Melody took off her own boots, hung her coat and hat on a coat tree and stepped out onto the gray carpeting in the living room, wiggling her toes into the deep pile. She sighed appreciatively at the elegant yet comfortable furnishings in Jason's home.

Picture windows on two walls of the living room let in the February sunshine. A dark blue sectional sofa curved at an angle between a native stone fireplace flanked by floor-to-ceiling bookcases on the third wall, and an entertainment center covered the fourth wall. Lighter blue drapes matched plump throw pillows on the sofa.

Carolyn bustled back into the living room, waving to Melody to come along as she headed through another doorway. Melody followed her through an airy dining room graced by an antique buffet and a round oak table and on into a shining modern kitchen. Carolyn opened the back door and let out a piercing whistle before saying to Melody, "The coffee's in that cabinet next to the stove. Go ahead and put on a pot while I feed the dog and water the plants. Then we can visit."

Melody did as she was told, and burst out laughing when a furry, obese animal that looked as if it couldn't decide whether it was a German shepherd or a Labrador retriever struggled through a swinging pet door and broke into an hysterical waddling dance of greeting for Carolyn. Its toenails clicked on the tile floor, and its tail wagged like a crazed metronome.

Carolyn obligingly petted the dog, crooning softly, "Yeah, I'm glad to see you, too, Jezebel. Settle down now, girl."

Jezebel gyrated over to greet Melody, as well, shoving her muzzle against Melody's legs until she received a good scratching behind the ears. While Melody acquainted herself with the dog, Carolyn opened a can of Alpo. The instant the food landed in the plastic dish beside the door, Jezebel streaked across the kitchen to gorge herself.

"Honestly, Jez," Carolyn scolded, "you're such a hog!"

While the coffee finished dripping, Carolyn filled a large glass and scurried around the kitchen watering plants on the counter and the windowsills. As she returned the empty glass to the sink, she asked Melody, "How's Lucky?"

It took Melody a second to realize that Lucky must be the horse. Though she didn't know a lot about horses, she described the animal's condition and answered Carolyn's questions about what the vet had said as best she could. Carolyn poured two mugs of coffee, handed one to Melody, then plopped into a chair beside the table.

"Poor Jason," Carolyn said when Melody joined her. "And that poor old mare. She can't have much time left when the heaves start gettin' this bad, but Jason's real attached to her—" she paused and nodded at Jezebel "—and to that old dog."

Recognizing a good source of information when she met one, Melody asked, "How old is Lucky?"

"I think she's about thirty, same as Jason. He got her for his ninth birthday, just before his mom died."

Carolyn picked a piece of lint off her black polyester slacks and let out a sad sigh before continuing in a thoughtful tone, "We started working for Jason's dad about a year after Mary died in that accident. Nathan was so full of rage and grief, he didn't pay any attention to his son. I didn't see as much of Jason as I'd of liked 'cause I had my own five kids to raise. He was an awful sweet boy, but even then I could see he was gonna be a loner."

"A loner?" Melody asked, raising her eyebrows at that description of Jason.

Carolyn grinned at Melody's surprise. "Oh, I know he's always been popular and that he's got kind of a wild reputation, but he doesn't let many people get close. His living with your family was probably what saved him from turning into a hermit."

"Why do you say that, Carolyn?"

Fidgeting on her chair as if she weren't comfortable with gossiping but couldn't help herself, Carolyn answered, "How much do you know about Nathan's second and third marriages?"

"Not much. Jason didn't talk about home a lot."

"No, he wouldn't. All Evelyn thought about was partyin' and havin' a good time. And that Becky, well, I'll tell you, she wasn't much more than a tramp. Nathan fought with 'em all the time, and neither marriage lasted more than a couple of years."

Carolyn pulled a tissue out of her sweater pocket and dabbed at her eyes. "Jason turned to Lucky and Jezebel for companionship, 'cause there wasn't anybody else who paid him any mind. I feel so bad for him. I know he felt abandoned after his mom passed away. And since his dad died last year, well, the way I see it, he doesn't have any other family but his pets."

"And now Lucky's sick," Melody murmured. Jezebel waddled over and laid her head on Melody's knee, her big brown eyes begging for another scratching session. Melody couldn't refuse.

"Yeah, and I don't know how Jason's gonna handle it when she goes. Harlan told him he oughtta settle down and get married, but he just said Lucky and Jez are the only two females who've never let him down." She tipped her head to one side and studied Melody for a moment, then sat forward with a calculating gleam brightening her expression.

"You and Jason must be pretty good friends for him to bring you to the ranch. He doesn't have much company out here."

Melody grinned. Carolyn had all the subtlety of a Mack truck. "We're good friends, Carolyn, but I wouldn't get my hopes up."

Carolyn heaved herself out of the chair. "I'll always hope, but I'd best get on back to our place. Some of our grandkids are comin' for dinner after church. I put a dish of stew and some rolls in Jason's fridge last night 'cause I knew he was comin' out today. Maybe you could help him warm it up. You know, it's funny. Jason's pretty handy around the house for a man, but he's a plain disaster in the kitchen."

Laughing her agreement, Melody walked Carolyn to the living room. The older woman yanked on her boots, then held out her hand to Melody.

"I sure enjoyed visiting with you. Have Jason bring you out again sometime."

"Thanks, Carolyn. I enjoyed it, too," Melody replied, struggling not to chuckle at the enthusiastic pumping her arm received.

Carolyn opened the door, stepped outside, then smacked her forehead with the heel of one hand before turning back to Melody. "I almost forgot. Will you tell Jason that tape he asked me to make is still in the machine?"

"I'll be glad to."

"Thanks, hon. Be seein' you."

"Bye, Carolyn."

After waving the older woman off, Melody closed the door and wandered back to the living room. She looked out a window that offered a view of the barn but didn't see any sign of Jason. Then she walked over to the entertainment center and found the cassette deck hooked up to a complicated AM/FM stereo receiver. Sure enough, there was a tape inside.

Melody rewound the cassette, ejected it and laid it beside a stack of Jason's mail on the dining room table. The wind rattled the storm windows. Melody shivered at the sound and decided to explore the house. She had never seen much beyond the living room and kitchen on her earlier visits.

She discovered four bedrooms, two bathrooms and a laundry room along the hallway Carolyn had used, and an enormous master suite at the end. Half expecting to find a sybaritic bachelor's playroom, she was pleased to see a regular king-size bed and dresser, a recliner, a floor lamp, and a small table stacked with books beside the fireplace. A peek into the bathroom revealed a Jacuzzi, but all in all it was a pretty functional-looking bathroom.

As she left the bedroom wing and headed back to the living room, Melody realized just how big and empty Jason's house must be for him with only Jezebel for company. It was a beautiful home, but it cried out for a family. She could ease that loneliness for him, give him the children he wanted, if only he'd let her. She wanted to be a permanent part of his life so much it scared her. But before she got carried away with visions of wedded bliss, she glanced at the clock on the mantel in the living room. Since it was half past noon, she decided to start fixing dinner.

Jezebel snored softly from a sun-warmed spot near the back door and didn't stir when Melody snooped through the refrigerator for the stew. She smiled to herself at Carolyn's assessment of Jason's cooking ability. The entire Hunter family knew from long experience that when it came to stoves the only setting Jason considered any good at all was the one marked Hi.

By the time Jason entered the house, the stew was bubbling gently, the table was set and Melody was preparing carrot sticks at the sink. At the solid thunk of the front door, Jezebel opened one eye, snorted, then struggled to her feet and charged toward the living room.

Hearing Jason's "Jez, darlin! I missed you. Yes, I know you missed me, too, sweetheart," and the dog's ecstatic woofing, Melody snickered and shook her head.

Jason stepped into the kitchen a moment later, followed by the besotted animal. He walked over to the sink, gave Melody a quick hug, then ordered Jezebel to go lie down when she tried to wriggle between them. He leaned over the stove, sniffing appreciatively.

"Sorry I was gone so long," he said, moving the spigot over to the empty side of the sink to wash his hands. "I didn't expect you to cook, but I'm glad you did."

"Carolyn Peters did all the work. I just heated it up."

Jason rolled his eyes at the ceiling. "She stopped by the barn. I suppose you know everything about me now?"

"Let's put it this way," Melody answered with a wry grin, "I wouldn't tell her any deep dark secrets. But she's a wonderful person, Jason."

"Yeah, I don't know what I'd do without her."

He dished up the stew while Melody took the homemade rolls from the oven. After sitting down together, they ate silently for a few minutes, but it soon became obvious that Jason didn't have much appetite. Melody set her stew aside.

"Is it Lucky, Jason?"

"Yeah." He sighed and shoved his own dish out of the way, propping his elbows on the table.

"What exactly is wrong with her? I didn't understand what the vet said."

"She's having a hard time breathing out. A horse's lungs are susceptible to dust, especially when they're cooped up in a stall a lot. And it's been such a hard winter, I've been keeping her in the barn too much. She's had the heaves for quite a while, but her conditions's gotten a lot worse."

Melody covered one of his hands with her own. "What did you decide to do?"

His free hand balled into a fist as he looked at her, a muscle twitching along the side of his jaw. "I'm gonna try to keep her going until spring. It'll be easier on her then."

"But if she's suffering, Jason—"

His eyes glinted, and he jerked his hand away. "Dammit, Mel, I can't have her put down. I won't!"

Jezebel whined at the anger in her beloved master's voice. Jason patted his leg, and the dog rushed to his side, laid her head on his thigh and gazed mournfully up at him. He petted her with long, loving strokes, and gradually some of the tension eased from his face.

He pushed back his chair then, leaned over and grabbed Melody's hand and, after pulling her to her feet, walked her into the living room. Jezebel followed. While Jason started a fire, Melody took a seat on the sofa and decided a change of subject was in order. Patting the dog's back, she asked, "Why on earth did you ever name her Jezebel?"

He closed the fire screen, smiling slightly, and came over to sit beside Melody. "I found her wandering in a pasture the summer I turned fourteen. Somebody probably dumped her out of a car when they decided they didn't want her. Dad wanted to have her spayed right away, but I promised to keep her penned up when she was in heat. But old Jez here was one determined lady. After her third litter of pups I had to give in and get her taken care of."

"Why, Jason," Melody teased gently, "all this time I've thought you were such a macho guy, and you're really just an old softy."

He shot her an appalled look. "You're not gonna tell anybody, are ya?"

Laughing, she reached up, looped her arms around his neck and gave him a noisy, smacking kiss on his left sideburn. "Nah, your secret's safe with me."

He put his hands under her armpits and lifted her onto his lap. Jezebel snarled when Melody nearly sat on her nose but sulked obediently over to the fireplace and curled up with her chin on her front paws at Jason's command. His arms wrapped around Melody's waist. She turned and hugged him back, wishing there was a way to absorb his pain.

Jason held her silently, stroking her curls and rubbing her back. Her presence made the house seem warmer, more inviting. And her quiet compassion eased the ache of knowing he was going to lose Lucky before long. He buried his lips in her glossy hair and held her tighter, feeling an unfamiliar burning sensation behind his eyelids for a moment.

He flipped a lever on the side of the sofa, lifted his feet onto the footrest that popped out and settled back, enjoying the quiet crackling of the fire and her company. He smiled when she shifted to a more comfortable position, her head nestled against his chest and her arm snaked across his waist as she snuggled closer.

Mel had always been a cuddler, and he couldn't think of anything he wanted and needed more. If he were in a better frame of mind, being this close to her would send his libido into overdrive. But what she was offering and what he was gratefully accepting was simple human contact, and it felt damn good.

He would never have allowed anyone else to see him like this—with his vulnerability exposed. But he trusted Mel, respected her intelligence and integrity. He liked her sense of humor and her sensitivity to other people, too. And he loved her warmth and her soft, feminine little body....

He stiffened at that thought, that word—love. It echoed in his mind. Melody looked up, giving him a quizzical look from behind her glasses, and his heart turned over. Was he falling in love with her? Was that why it felt so good to have her here with him and why he felt jealous enough to start punching out other men when she turned one of her special smiles on them?

He sighed and pressed her head back against his chest, his hand lingering to fondle her silky hair. He'd always thought falling in love would be an earthshaking event, something he could look back on later and say, "It happened then." But if what he was feeling for Melody was love—and he thought it just might be—it had snuck up on him like the gradual coming of spring after a long, hard winter.

They sat quietly together another half hour, which was quite an accomplishment for Jason, since he was usually too restless to sit around. But with Melody in his arms he felt relaxed, content, complete. And at the end of that brief healing respite from his worries, there wasn't a doubt in his mind that he loved Melody.

It was too soon to tell her, of course. He was painfully aware that even though she had lovingly given him what he needed today, Mel was still wary of him and the kind of commitment he was beginning to want from her. He'd have to take it nice and slow, but he wasn't about to let her go, not now—not ever.

She shifted position then, and he knew it was time to head back to Cheyenne. He'd promised to get her home in time to work on her report cards. Mel took her responsibilities as a teacher seriously, and he wouldn't have had her any other way. Much as he hated to move, he gave her one last warm squeeze and said, "It's about that time, Mel."

She sat forward, stretching her arms over her head and bending her neck forward. "I suppose so."

He couldn't resist pressing a sneaky little kiss on her nape, and when she turned in surprise and smiled at him he couldn't resist grasping her waist and flipping her flat on her back on the sofa. And when he saw her dark eyes widen and felt her breath quicken with anticipation, he just plain couldn't resist her.

David was right, he thought, savoring the sweet taste of her lips, relishing the feel of her slender curves with his hands and reveling in the gasps and soft moans of pleasure she made as he kissed and caressed her. *Love makes it all more exciting*.

Then he heard an indignant whine and felt a rough, slobbery tongue wash over the side of his neck. Turning his head, he received a blast of doggy breath in his face. Jezebel put her front paws on the edge of the sofa, slurped him across the mouth and, before he could stop her, jumped up onto his back and stomped back and forth, shedding hair from her swishing tail all over him.

Melody's sudden burst of laughter distracted him for a second, and Jezebel got in another slurp, this one on his ear.

Cursing, Jason rolled over, put his hands under Jezebel's rump and shoved her onto the floor, roaring, "Jezebel, go lie down!"

Her tail between her legs, Jezebel slunk off to the kitchen.

"Uh, Jason," Melody gasped between giggles, "I can't breathe."

Feeling about as awkward as the first time he'd been dumped by a horse, Jason scrambled off the sofa and, when he'd caught his balance, reached down to help Melody up.

"Did I hurt you?" he asked anxiously. "Lord, I could have squashed you like a bug."

Still laughing, Melody shook her head. "I'm fine. But I think you really hurt poor Jezebel's feelings."

"Mangy mutt," he muttered, but his mouth twitched with the beginnings of a smile. "She's not used to seeing me with women—except for Carolyn, of course—and I don't kiss her."

Taking his hand, Melody led him toward the kitchen and the cowering Jezebel. "You'd better make up with her."

While Jason hunkered down beside the dog and began to do just that, Melody started cleaning up the kitchen. Jason came over to help a few minutes later, but, aware of the time now, she suggested, "I'll finish up here, Jason. Why don't you get your stuff together and check on Lucky?"

Thinking that sounded like something a wife would say, Jason smiled to himself and agreed. It didn't take long to get ready to leave then, and when he found Lucky's breathing had eased after the vet's medication and some time out in the pasture his spirits improved even more.

He helped Melody into the Blazer, hurried around to the driver's side and dropped the stack of mail and the cassette he'd picked up during a last check of the house onto the seat between them. When he rounded the curving ramp onto the interstate, the mail toppled over and Melody had to grab for it to keep it from sliding to the floor.

"Would you mind sorting through that mess and digging out all the little square envelopes for me?" he asked. "Those'll be the invitations."

Melody obliged, rolling her eyes when she saw how many there were. "Good grief, Jason. You're nothing but a social butterfly."

He shrugged. "Only when the legislature's in session. Open 'em up and read 'em to me, and we'll decide which ones to accept."

She did as he had asked, laughing at his pithy but no doubt accurate descriptions of the events he'd been invited to. When she read the last one to a formal party at the governor's mansion, however, his expression sobered and he said, "We've gotta go to that one. When is it again?"

"Next Saturday night. Eight o'clock."

"I'll pick you up at seven forty-five."

"Wait a minute, cowboy. I didn't say I'd go," Melody protested.

"Got another date?" he asked, a hint of suspicion in his voice.

"No. I just hate big parties like that."

"But you'd love this one, Mel. You enjoy politics, you're articulate and informed about the issues. This will be the biggest party in Cheyenne for the whole year. David and Liz and Alan will all be there, and so will a lot of other people you know."

"I enjoy reading about politics and listening to the news. But that doesn't mean I like getting right into the arena with all the back-stabbing and bootlicking, Jason."

"Aw, come on. I don't want to go to this thing by myself."

"I'm sure you can find another date."

She didn't want him to find another date, of course, but she'd been to enough bashes like this to know she would feel out of place. As one of the younger state senators from the governor's party, Jason would be busy "working the room," and she would no doubt be left to make small talk with the party hacks.

He braked for a stoplight on the western edge of town and used the opportunity to reach across the seat and tip her chin up. When she met his eyes he said quietly, "I don't want another date. I want you."

She gulped. When he put it like that and smiled at her as if she were the only woman in the world, what did a long, boring political evening matter? Her tentative hopes for a future with Jason, encouraged by their closeness at the ranch, expanded even more, and her heart pounded with elation.

"All right. I'll go."

"Thanks, Mel."

The light changed to green. Jason turned his attention to the traffic on Sixteenth Street while Melody restacked his mail. As she laid it on the seat, her hand brushed against the cassette, and on impulse she stuck it into the tape player on the dashboard. Before Jason could react, a familiar voice filled the Blazer.

"Howdy, folks! This is Wendy Wyoming, coming to you on another cold February night from KBOY, Cheyenne's home of country music. Are you ready for a good time?"

Jason smacked the steering wheel with the heel of one hand and muttered, "Damn," before ejecting the cassette.

Melody didn't say a word, even though her romantic dreams of a life with Jason were melting like pristine snow that falls on a street and turns into dirty slush. Who had she been trying to kid, she wondered, to think Jason could be seriously interested in her.

"I asked Carolyn to tape that for me last Thursday, Mel."

"You don't have to explain, Jason."

"Well, shoot, I can't help being curious, especially since you told me I already know her."

He turned onto Melody's street, and she remained silent as he parked in front of her apartment. With a coaxing grin, he drawled, "Since we're gettin' to be such good friends and all, why don't you just tell me who she is? Then you won't have to worry about her anymore."

Melody considered telling him. But what if he laughed and didn't believe her again? Gooseflesh broke out on her forearms at the thought of facing an encore of that humiliation. It would be so much worse a second time around, especially now that she'd admitted to herself that she loved him. Desperately holding on to a light tone, she offered, "I'll give you another hint."

He laughed but shook his head. "No thanks. I don't think I could stand it." Then he leaned across the seat and, cupping her face between his big hands, kissed her. "I'll call you, Mel."

An hour later, Melody sat on her own sofa, grade book and calculator in her lap, stockinged feet on the coffee table, the television tuned to an old movie for company, while she struggled to concentrate on averaging grades. But she couldn't get Jason to stay out of her head long enough to make much progress. It was a relief when the doorbell rang and she found her sister standing on the front step.

Barbara stepped into the apartment, flushed with cold and an air of excitement. "Just thought I'd stop in and say goodbye and find out how it went last night."

Melody took her coat and waved her into the living room, giving a brief synopsis of her evening and day with Jason.

Barbara plopped into the big overstuffed chair and crossed one long, slender leg over the other.

"I'm glad you had a good time, sis. I had an interesting evening myself."

Melody turned sideways on the sofa, one arm resting along the back. "Oh, really?"

"Really. I barged into Alan's apartment and had a long talk with him."

"And what did you decide?"

"About what I expected. I'm going back to Washington for now, and Alan's going to start dating other people. But I think we managed to salvage our friendship." Barbara paused to examine her fingernails for chips in the polish, then looked back at Melody, a wry, almost wistful smile on her face. "Who knows? Maybe I won't like this new assignment and I'll come back and steal him from his current girlfriend someday."

Melody raised a doubtful eyebrow. "Somehow I can't see you being happy in Cheyenne for the rest of your life."

Barbara chuckled and stretched her arms toward the ceiling. "You're probably right, but I'm glad he doesn't hate me. I still love him, in a way."

Melody tried to pay attention as her sister chatted on, but her eyes kept wandering to the window behind the sofa and to the spot at the curb where Jason's Blazer had been parked. Her thoughts skittered from what she'd learned about Jason from Carolyn to his continued curiosity about Wendy Wyoming to what Barbara was saying and back to Jason again. Finally Barbara stood, leaned across the coffee table and tapped her on the shoulder.

"Have I suddenly become a boring person?"

"Huh? Oh. I'm sorry, Barbara," Melody answered, flushing in embarrassment.

"Why don't you tell me what's bothering you?" Barbara suggested. "And don't say it's nothing."

Melody ran both hands through her curls and looked out the window again. Hesitantly she admitted, "It's about Jason."

"I thought you had a good time last night and today."

"I did. But Jason and I are just so . . . different. I'd feel a lot better about getting involved with him if I knew what he sees in me. I mean, shoot! He can have any gorgeous woman he wants and—"

"Melody Jane, you stop that sniveling this minute," Barbara ordered.

"I'm not sniveling—"

"Oh, yes, you are." Barbara stood, hands on her hips, glaring down at Melody. Shaking her finger, she lectured, "Jason has already *had* any gorgeous woman he wants, but he hasn't gotten serious about any of them, has he? Your lack of self-confidence is your worst enemy in this situation, not some other woman."

"But—"

"Don't give me your *but*s. You're pretty darn gorgeous in your own right, Melody. Especially where it really counts." Barbara thumped her chest. "In here. You've got warmth and passion and a ton of love to give. And Jason needs that in his life, just like anybody else.

"But—" Barbara stepped around the coffee table, moving Melody's grade book aside and sat down close enough to pat Melody's knee. Her voice lost its strident tone, and her mouth curved into a rueful grin.

"You have to make your own decisions, but I think you should give Jason a chance. Don't go looking for problems when you've just started dating. Play it by ear, and don't be afraid to tell him what you're feeling. He's really a pretty sensitive guy, you know."

"I know he is," Melody answered quietly. Then, looking her sister in the eye, she asked, "But why are you so concerned about this, Barbara?"

Barbara hesitated a moment before saying thoughtfully, "I've learned some things about myself on this trip home. I've taken a lot of people I love for granted besides Alan. I've always been so wrapped up in my own concerns, I haven't taken the time to show I care about you or David, or even Mom and Dad. But I do care."

"We know that," Melody assured her.

"Well..." Barbara glanced away, sighed and looked at Melody again. "I just don't want you to pass up a good thing with Jason. Look at it from my point of view, Mel. I've had to choose between Alan and my career, and now, at thirty-five, I'm not sure I'll ever have my own home and family. I may not be cut out to be a wife and mother anyway, but you are. You can have it all, sis, if you're not too scared to take a chance on Jason."

"I don't think he's that serious, Barbara."

"But you want him to be, don't you?" When Melody looked away, Barbara couldn't contain her impatience. "For heaven's sake, Melody, you've been in love with Jason for years!"

"How did you know?" Melody whispered, feeling a sickening sense of panic churning up from the pit of her stomach. Did the rest of the family know? Did Jason?

Barbara bit her lip in contrition for her tactlessness, then reached over and held her sister's cold hand. "Hey, relax. I'm the only one who knows. It was something I sensed, not anything you did. And I didn't tell anyone."

"I tried so hard not to love him."

"I know you did, Mel. But don't you see? Maybe you don't have to fight it anymore. I think Jason's darn serious about you, but you'll never know if you chicken out, will you?"

Melody slowly shook her head. "No, I guess not."

Barbara stood then and studied Melody for a moment. "Are you all right?"

"I'm fine."

Barbara pulled Melody to her feet and hugged her, saying quietly, "Okay, end of lecture. I need to get back to the house for dinner. Want to come?"

Pulling away, Melody shook her head again. "I've got to work on report cards."

Barbara walked to the front door with Melody keeping pace beside her. While she put on her coat, she said, "Keep in touch? I'll be dying to hear how this turns out."

Melody shrugged. "I will if you will. You know, a phone call once in a while would be nice. And there's this neat invention called the letter. . . ."

"Awright, you smart-mouthed brat. I get the message." She leaned down and kissed Melody's cheek before heading out the door.

"Barbara," Melody called from the doorway as her sister unlocked Karen Hunter's Volvo. "Thanks."

"Anytime, kid. You'll be hearing from me."

Melody shut the front door with a smile on her lips, but once she was back in her living room, alone, her doubts came rushing back. She appreciated her sister's lecture and the concern behind it, but it was easy for Barbara to wave Jason's history with women aside. Barbara was so gorgeous, she'd never been a wallflower, never had to worry about competition, never dated anyone who was more physically attractive than she was.

There were a few things she hadn't told her sister; nasty, nagging suspicions she hadn't wanted to admit. Barbara was so certain Jason was really interested in her. But Melody couldn't help wondering since she'd heard Jason's cassette in the car, if perhaps, maybe even subconsciously, he was dating her as a way to get to Wendy Wyoming.

And in light of what she'd learned about Jason's attachment to Lucky and Jezebel, she couldn't help wondering if maybe he saw her as a replacement for his aging horse and dog. It was an outlandish and unflattering thought, but one she couldn't completely ignore.

But the real kicker, the one truth that refused to let go of her no matter how hard she tried to push it from her mind, was the look on Jason's face when Wendy Wyoming's voice had blared from the car stereo. That look had only been there for a second, but it had been there, a look of longing and desire she had foolishly hoped he would feel only for her.

Much as it hurt, she had to face facts. Jason's hormones would always go wild around an attractive, sexy woman. With his popularity and his political career, he would always have contact with Cheyenne's version of the jet set. And over the long haul, plain little Melody Hunter would never be able to compete.

He was interested in her now, but sooner or later—probably sooner—he would find some other woman he wanted to chase. He might very well take Melody to bed and, having satisfied his curiosity or lust or whatever it was he felt for her, end the affair the next day. Could she stand that?

Oh, dammit, why had she ever played that stupid cassette? Why did she have to love that big dope, anyway? She had felt so close to him out at the ranch, so special. She'd seen a side to Jason she had never dreamed existed, and she still wanted to make love with him more than she'd ever wanted anything in her life. But could she have an affair with him, enjoy it and maintain her dignity when it ended?

Melody paced over to the picture window, wrapped her arms across her midriff and once more gazed at the spot where Jason's Blazer had been parked. She was probably being ridiculous, trying to analyze Jason's motives and emotions. If it were anyone but him, she wouldn't be doing this to herself. But it *was* Jason. He was so special to her and had been for such a long time, how could she hope to view him or their relationship objectively?

The truth of the matter was, she couldn't give him up—not just yet. She was going to feel pain when they broke up, no matter when it happened and no matter who decided to call it quits first. But there had to be a way to protect herself from the deep emotional devastation an affair with him would bring.

A moment later, her decision made, she turned away from the window, marched into her bedroom and searched through a stack of papers on the small desk where she kept her personal files. After finding the application for a teaching job in Denver she'd sent for last December, she marched back to the kitchen, fished a pen out of the depths of her purse and sat down at the table.

She would have her affair with Jason Wakefield and enjoy every single minute of it. But she would remind herself frequently that the relationship would end in a few weeks, and that knowledge would be her protection. There would be no more daydreams of marriage and children, no more foolish romantic hopes. She was an adult and could handle it. Leaving Cheyenne for a while had apparently healed Vic Grant's broken heart. Perhaps it would do the same thing for her.

But as she doggedly filled in line after line on the application, other images haunted her. Jason and Lucky in the barn, Jason and Jezebel wandering around in that big, empty house, Jason cuddling her on his lap in front of the fire. She could have given him so much love. And the big lug was too blind to see it.

Chapter Seven

With light pouring out from every window and spotlights illuminating the native stone exterior, the governor's mansion glittered like a fairy-tale palace against a dark backdrop of stately pines. An inch of fresh snow frosted the massive wrought-iron gates, opened wide for the steady stream of arriving party guests. In deference to Melody's long dress and evening shoes, Jason let her out in front of the entry, then drove off to park the Blazer.

Melody smiled and nodded at a state representative and his wife, hugged her fake-fur coat tighter against her sides in an attempt to thwart the February breeze sneaking up her skirt and wished Jason would hurry. Watching more elegantly dressed couples enter the building, she sent a silent thank-you to Barbara for her helpful makeup tips. Of course, she wasn't about to go through all that rigmarole every day, but for an evening like this, knowing she looked more sophisticated had given her self-confidence a boost.

She shifted from one foot to the other to keep her toes from going numb but forgot all about the cold when Jason strode into view. Dressed in his usual jeans and shirt, he made her heart race; dressed in a tuxedo, he took her breath away. The rough, endearing cowboy was gone, his place taken by a man handsome and polished enough to qualify as any woman's idea of Prince Charming.

After entering the mansion and disposing of their coats, Jason escorted Melody into a spacious living room to greet the governor and his wife. They exchanged pleasantries for a moment, but when Jason and Melody turned to leave and allow the guests arriving behind them to greet their host, the governor tapped Jason on the shoulder and whispered something in his ear. Jason chuckled and glanced at Melody before answering, "I couldn't agree more."

Heads turned as they moved into the crowd, and Melody felt a flash of pride at being Jason's date, followed by an instant of irrational fear that her halter-style black evening gown left too much of her exposed. She resolutely straightened her spine and pushed the fear aside; though her back was bared to the waist, she had more fabric covering her front than a lot of the other women present did. Smiling, she asked Jason, "What did the governor say to you?"

Jason put his arm around her shoulders and smiled down at her. "He said you were a lovely young woman and I ought to hang on to you."

Melody flushed with pleasure and gave Jason a cheeky grin as she accompanied him to the bar. "The man obviously has excellent taste."

By the time Jason had ordered a glass of wine for Melody and a Scotch for himself, Ed Simmons, the state party chairman, had attached himself to Jason's side like a barnacle and was steadily gathering a group of influential party officials around them. Melody smiled and made appropriate responses when Jason introduced her, and answered polite questions about her family for those who were acquainted with the Hunters. But inevitably the conversation turned to politics, and as people left the group and new people joined it, Melody gradually found herself separated from Jason.

Glad to escape from an extremely talkative state representative who had now cornered Ed Simmons, she wandered through the room. She listened to a debate between an oil company executive from Casper and the president of an environmental group. She witnessed an argument between two state senators over a bill to increase the sales tax. She found herself defending the state's allotment for education to the chairman of a budget committee and was surprised to realize she was almost enjoying herself.

Still, after an hour of being on her own she was glad to see David and Liz and Alan Jordan talking together in front of some large windows overlooking the golf course adjacent to the governor's mansion. Melody excused herself from the committee chairman and joined them.

"Mel, you look great," David said, stepping back to widen the circle and include her.

"Thanks. So do all of you," Melody replied.

"I thought you didn't like political functions," Alan teased, "especially not for this party."

Melody shrugged and wrinkled her nose at him. "Jason talked me into coming."

"Where is Jason?" Liz asked.

Melody waved one hand toward the bar. "Over there somewhere, surrounded."

David and Alan shifted position and looked in the direction Melody had indicated. "Get a load of who he's talking to," David muttered, "the governor, a U.S. senator and—who are those other guys, Alan?"

"The taller one works for the national party organization, and I think the other guy was a candidate for governor back in the fifties. If he's who I think he is, he's still got a lot of clout in the party."

The two men looked at each other and smiled the same exuberant smile. "What did I tell you?" David asked, slapping Alan on the back. "What do you want to bet they're grooming Jase for a higher office?"

"I wouldn't be at all surprised," Alan answered. "He's made quite a name for himself already. In another ten years he could be our governor."

"Or a congressman or senator," David agreed, then finished the rest of his drink. Holding up his glass, he said, "I could use another one of these. Anyone else?"

Alan agreed, but Melody and Liz declined. While the men went off to the bar, Liz glanced around, located a love seat angled into a corner and said, "Come on, Melody. Let's sit down for a minute."

Melody followed her and once they were seated, found they had an excellent view of the entire room. She saw David and Alan greet Jason, who grinned at something David said before turning back to the group surrounding him. She studied the faces of the people Jason was speaking with and felt another tingle of pride at the respect and admiration they showed him.

"I was right about you and Jason, wasn't I?" Liz remarked, pulling Melody's attention away from her study of Jason.

"What do you mean?"

"You feel more for him than friendship, Melody."

Melody nodded, but she didn't intend to get into a discussion about her relationship with Jason at this point. Instead, she asked Liz, "How are the wedding plans coming along?"

"Not very subtle, but I get the message," Liz answered with a chuckle. "Well, let's see. Did I tell you my mom started making my dress?"

"No. What's it going to look like?"

After Liz described the dress and chattered on about the wedding arrangements, Melody's attention drifted back to Jason. As the group around him expanded to include a federal judge and a Wyoming congressional representative, Melody's conviction that David and Alan were right about Jason's future deepened.

Jason had enough charisma for two politicians, intelligence and integrity and a deep commitment to the well-being of the people of Wyoming. In addition, he represented the third generation of Wakefields to serve in the state legislature. The officials of his party would have to be blind not to notice his potential. And it was obvious from Jason's bearing and the animated expression on his face that he enjoyed being in the thick of things.

Just how far did Jason intend to go with his political career? He'd always been ambitious, but she hadn't really thought much about his political goals. Before Melody could follow that train of thought any farther, Liz inhaled an angry gasp and her body suddenly became rigid.

Following Liz's gaze, Melody stifled a groan. Two of David's former girlfriends had cornered him at the bar and were taking turns vying for his attention. Melody could have kicked her brother when he turned, braced one elbow on the back of a stool and talked to the two women, a look of masculine admiration in his eyes that was obvious clear across the room.

Melody glanced back at Liz, whose complexion had paled beneath her makeup, and muttered an unladylike description of her brother's character and intelligence. Alan said something to David before turning and heading back to-

WE EVEN PROVIDE FREE POSTAGE!

It costs you *nothing* to send for your free books — we've paid the postage on the attached reply card. And we'll pick up the postage on your shipment of free books and gifts, and also on any subsequent shipments of books, should you choose to become a subscriber. Unlike many book clubs, we charge *nothing* for postage and handling!

ward Melody and Liz. David nodded and went right on smiling that charming smile at his companions.

Before Alan got within earshot, Melody asked Liz, "Want to go over and break it up?"

Liz gave her head one quick, emphatic shake and answered tersely, "No. If that's the way David wants to spend the evening, let him. Excuse me, Melody. I need to visit the rest room."

While Melody worriedly watched Liz stalk away, Alan joined her on the love seat. Gesturing in Liz's direction, he asked, "Trouble in paradise?"

"I'm afraid so," Melody answered, giving him a rueful smile.

"Have you heard from Barbara?"

"Not yet. She's only been gone a week."

"Funny. It seems longer than that to me." Alan tugged at his tie and cleared his throat.

"Give it some time, Alan," Melody suggested gently. "I thought you were going to start dating other people. Why did you come alone tonight?"

"Oh, well... I, uh, couldn't think of anyone I wanted to ask. But I will. Soon." He sent her a long considering look before confessing, "Uh, I was thinking about asking you out, Melody, but I guess you're interested in Jason now."

Melody answered, "We haven't made any commitments, Alan. But don't you think you should be looking for someone who wouldn't remind you of Barbara all the time?"

"You're probably right." He sighed. "But you know, Melody, I really do like you."

"I like you, too, Alan."

He leaned over and quickly kissed her smiling lips, then stood, took her hand and pulled her gently to her feet beside him. "Come on. I need to circulate some more. And I think they're setting out a buffet in the other room, so you'd better get back to Jason."

"All right." She gave his hand an affectionate squeeze. "I'll see you later, Alan."

Melody turned and walked toward Jason, then caught a glimpse of her brother at the bar, still entertaining his former girlfriends. Hesitating for only a moment, she veered off course, tapped her brother on the shoulder and whispered in his ear, "I'd go find Liz if I were you, brother dear."

When her message registered, David's head jerked up and swiveled around in search of his fiancée. A red flush climbed the back of his neck, and his mouth dropped into a tight, grim line when he couldn't locate her. With a muttered "Thanks" to Melody, he excused himself from his two admirers and hurried off into the crowd.

Satisfied she had tried to be helpful, Melody turned back toward the spot where she'd last seen Jason and collided with a hard masculine chest. A hand shot out to steady her, and Melody found herself looking up into Vic Grant's amused brown eyes.

"Oh. Excuse me, Vic."

He studied her up and down for a moment, then let out a low whistle as his eyes returned to her face. "You look beautiful, Melody."

"Thank you," she answered, flushing slightly at his compliment and at the look in his eyes. Despite what he'd said about wanting a friend, it was evident that not all of Vic's feelings for her were strictly platonic. Putting on a bright yet impersonal smile, she said, "I see you didn't waste any time getting back into politics."

He shrugged. "You know how it is when you're starting up a business. I've already made several helpful contacts here tonight."

"I'm glad to hear that. Well, I guess I'd better go find Jason."

Vic's expression hardened, and he reached out and gripped her wrist to detain her. "You're here with Wakefield?" When she answered him with a stiff nod, he asked, "You're not seriously dating him, are you?"

Her eyes narrowed and her chin rose at the incredulous, disapproving note in his voice. She pulled her arm from his grasp and stepped away. "That's none of your business, Vic. Excuse me."

"Melody, wait. Please."

She hesitated, then turned back, one eyebrow raised in query. He shoved his hands into his trouser pockets, shifted his weight to the opposite foot and looked back at her, a concerned frown wrinkling his forehead.

"You're right. It's none of my business, and I admit I've always been a little jealous of your relationship with him," Vic said slowly, as if he were carefully considering each word. "But regardless of what happened between us, I know his reputation and I'd hate to see you get hurt."

Melody nodded and tried to swallow down a hard lump of emotion in her throat. It was impossible to stay angry at Vic when he was only showing he still cared about her. But his warning about Jason's reputation stung. And seeing that loving look in Vic's eyes again brought back painful memories and a trainload of guilt over the way she had hurt him.

Lifting a hand to gently stroke her cheek, he continued, "If you ever need me, Melody, I'll be around. Be careful, will you?"

A small part of her wanted to reach out and respond to Vic. He was a good man and much safer than Jason. But she'd been down that road before, and it had only led to heartache for both of them. She was committed to Jason now, at least for a while, and she couldn't, wouldn't, use Vic as a safety net. Finally she said softly, "Don't worry about me, Vic. I can take care of myself." Then, before he could answer, she moved off into the crowd to find Jason.

Jason stifled a relieved sigh when he saw Melody walking toward him again. Damn, but he wished this party was over. He'd had more than one uneasy moment when Melody had been talking to Alan Jordan. In fact, he'd seriously considered giving Jordan the Wakefield version of a nose job when he'd kissed her—and he would have done it if that kiss had lasted more than a second.

Then Melody had started walking toward him and he'd thought everything was going to be all right, and who had she run into? Vic Grant, of all people! He didn't know what Grant had said to her, but whatever it was, Jason doubted he'd have liked it. The worm was probably trying to get her to come back to him, and Mel was too damn softhearted for her own good.

Melody looked up at that moment, and Jason shot her a welcoming smile over the top of the senator's head. When she smiled back at him, Jason wanted to tell all these blowhards that if they'd get the hell out of his way and quit harping at him about how much a candidate needs a wife and family he just might be able to convince Melody to marry him.

She'd make a darn good wife, though not for the reasons these jokers were singing her praises to him. Jason didn't give a damn about her media connections, her family name or any of the rest of that garbage. No, he thought she'd make a good wife because she was warm, loving, intelligent and sexy and he loved her. And if he didn't get a few minutes alone with her soon, he was going to shock everyone and carry her out of this party like a caveman!

He'd been planning a slow courtship of Melody Jane Hunter, but after watching two other men come on to her in one evening he knew he would never be able to be that patient. Like any rancher, he wanted his brand on what was his, and dammit, Melody did belong to him. She just didn't know it yet.

When she reached his side, Jason automatically wrapped an arm around her shoulders and pulled her against him. It was agony having her so close and not being able to kiss her, but it was a sweet agony. After he introduced Melody to the people in the group she hadn't met, he stepped back a little and simply enjoyed watching her.

Inside of five minutes she had charmed even the crusty old party fund-raiser, just as Jason had known she would. She was laughing at one of the old man's corny jokes right now. And there was something awfully familiar about that laugh. Of course, he'd heard Mel laugh a million times, but...

Jason shut his eyes for an instant and put all his concentration into listening. His heart started pounding when he realized it wasn't just Melody's laugh he was hearing, but Wendy Wyoming's, too. He looked down, studying her posture, her gestures, her warm responses to the others in the group, and suddenly he knew he'd been right. The squirt really was Wendy Wyoming!

At first he wanted to throw back his head and laugh with delight. Of course Mel was Wendy! It couldn't be anyone else. He should have guessed it right away. No wonder she'd gotten so mad at him the day after Wendy's first broadcast. No wonder she'd let him freeze his behind in the parking lot that night. No wonder Dave had always acted so damn smug about Wendy's identity...

Wait a minute, he thought suddenly. His heart skipped a beat as his mind jumped back to the first time he'd asked

Melody about Wendy Wyoming. He could see her shrug, her teasing grin as she told him she was Wendy, and then he'd— Oh, damn, he'd laughed his fool head off at her. She must have hated his guts for that.

She'd made a lot of changes in her appearance lately—new glasses, new clothes, new makeup and hairstyle. Had he made her feel so rotten about herself that she'd done all that? Lord, he hoped not. Mel had been beautiful all along. He'd just been too damn stupid to notice.

Filled with regret, he moved his hand up to her shoulder and gave it a gentle, apologetic squeeze. She glanced up at him and smiled that sweet, heart-melting smile of hers, and he felt like a horse's rear end. Had she forgiven him? She must have, or she wouldn't be going out with him. Would she?

He needed to be alone with her, needed it in the worst way. Glancing around the room, Jason saw an opportunity to move away from the group. Waiters were directing people to the buffet. At the next break in the conversation he stepped forward, tucked Melody's hand into the crook of his arm, then said, "They're starting to serve dinner, and all this talk has made me hungry. Excuse us, will you folks?"

They'd only gotten a couple of steps when the party fund-raiser clapped Jason on the back. Jason, with Melody in tow, stopped and turned back to him.

"I meant what I said a while ago, Jason," the white-haired gentleman said, gesturing with his cocktail glass. "Whenever you're ready to make a run for the big time, give me a call. I still think you'd have a better chance if you were married, of course—" he paused and gave Melody a sly grin "—but I'd be willing to give it a shot no matter what."

Jason shook the man's hand. "Thanks. I appreciate the offer. I'll give it some thought and let you know."

"You do that. I'll be waiting to hear from you."

The fund-raiser walked away then, and Jason escorted Melody into the buffet line. The sooner they ate, the sooner they could leave. He didn't plan to stay for the dancing; he was in no mood to share Melody with anyone.

After they had filled their plates with rare prime rib and fancy vegetable casseroles and salads, he led the way to an empty table at the back of the room, hoping he'd get lucky and they could eat by themselves. But a few minutes later David and Liz joined them. The hostility between the engaged couple was thicker than congealed gravy, effectively cutting off all attempts at conversation.

Finally, when the silence at the table passed from merely uncomfortable to downright unbearable, David cleared his throat and asked Jason, "So what did the big shots have to say? They want you to run for Congress?"

"Yeah."

"No kidding?"

"Yeah."

"Are you going to do it, Jason?" Liz asked, clearly making an effort to help lighten the atmosphere.

Jason chewed on an bite of meat thoughtfully, swallowed, then shook his head. "Not this time, Liz. I'm not ready yet."

"But you will be someday?" Melody asked.

"I might. It's certainly flattering to be asked. I'm not sure how much I'd like living in Washington, but I think I could do some good for the people of this state."

"Hell, yes, you could," David agreed enthusiastically.

For the rest of the meal, David tried to convince Jason to run in the next election and Liz and Melody chimed in with teasing questions and observations about his chances. But when the two couples split up to leave the party, David and Liz were being awfully careful not to touch each other, and Melody seemed preoccupied.

Jason located his coat and Melody's, then left her standing inside by the entrance while he went to get the car. It bothered him that David and Liz weren't getting along. Somehow it seemed like a bad omen for his own relationship with Melody. But that was silly. Mel wasn't Liz, and he wasn't David.

Still, he had to admit the evening hadn't gone quite the way he'd planned it. He had hoped Melody would have a good time, and he thought she had—up until about the time she'd run into Vic Grant. Oh, she'd carried on like a trouper for the rest of the evening, but sometime after she'd talked to Grant the party had gone sour for her.

He started the Blazer, dug the snow scraper out from under the driver's seat and stepped back out to brush off the half inch of new snow that had fallen while they'd been inside. As he moved around the vehicle, he wondered again what Vic Grant had said to Melody. Was it possible she still loved him and wouldn't admit it? And what could he do about it if she did love Grant?

Jason climbed back into the Blazer and turned up the heater another notch. While he waited a couple of minutes for the car to warm up, he answered his own question. He was going to stake his claim to Melody tonight.

He would have enjoyed courting her a while longer, but he couldn't afford to wait now. Once Mel made love with him, she would feel committed. It might not be entirely fair to her, but he couldn't let her get involved with Vic Grant, Alan Jordan or anyone else. He would make love to her, show her how he felt about her and drive all thoughts of other men right out of her mind.

Chapter Eight

After parking in front of the entrance, Jason left the engine idling and hurried back inside. A band had started playing in the room next to the dining area. He found Melody peeking around the corner to the hallway from which the music was coming, hands in her coat pockets, one foot tapping in time with the beat.

She turned toward him when she heard his approach, and he felt a moment's guilt for taking her away from the party early. But when he offered to stay for a while, she smiled and shook her head.

"No, I'm ready to go, Jason. You'll never get a minute's peace in this crowd."

"Thanks for understanding, Mel," he answered. "And thanks for coming with me tonight. I know it wasn't your kind of party, but I'll make it up to you sometime."

She tucked her hand into the crook of his arm and said, "I'll remember that promise the next time I have to chaperon a school dance."

Jason chuckled, then escorted her out to the Blazer. Once they were cruising down Central Avenue, he asked, "How about going back to my place for a nightcap?"

Melody hesitated. If she went to Jason's apartment with him, they would make love. There had been an exquisite tension between them all evening that had had nothing to do with the party. She wanted him, whether they had a chance for a future together or not. But it didn't have to be tonight. It might be better to wait a little longer.

They stopped for a red light at Pershing Boulevard. The streetlights' illumination allowed her to see Jason's face more clearly. She swallowed at the intense expression in his eyes.

"I want to be alone with you, Mel," he persisted in a deep, gritty tone that sent a shiver of anticipation up her spine. "Nothing will happen that you don't want to happen."

Nodding her acquiescence, she thought, *But I do want it to happen. Maybe I want it to happen too much.*

He reached across the seat then, picked up her hand and tugged. "Scoot on over here and sit by me. I won't bite very hard."

Melody laughed at the awkwardness of scooting in a long dress and let out a small, contented sigh when he laced the fingers of his right hand through the fingers of her left hand and rested both hands on his thigh. Jason's palm felt warm against hers. She squeezed his hand. He looked down, smiling a slow, sexy smile at her.

She laid her head against his arm and closed her eyes, inhaling the scent of his after-shave as she rubbed her cheek against the woolly texture of his overcoat. While Jason negotiated his way through the Saturday-night traffic, she floated along on a cloud of bliss. Time lost all meaning; what was only a five-minute drive seemed to take hours.

It didn't matter. Nothing mattered as long as she was with Jason. To heck with tomorrow. She was exactly where she wanted to be. And for once in her life she was going to forget the future and enjoy whatever time she had with him.

He parked in his spot at the apartment complex, lifted her down from the vehicle and escorted her inside. He hung their coats up in a small closet by the front door, then led her into the living room. She kicked off her shoes and curled up on the sofa while he started a fire in the fireplace, tuned in a station on the radio and poured a glass of burgundy for her and a Scotch for himself.

Melody sipped her wine and watched Jason's every move as he shed his jacket, unhooked his bow tie and tossed them both over a chair and unfastened the top button of his shirt before turning back to the fire. She felt her heartbeat pick up speed when she saw the muscles in his arms and across his shoulders flexing as he hefted a log and dropped it onto the burning kindling.

He straightened and turned back to her, and she felt her mouth go dry as the flames behind him boldly silhouetted his body. He looked so big, so handsome, so virile, that her fingers itched to touch him. He moved toward her, removed the wineglass from her unsteady fingers and placed it beside his Scotch on the coffee table.

She would have followed him into the bedroom then and there, but instead he extended a hand to her and said, "May I have this dance, Miss Hunter?"

"Certainly, Mr. Wakefield," she answered, accepting his invitation.

He pulled her gently to her feet, guided her to an open space in front of the coffee table and then, singing along with the radio, waltzed her around the room. Melody looked up into his face, and a gurgle of laughter escaped her lips. The only thing worse than Jason's cooking was his singing, but oh, dear, even his flaws were endearing.

He flashed her an unabashed grin. "Off-key again, huh?"

"A little."

"You're a cruel woman to laugh at my tin ear."

"I'm sorry, Jason."

"I'll forgive you this time, but it'll cost you."

"How much?"

He stopped dancing then, stepped back and thoughtfully rubbed his chin, his eyes laughing down into hers as he sternly pronounced, "Three kisses."

"Well," she answered with phony reluctance, "I guess I'll have to pay, then." She shut her eyes tight, puckered her mouth and stretched as high on her tiptoes as she could.

Nothing happened. She cracked one eye in time to see Jason's backside disappearing into the bedroom. "I said I'd pay, Wakefield, but I didn't say I'd do it in your bedroom," she called indignantly, and was rewarded by a snort of laughter that made her blush when she realized how that had sounded.

"Hang on, Mel. I've got a present for you."

She watched him warily when he reappeared, both hands behind his back, his stride made awkward by whatever he was carrying.

"What have you got there?" she asked not trusting the boyish, eager smile on his face for one second.

"Remember the morning I picked you up to go out to the ranch?"

"Yes."

"You were standing on a chair and I kissed you and it was fun?"

"Yes."

"Well, uh..." He shifted his weight from one foot to the other, looking like a kid expecting to get detention for a misdemeanor of some sort. "You see, that's what gave me the idea. So when I went out to the ranch to check on Lucky again last week I, uh, fixed this up for you. Promise you won't laugh?"

Wishing she could turn on more lights and find out if Jason was really blushing or if her eyes were playing tricks on her in the firelight, Melody nodded cautiously. Jason studied her for another long moment. Then, apparently satisfied with her response, he released his left hand from whatever he was holding and set the object on the floor in front of her with his right.

Melody stared at it, swallowed down another bubble of laughter and was glad she did when she glanced up and caught an anxious expression in Jason's eyes. Then she looked back at the sawed-off wooden bar stool and stepped closer to read the writing painted on the seat. Picking it up, she carried it over to the end table, turned on the lamp and read the bright red letters.

"Mel's... something... stool?"

Jason stalked over to stand behind her, took the stool away from her and pointed to the lopsided blob of paint in the center. "That's a heart, Hunter. Can't you tell?"

"Of course, Jason."

He flipped the stool over and indicated the rubber tips on each of the four legs. "And see these? I put 'em on for safety on tile floors. It won't skid."

"That was thoughtful of you, Jason."

"You still don't get it, do you?"

"Well, no, but I'm sure you'll tell me what it's for any day now."

Shaking his head in disgust at her, he turned the stool over again, set it on the floor in front of him and, putting his hands under her armpits, lifted Melody onto it. She put her hands on his shoulders and faced him, eyeball-to-eyeball, smiling lips to smiling lips.

"I'm beginning to see the possibilities," she said softly, running her fingers through his hair, just above his ears.

"Shut up and pay off, Hunter."

"Gladly, Wakefield."

He kissed her then, ever so gently, once, twice, three times. Her heart opened, then overflowed as she realized the enormity of his gift. He'd given her more than a stool. He'd given her the next best thing to physical equality, a chance to kiss him without feeling overwhelmed by his size and strength.

"Forgive me now?" she murmured, her voice hoarse with emotion.

Jason answered in the same hushed tone, "There was nothing to forgive, sweetheart."

He carefully removed her glasses and set them on the coffee table. He kissed her eyelids, the tip of her nose, and her temples while his big hands cradled the back of her head and his thumbs traced her collarbones. Melody left coherent thought behind and surrendered herself to sensation.

Shivers of excitement radiated from wherever his thumbs stroked, up her neck and down into her chest. Impatient to kiss him again—and not so gently this time—she clasped his head on both sides and sealed his lips with her own, darting her tongue out to meet and mingle with his, tasting the Scotch on his tongue and absorbing the groan of pleasure that rumbled out of his chest.

His hands began to move then, spreading a tingling heat as he caressed her neck, her bare shoulders and the naked length of her spine. His arms closed around her waist, pulling her so close against his hard body that she felt his heart pounding against her breasts. Then it was her turn to feather kisses across his wiry eyebrows, down the bold ridge of his nose and across his cheekbones.

He eased his hold on her waist, cupped her chin with one hand to hold her head steady and kissed her lips again, plunging his tongue deep into her mouth. She clutched at his shoulders, feeling as if she might float right off the stool. His other hand skimmed over her hip, past the indentation of her waist, and found her breast.

Her breath caught in her chest, then rushed out on a sigh of pleasure as he teased the sensitive tip through the thin silk of her dress and moved on to minister to her other breast, as well. He released her mouth, leaving her head spinning as he trailed hot, moist kisses down her throat and into the deep V of her bodice.

She buried her lips in the softness of his hair, closed her eyes and inhaled deeply of his musky, masculine scent. Her breasts felt full, aching for more of his touch, his mouth. She felt his fingers at the back of her neck, an increase of pressure as he manipulated the clasp holding up the halter, then a release as the clasp gave way and the top of her dress slithered to her waist.

He stepped back. She raised her head as she felt the heat of his gaze burning over her torso. With unsteady fingers he traced her delicate curves, murmuring, "Ah, Mel, you're beautiful. So beautiful."

He bent his head then and tenderly kissed her erect, rosy nipples. Her knees buckled. He caught her before she could fall and held her snugly against his body, arching her back across his arm as he began to suckle. She moaned, feeling delightful yet almost painful contractions in the depths of her belly. Her body ached with emptiness, an emptiness only Jason could fill.

Pausing a moment, he said in a shaky voice, "I want you, sweetheart."

"Oh, Jason," she sighed, clutching his head against her with both hands, "I want you, too."

Placing his free arm behind her knees, he lifted her up high against his chest and carried her into the bedroom as if she were a priceless treasure. He set her on her feet beside his big bed and slowly removed the rest of her clothing. After turning back the gray-and-white quilted comforter, he scooped her up again and carefully lowered her onto the crisp cotton sheets.

He unfastened his cummerbund and tossed it on the floor. His shirt followed. He sat beside her then, gliding the tips of his fingers over her shoulders and across her chest.

"Are you protected, Mel?"

"I've, uh—" she felt a hot blush climb her neck "—I've got something in my purse."

He pushed her back down on the bed when she tried to rise, chuckling as he said, "That's all right. I'll take care of it."

She looked away, feeling like an idiot. It wasn't the first time she'd discussed such things with a man, after all. And she wasn't ashamed to admit she had come "prepared" this evening. But this was Jason, and it felt strange to be lying here naked while he nudged off his shoes without bothering to untie them.... Then she felt his fingers stroke the side of her cheek, gently but insistently turning her to face him. His gaze was steady and direct, his tone sincere and tender.

"Don't feel embarrassed with me, honey. Not about anything. I only want to love you."

Her tension drained away. Maintaining eye contact with him, she turned her face just enough to kiss his palm. "All right."

He yanked off his socks, then stood and shucked off his trousers and underwear in one quick motion while she watched with brazen interest. Living in the same house for four years, she'd accidentally caught glimpses of Jason undressed a time or two. But never this close. Or for this long. And never...aroused.

She reached out shyly and touched his hip, letting her hand ride softly over the smooth skin and on down to encounter the soft golden hair on his muscular thigh. He sucked in a ragged breath, and then he was in the bed beside her, holding her, kissing the breath right out of her.

His head swiming, Jason pulled back for a moment, reminding himself he had to stay in control. Mel felt so soft and warm and inviting in his arms, and he'd wanted her for so long, it was all he could do to stop himself from plunging into her right away. But that wasn't how he wanted their first time together to be. He wanted to make it a memory she'd treasure the rest of her life.

Hoping to slow himself down, he shut his eyes and inhaled a deep breath and felt seduced by the light floral fragrance that had driven him nuts all evening. He sighed and opened his eyes, unable to resist touching his lips to the incredibly soft skin at the base of her neck, her shoulders, her breasts.

Her breasts enticed him. He, who had always thought he loved big-breasted women, found he couldn't keep his hands or his mouth away from her gentle curves for long. And her thighs. Lord, he loved her soft white thighs, and her dainty ankles, and her sassy little fanny. For such a small woman, she had a lot of delectable places. He intended to touch and caress and taste every one of them.

She was touching him back now, exploring the muscles in his back and shoulders, his neck and chest, sending fiery signals to his groin from every spot her clever little hands stroked. He didn't remember his neck being so sensitive before, or the backs of his ears, or his nipples. She seemed entranced by the pattern of hair on his chest and stomach. His control was nearly shot now. If her hands moved any lower...

"Sweetheart, no," he groaned as her hand closed around him.

"Why not?" she asked, giving him a smile as seductive and tempting as Eve's must have been.

"I'll never be able to last," he gasped, grabbing her hands and anchoring them above her head with his big left hand.

He paid homage to her breasts with his mouth again, while his right hand stroked her thighs in a motion that coaxed them to part. She tasted luscious. She made little purring, whimpering noises as his fingers moved higher and higher. She cried out in delight when he found the very core of her passion.

Her responsiveness pleased and excited him almost beyond endurance. She called his name, and he felt like the world's greatest lover. She was hot and slick and ready for him, but still he held off, driving her closer to fulfillment with his loving touch.

She pulled one of her hands free and hooked a finger under his chin, demanding that he look up at her. "Jason, please. I want you now!"

He gave her a long, searing, soul-touching kiss before answering, "All right, honey."

He took care of protecting her, rolled onto his back and lifted her above him. She started to speak, but he silenced her with another kiss and said, his breathing harsh, "I want you to be in control this first time, Mel. I don't want to hurt you."

She nodded, sent him a wicked smile and, with his help, slowly eased him inside her. The sensations were unbelievable. She was so hot and tight, he nearly lost all restraint immediately. And the expression of wonder in her eyes at the contact touched him as nothing before ever had.

She leaned forward, resting her weight on her hands on either side of his head, and began to move, slowly at first, and gradually with more vigor. He clamped his hands on her hips in an attempt to slow her down, but she would not be denied. And then his own need became too urgent to ignore and he started to move with her.

Her eyes closed tightly and her head fell back. Her spine arched. Her breathing became labored. Her face contorted as if she were in pain, and she gasped, "Jason. I can't... fast... enough. Please."

He wrapped his arms around her and rolled over. Her legs clamped around his hips. He paused only long enough to murmur, "You're wonderful," and then his control evaporated and he thrust into her again and again.

Their hearts thundered in unison. Their cries of pleasure mingled. He was reaching, reaching right inside her, touching her heart and soul and mind as she was touching his. She stiffened, called his name and shuddered, gripping him so tightly that he followed her into ecstasy.

His arms gave way, and he slumped against her to catch his breath. After a moment, he supported his weight on his forearms and gazed down at her still form with growing concern. She was so small. Had he been too rough with her? He stroked her hair away from her forehead and whispered, "Mel? Honey, are you all right?"

Her lips curved into a captivating smile. Her eyelids fluttered, then lifted, revealing misty brown eyes that looked up at him with such joy and satisfaction that he felt as if he'd been given a rare gift.

"I'm fine," she purred.

"Oh, you are, huh?" he asked, smiling at her husky voice. He started to pull away, but she wrapped her arms around his back and reached up to kiss his chin.

"Don't. Not yet."

Cradling her in his arms, he kissed her long and lovingly, then rolled them onto their sides, facing each other. They traded a few more light, teasing kisses and ended up with Jason flat on his back and Melody cuddled close against his side, one arm draped across his chest, slowly twirling tufts of chest hair around and around her index finger.

He sighed with contentment and lazily stroked her hip and fanny. He felt totally satisfied, happy, complete. He didn't care if he ever got out of this bed as long as Melody stayed right here beside him. Brushing his lips against her soft, silky hair, he gave her a quick one-armed hug.

She met his eyes and grinned. "You look so smug."

"I'm feelin' mighty smug."

"About what?"

"About you, me, us. Mel, we were dynamite together."

"Oh yeah?"

"Yeah. And you know what else?"

"What else, Jason?" she asked, giving his chest hair a playful tug.

"Stop that." He grabbed her hand, lifted it to his lips and kissed each fingertip. "I think we oughtta make this relationship permanent."

She froze for a moment, looked away, then looked at him again. "What do you mean?"

He hesitated. Shouldn't she be smiling? But dammit, this was not the time for beating around any stupid bushes. "I think we should get married."

She raised up, balancing on one elbow, disbelief—or maybe shock—replacing the relaxed, happy expression of a moment ago. "You what?"

"I think we should get married," he repeated, feeling a sick dread start growing in the pit of his stomach. She really should be smiling now, but she wasn't. "What's the matter, honey?"

Her eyes fell away from his. Then, as if she'd just noticed they were both naked, she scrambled around in the bed and pulled the top sheet and a blanket up over them, settling at least a foot away from him. Finally she looked at him again and said calmly, "Jason, you don't have to marry me."

"Melody—"

"I know David is your best friend, and you told him you'd keep your hands off me or some idiotic thing like that," she continued, as though he hadn't spoken, "and it's very noble of you, but it's not necessary."

"Oh, but it is necessary, Melody Jane."

"No, it's not. I won't get pregnant. And even if I did, it's nobody else's business."

He closed the distance between them, lifted her chin with his index finger and looked deep into her wary brown eyes. "I love you, Mel."

She sighed and inched away until his hand dropped of its own accord. Then she scooted into a sitting position, propping her back against a pillow and rearranging the blankets to cover her up to her neck.

Resting his weight on one elbow, he stared at her, his eyes wide with disbelief. "You don't believe me."

"Why should I believe you?" she began calmly, meeting his affronted stare with an unwavering gaze of her own. "It wasn't all that long ago you told me you wanted to marry Wendy Wyoming."

The lines of strain around his nose and mouth relaxed. His eyes lighted up with sudden mirth. "And I still do."

She jerked one arm out from under the covers to wave an exasperated hand at him. "Did you hear what you just said, Wakefield? I don't believe you, you rotten—"

He grabbed her hand and gave it a good hard jerk, tumbling her over onto her side. Her eyes were still flashing sparks of fury at him. He loomed over her, a smirk on his lips. "Don't you think your little game has gone on long enough, Wendy?"

Melody became very still, then raised her head and stared at him, her mouth opening and closing like a goldfish's. Then she asked, "How did you find out?"

He threw back his head and laughed and hauled her into his arms, ignoring her feeble attempts to put some distance between them again.

"I know I should have figured it out sooner, but give me a little credit, Mel. I've been suspicious for quite a while now, but I was finally sure tonight at the party. Your laugh tipped me off."

"I see."

She rolled onto her side, her back to him. He stroked her hair, her neck, her rigid shoulders. Then he took a deep breath and said, "I can't begin to tell you how sorry I am that I laughed when you told me the first time. You've always been a special lady to me, but I'd just never thought of you that way, and—"

"I know, Jason. You don't need to explain." She glanced over her shoulder at him. "I'm sorry I was so mean to you."

"I don't blame you. I had every bit of that coming and more." He rolled her over to face him again and, after gently kissing her forehead, said, "I really do love you, Melody. Marry me."

She wanted to say yes. He could see it in her eyes. But there was something else there, too—anxiety, distrust, fear? He wasn't sure what it was, but he knew she was going to refuse him before she opened her mouth. His mind raced, desperately seeking something to change her mind. Her eyes turned all misty and sad. She touched his cheek.

"Jason, it's too soon to know how we really feel about each other."

He closed his eyes for a moment, grateful she hadn't said no, absolutely not, never in a million years. It wouldn't have mattered to him if she had said all those things, because he wasn't about to give her up. But if all she needed was more time, he would try to be patient.

Reluctantly he admitted, "Maybe I am rushing it a little."

She shook her head, but smiled when she said, "No, you're rushing it a lot, Jason."

"You think so?"

"Yup."

"Well, then, I guess we'll have to keep on dating awhile and see what happens. All right?"

Melody wavered only a second. Her brain told her to get out of the relationship now. But her heart and body told her to stay and collect a few more wonderful memories with Jason. Her heart and body won. Jason would come to his senses soon enough. But for now she wanted to spend as much time with him as she possibly could.

"All right, Jason."

He moved closer, pulled her into his arms and just held her, savoring the feel of her warm, naked body against his. Mel loved him; he knew she did. She wouldn't have made love with him if she didn't. But her doubts about marrying him hurt. She probably still thought he was too fickle or some such nonsense.

But what if he was wrong about her feelings for him? Was he seeing love in her eyes only because he so much wanted to see it? She was a lot more complicated than he would have believed a few short weeks ago. What if she really didn't love him?

His arms tightened around her in denial. She kissed his chin, his mustache, the tip of his nose. He claimed her mouth in a deep, searching kiss, finding reassurance in her instant response. And then his doubts and worries faded away and they were off on another journey into passion.

Chapter Nine

A muted chirping woke Melody from a sound sleep. She stretched, then started a bit when her backside encountered warm, bare flesh. She glanced over her shoulder and smiled. It was dark in the bedroom, but she could see Jason fairly well. He was still asleep, and he looked as if he might be having a particularly pleasant dream.

She settled back on the pillow, sighing contentedly when his arm tightened around her waist and his left hand unconsciously moved up to cup her breast. She closed her eyes and would have gone back to her own dreams, but that funny chirping noise sounded again.

Rising up on one elbow, she listened carefully and squinted into the darkness. There it was again. And it sounded as if it had come from the digital clock radio on the nightstand. After freeing herself from Jason's loving arm, Melody scooted across the king-size bed and discovered a cordless telephone built into the radio.

A green *4*, a *3* and a *0* blazed out at her, and she blinked as the phone chirped again. She reached for the receiver but faltered at the last moment. Who would be calilng Jason at 4:30 in the morning? If it was another woman, she didn't want to know about it.

The next chirp sounded almost angry. Jason let out a muffled grunt and stirred. Melody grabbed the phone and muttered a terse "Hello."

"Hello?" a familiar male voice answered in slurred syllables. "Melody Jane, is that you?"

"Yes. David?"

"Well, shoot. I thought I wuz callin' Jashon—er, Jason. But tha's okay. I wuz gonna call you, too."

"David, do you know what time it is?"

"I don't care, Melody Jane. She did it. She did it an' I think I'm gonna die it hurts so bad."

Melody's mouth dropped open when she heard her brother sob. Gripping the phone tighter, she demanded, "David, what are you talking about? Are you all right?"

"Hell, no, I'm not all right. Didn' I just tell you she hurt me real bad?"

"Who hurt you, David?"

"Aw, hell, whadda you care? I'm gonna call somebody else."

"David. David." The receiver clicked. "David!"

Jason groaned, then propped himself up on one elbow and asked groggily, "What's goin' on, Mel?"

She slammed down the phone, switched on the lamp and started collecting her clothes as fast as she could. "David just called. Jason, we've got to go over there. He sounded weird, and I couldn't understand half of what he said. But he said somebody hurt him."

When Melody's words registered in his sleep-befuddled mind, Jason sprang out of bed and started pulling on jeans and a sweater. In five minutes flat they were out the door and speeding north toward David's apartment in the Buffalo Ridge subdivision. Jason slammed on the brakes and parked behind David's car. He and Melody jumped out of the Blazer and raced up the three flights of steps.

Breathless, Jason pounded on the door and shouted, "David! Let me in. It's Jason, David."

By the time Melody caught up with him, heads were popping out of doors up and down the hallway, more than one angrily demanding if they knew what the hell time it was. Melody paused a second to catch her breath, then dug into her purse for her key ring.

"Shhh, Jason, I've got one of his keys on here somewhere."

He gave the disgruntled neighbors an apologetic nod, then turned his attention back to Melody, who had finally located the correct key. He took it from her, shoved it into the lock and almost sprawled into the apartment when David unexpectedly opened the door. David smiled benignly and waved them inside, a fifth of Jack Daniel's in his hand.

"Jason. Mel. Glad you dropped by. Wanna have a li'l drink?"

Melody groaned. Jason cursed under his breath. David weaved across the room, picked up the phone, which was dangling on the floor, said, "I gotta go 'cause I got comp'ny," and plopped into a chair as he hung up, cuddling his bottle the way a toddler holds his favorite blanket. He gave them another benign smile, then leaned his head back against the chair and closed his eyes.

Jason looked at Melody. Melody shrugged and shook her head. David belched and tried to sit up a little straighter. Melody approached her brother, knelt down in front of him and carefully removed the Jack Daniel's from his grasp. She handed it to Jason and said softly, "All right, David. Now what's going on?"

He looked at her with bleary, bloodshot eyes that rapidly filled with tears. He put his arms around Melody, laid his head on her shoulder and sobbed, "It's Liz, Mel. She did it."

Melody hugged him and stroked his rumpled hair back from his face. "What did Liz do, David?"

"She...she gave me...b-back her engagement ring. She w-won't m-marry me, M-Mel."

"And getting drunk will solve your problem, Dave?" Jason asked.

David reared back and frowned up at his friend. "I s'pose not," he replied, punctuating his statement with another belch. "But it seemed like a helluva good idea at the time."

Jason held the bottle up to the light and whistled at how much was gone. "Tell me you didn't buy this bottle tonight."

"Well, sure I did, Jase. I don't keep that stuff around all the time, y'know. But you can have whatever's left."

Jason leaned down and disentangled Melody from David's embrace, then draped one of David's arms across his shoulder and got him on his feet. "Come on, pardner. Let's get you into the shower. You're gonna be in a world of hurt tomorrow."

"I don't wanna take a shower, Jase. I wanna have a party."

"You've had enough of a party for one night, Dave." Jason started him walking toward the bathroom, whispering to Melody as they passed her, "See if you can fix him something to eat."

Melody nodded and headed for the kitchen, flinching at David's slurred speech as Jason marched him down the hallway.

"She doesn't love me anymore, Jase. I tol' her an' tol' her I love her, but she jus' wouldn't believe me."

The bathroom door banged shut. A moment later Melody heard the sound of water running, then a lot of colorful language she'd never heard David use before. As she opened the refrigerator door she thanked heaven Jason was here to handle him.

By the time Jason returned, Melody had made coffee and toast and was dishing up cheese omelets and hash browns. She eyed the wet splotches on Jason's jeans and the soggy sweater cuffs at his wrists and asked, "How is he, Jason?"

"He'll live."

David stomped into the kitchen then, wearing a terrycloth bathrobe and a scowl. He poured himself a cup of coffee and sat down at the table, his face turning a little green when Melody set his plate in front of him. He gulped and pushed the plate aside, mumbling, "I don't think I can eat anything."

Jason pushed the plate back in front of him and ordered, "Chow down, pal. Your sister went to a lot of work, and it just might save you from a hangover worse than death."

Melody pulled back the curtains, letting the sunrise into the kitchen, while Jason carried the other two plates to the table. They ate in silence until David looked up from his plate and stared at Melody's dress—the same one she'd worn to the party—and at her wildly tousled hair. Then he turned on Jason.

"You bastard. I knew I'd dialed your number, but I figured I was so drunk I'd dialed Melody's instead. But I didn't, did I? She spent the night with you."

"David, stop that this minute!" Melody commanded. "It's none of your business."

"It sure as hell is my business when my best friend seduces my sister."

"For heaven's sake, he didn't seduce me. I'm not that naive, David."

"I asked her to marry me," Jason offered, drawing David's attention away from Melody.

"You did?" David's head swiveled back to Melody. "He did?"

"Yes."

"She turned me down, though."

"She did?" David glared at Melody. "You did?"

"It's none of your business, David," Melody repeated.

"Why in the hell did you do that? Jason's a great guy!"

"Shut up and eat your eggs, David."

"Thanks, Dave."

David let out a long-suffering sigh, muttered, "Women!" and proceeded to clean his plate. Melody poured him a second cup of coffee. When he'd finished he got up, walked around the table and dropped a kiss on her forehead. "I've gotta get some sleep. Thanks for feeding me, Squirt."

She stood, put her arms around his waist and gave him a sisterly hug. "Let me know if you need to talk later. Maybe you and Liz could still work it out."

"I don't think that's possible." He held her away from him then and looked her square in the eye. "It may not be any of my business, sis, but I've got to tell you, you're a damn fool not to accept Jason's proposal."

"David..."

"All right. But sometimes I think you're too much like Liz for your own good, Mel."

"Good night, David."

"Good night, Mel. Night, Jase."

Hands propped on her hips, she watched David walk away before turning back to start stacking the plates. Jason took the dirty dishes from her hands and set them back on the table.

"Come on, honey. You didn't get much sleep last night, either. David can clean this up later."

"Oh, but Jason, he's going to feel so rotten," she protested.

"Serves him right."

"I'd do the same for you."

"Well, all right. But I'll help, and then I'll drive you home so you can rest up before school on Monday."

They finished cleaning the kitchen in a few minutes. While Melody switched on the dishwasher, Jason went into the living room and returned a moment later carrying the bottle of Jack Daniel's. He dumped what was left down the drain, ran water to wash the strong odor away and dropped the empty bottle into the trash can.

Melody couldn't hold back her concern for her brother any longer. "Uh, Jason..." she began tentatively.

"What, Mel?"

"As far as you know, David doesn't usually get drunk when he has a problem, does he?"

He turned to her, a gentle smile on his face. "What you really mean is, does David have a drinking problem."

"Well, yes. I mean, sometimes people can hide things like that from their family, you know, and..."

He shook his head and chuckled. "I understand, little mother. But you don't have to worry about Dave. He's never done this before that I know of, and he's gonna have such a headache tomorrow—and probably the next day, too—he won't want to even smell hooch again for a month."

"Are you sure?"

"Positive. I think he just couldn't handle losing Liz."

Melody sighed with relief and gratefully went into Jason's open arms for a quick hug. "Thank goodness."

They went out to the Blazer then, and once they were underway Melody said, "I'm sorry this is so painful for David, but I'm glad to know he really loves Liz."

"They were engaged," Jason pointed out dryly. "Why wouldn't you think he loved her?"

Melody shrugged. "He's so nonchalant most of the time—except about work, of course—that I didn't think of him as a man deeply in love. Do you know what he meant about my being too much like Liz?"

Jason considered her question for a moment, then briefly related the conversation he'd had with David on the night of their first date, ending with, "Because of his reputation, Liz couldn't trust him enough to make the relationship work."

"He was flirting with a couple of his old girlfriends right in front of Liz last night, so I can't say that I blame her," Melody said thoughtfully.

"Yeah, I saw him. But you know, David didn't see it as flirting. He just really likes women and enjoys talking to them. I don't think Liz or anyone else could expect him to change that part of his personality."

"You're probably right," Melody murmured. As she studied Jason's profile in the pale light of dawn, she thought, *And you're so like him, Jason.*

They fell silent then, and the silence lasted until Jason turned onto Central Avenue. He shot her a sideways glance and said, "You know, Mel, David warned me that you might not be able to trust me any more than Liz trusted him. Is that why you rejected my proposal?"

"Partly," she admitted. "I hope I'm not as jealous as Liz, but it's hard to imagine either one of you as a happily married man."

"Will you believe me if I tell you we've never been as wild as the rumor mill says we are? We're not exactly virgins, but

I sure as hell didn't sleep with every woman I dated, and neither did your brother."

"It's really none of my business, Jason."

"No, it's not," he agreed. "But Liz couldn't help worrying about it. And you once told me I was too fickle, so I'm not sure you can, either. How can I convince you that I love you?"

"I don't know. All I can suggest is to give it time."

"How much time?"

"I don't know that, either."

He parked in front of Melody's apartment, shut off the engine and turned toward her. "Well, then, I guess we'll just have to take each day as it comes."

Jason walked Melody to her front door, picked up her Sunday newspaper from the step and stepped inside with her. But when she offered to make coffee, he refused. "I'd better not. You need some rest, and you won't get any if I hang around."

"I suppose you're right," she agreed, stifling a yawn, then laughing. "Oh, dear. Excuse me, Jason."

He enveloped her in a fierce hug and said softly, "Last night was special to me, Mel. And so are you. Don't ever doubt that."

She tilted her head back to look up at him and he kissed her with all the passion, all the love, he felt for her, trying to communicate with his lips and tongue all that she meant to him. The dazed expression on her face gratified him when he finally released her and opened the front door.

"Call me tomorrow after you've taped your show and I'll take you out to dinner."

She gave him a shaky smile. "Sounds good."

He bent to give her one more quick kiss, muttered, "I need to make another kissing stool to keep at your place," and stepped outside, closing the door behind him. He walked slowly back to his Blazer, climbed in and looked up at Melody's big living room window. She was standing there watching him, a pensive expression on her face until she noticed he was looking at her.

She smiled and waved. He waved back. And though she couldn't hear him, he said "Hang onto your hat, Melody Jane. This cowboy's gonna court you in style."

Melody turned from the window when Jason drove off, her emotions in such turmoil that she didn't know whether to laugh or sit down and have a good cry. So much had happened in the last twenty-four hours that she felt overwhelmed and exhausted. About the only thing she knew for certain was that she loved Jason Wakefield, loved him in every way there was to love a man.

She had read about passionate relationships in books but had never expected to actually feel the exotic sensations described by the authors. Making love with Vic, while not unpleasant, certainly hadn't prepared her for the delicious ecstasy of Jason's lovemaking. Comparing the two experiences was like comparing tap water to tequila.

She closed her eyes, and her skin tingled anew at the memories flooding her brain—his mustache, soft yet wiry against her breast; his voice, dark and hoarse, praising her encouraging her, exciting her; his hands touching her gently, tenderly, demandingly.

Melody shivered, looked down and groaned when she discovered she was hugging herself. She picked up the newspaper and headed for the bedroom, wondering if she had made the biggest mistake of her life in turning down Jason's proposal. Maybe he really did love her. And if he did she might have hurt his pride so much he would never ask her again.

The problem was, Jason wasn't acting the way she had expected him to. It was almost as if they were playing a game together but using different sets of rules. Though she had known they would make love, his sudden proposal had shocked her. Why on earth had he done that?

"Oh, for pity's sake, Melody," she muttered. "You're so tired you're not even halfway rational. Get some sleep, and then try to figure it all out."

She was passing through the kitchen, debating whether or not she had enough energy left to take a shower before climbing into bed, when the phone rang. She looked longingly toward her bedroom for a moment, then plunked the paper down on the table, sighed and answered the phone.

An anxious female voice said, "Melody, thank God you're finally home!"

Melody rolled her eyes heavenward, wondering why her brother and sister couldn't find somebody else to call before eight o'clock on a Sunday morning. "What's wrong, Barbara?"

"I got the weirdest phone call from David about a quarter to six this morning, which would have been a quarter to four your time. He sounded as if he were drunk. I tried calling him back a couple of times, but his line was busy. And I thought about calling the folks when I couldn't reach you, but I didn't want to worry them. Will you go check on him and call me right back?"

"He's fine, Barbara. Liz gave him back his ring last night, and he was drowning his sorrows in Jack Daniel's."

"Oh. Poor David. What happened?"

Melody briefly told her sister what had happened at the governor's party and braced herself for Barbara's inevitable next question. It wasn't long in coming.

"So where were you when I tried calling you at four o'clock this morning? And don't tell me you were with David, because he was whining about being all alone."

"Uh, I was in bed."

"With Jason?"

"Don't ask nosy questions."

"Hah! I knew it!" Barbara crowed. "So how good was it?"

"Barbara!"

"Come on, sis, you can tell me. On a scale of one to ten, it was—"

"A twelve."

"If it was that good, why don't you sound ecstatic?"

"I don't believe this conversation."

"What's the matter, kid?"

"Nothing important. He, uh, found out about Wendy Wyoming."

"So what's wrong with that? You knew he'd find out sometime. Cripes, he didn't get mad, did he?"

"No. But, you see, now I'm not sure if he was making love to me or to Wendy."

"That is without a doubt the most asinine thing I've ever heard you say, Melody Jane. Wendy Wyoming is just a part of your personality. You're not divisible."

"Come on, Barbara. She's a figment of my imagination a separate entity, not part of me. I couldn't be Wendy Wyoming in real life if I died trying."

"I wouldn't be too sure about that. And, if I'm right don't you think it's sort of ridiculous to be jealous of yourself?"

"Is that how you see it? That I'm jealous?"

"Well, aren't you?"

"Oh, poop." Melody sighed. "I guess you're right. David said I was too much like Liz for my own good, and I guess he was right, too."

"Hey, don't be so hard on yourself. We all feel pretty vulnerable when we fall in love. I'd probably feel the same way in your position."

"You think so?"

"Sure. The trick is to keep it in perspective."

"How do I do that?"

"Give it some time."

"Gee, that sounds familiar."

"What does that mean?"

"Never mind. It's a long story."

"Okay. Hang in there, sis. Keep an open mind about Jason, and don't forget to keep me posted."

"I'll try."

"Give my love to the folks and David. And . . . Alan."

"I will. Bye, Barbara."

Melody hung up the receiver and walked slowly into her bedroom, feeling restless and edgy. She also felt a little guilty for not telling her sister about Jason's proposal, but Barbara would have lectured her unmercifully, and Melody simply did not feel up to dealing with that right now. After stripping off her clothes, she stepped into the shower, hoping the hot water would relax her enough to sleep.

It didn't work. In fact, she felt even more restless and edgy when she'd dried herself off than she had before she'd gotten wet. Something was tugging at her memory, something about the party last night that she couldn't quite put her finger on. She went into her bedroom, shook her head at the bed and put on a pair of jeans and her favorite old pink sweater.

She would never be able to sleep now, so she might as well go over her lesson plans for tomorrow. She could always catch a nap later. She trudged into the kitchen, put some water on the stove for tea and glanced through the paper while she waited for the water to boil.

There wasn't much exciting news in the first section, but a photograph three columns wide on the first page of the second section momentarily stunned her. It was from the party last night. She was standing a little in front of Jason, talking to that man from the national party headquarters.

A former governor and a U.S. senator flanked Jason. They all looked glamorous, the men in tuxedos and she in her evening gown. The three older men were looking at her as if they were hanging on her every word. And Jason was gazing at her with something that looked pretty darn close to pride of ownership in his expression!

The teakettle let out a piercing shriek. Melody dashed across the kitchen to the stove, set the kettle aside and turned off the burner before hurrying back to the photograph. As she studied the picture again and scanned the brief article accompanying it, she got a sick feeling deep in her stomach. It was the man from party headquarters, the man with the drink in his hand— That was what she'd been trying to remember.

Jason had excused them to go eat, and the older gentleman had stopped him and . . . Melody shut her eyes tightly and could see the man clearly, waving his drink and saying something like "Whenever you're ready to make a run for the big time, give me a call. I still think you'd have a better chance if you were married, but I'd be willing to give it a shot no matter what."

Melody dropped the paper as if it had suddenly turned into a black widow spider. Her heart protested that Jason would never do such a thing. But her brain insisted she had to consider the possibility.

She sighed and crossed her arms across her midriff and paced the limits of her small kitchen. Her eyes stung with dryness from trying not to blink because every time she blinked she would see that old man again and hear him say, "I think you'd have a better chance if you were married," and then she would remember the sly way he'd smiled at her.

Melody knew she'd made a good impression on Jason's political friends; she had intended to. Though she didn't particularly enjoy political functions, she did know how to behave at them. And she really was pleased for Jason that his political career was going so well.

Seeing him with all those officials last night had convinced Melody that he was on his way up in the party. And from his remarks at dinner she could only conclude he was willing and eager for a chance to go to Washington. But Jason wouldn't marry someone to improve his chances of winning an election, at least not consciously. And even—just supposing, of course—if Jason would do such a rotten thing, even unconsciously, Melody Jane Hunter was not the woman who could help his career.

Oh, on the surface Melody supposed she might appear to be an excellent choice for Jason. She was presentable, reasonably intelligent and quiet enough not to steal his thunder. And politicians needed the media to get elected, and she did have media connections in Wyoming and in Washington, if you wanted to count Barbara as a connection.

But in reality she would make a terrible wife for a politician. If Jason married her, she would only hold him back. She had survived the party last night just fine, and had even enjoyed herself more than she'd expected. But she'd already been acquainted with quite a few of the people attending. Wyoming's population was small enough that if you attended the University of Wyoming or had a highly visible family like hers you simply knew a lot of people from all over the state.

Maybe she could handle Jason's political events in Wyoming. But in Washington? Not likely. She didn't know anything about gracious entertaining beyond what her mother had taught her at family dinners. And furthermore, she didn't much care about learning to entertain graciously either.

In a fit of temper, Melody rolled up the paper and drop-kicked it into the living room. Darn that old man for making her doubt Jason! She would have completely forgotten his remark if Jason hadn't proposed to her last night. And she probably would have caved in and said yes before very long if Jason had persisted with his proposal; her jealousy about Wendy Wyoming or any other woman wasn't *really* such a big problem. She could have learned to control it. And she would have married him and had his babies, and somehow she would have found a way to learn to be a good politician's wife, but now... Now she would always wonder if Jason had proposed to her to further his political career. Damn!

Breathing raggedly, Melody collapsed onto one of the chairs at her kitchen table, put her head in her hands and fiercely held back the tears burning behind her eyelids. She had promised herself there would be no more foolish romantic hopes about a future with Jason. What a joke! She couldn't keep that promise any more than she could suddenly grow another seven or eight inches.

After several long, deep breaths, Melody squared her shoulders, raised her chin and marched resolutely to her desk. She picked up her lesson plan book and turned back toward the kitchen but stopped after she'd taken one step. The envelope with the application for the job in Denver was still sitting there, just as she had known it would be.

She had told herself that she would mail it as soon as she found the time to locate a stamp. But she'd never made the time, and now she had to admit that finding a stamp was not the real reason she hadn't mailed the application. No, she hadn't mailed the application because, deep down, she couldn't stand the thought of ever leaving Jason.

"Well, it's time to grow up and face reality, Melody Jane," she muttered.

She had promised Barbara she would keep an open mind about Jason, and she would. Maybe miracles still happened once in a while. She certainly wasn't ready to give Jason up—please, God, not yet. It would be so easy to let him sweep her away on a magical cloud of romance and desire, but she had to keep her feet on the ground—for Jason's sake, as well as her own. She needed to do something, make some positive step to take charge of her own future in case things didn't work out with Jason.

After hesitating only another second, she scooped up the envelope, grabbed her purse and fished a stamp out of her wallet, licked the stamp and mashed it against the envelope. Then she put on a coat and, without waiting to zip it up, hurried out the door and ran down the sidewalk to the mailbox on the corner.

Chapter Ten

"Hey there, pardners, this is Wendy Wyoming coming to you on an absolutely gorgeous March twenty-fifth from KBOY, home of the best country music in Cheyenne, Wyoming. We're right at the top of the hour, it's a beautiful warm day outside and, best of all, it's Friday. Let's get this party rolling with Hank Williams, Jr.'s new single."

Jezebel perked up her ears, tilted her head to one side and whined, her tail thumping the floor. Jason shoved the mammoth portion of lasagna Carolyn had left for his supper into the new microwave Melody had talked him into buying, programmed the machine and leaned down to pat the dog's head.

"Yeah, you know that voice, don't you, girl? That's our Melody. She never would have fooled you, would she?"

Jez woofed her agreement, and Jason went back to fixing his meal. He poured a big glass of milk, buttered a slice of bread and scrubbed an apple for dessert, then smiled to himself when Wendy came on the air again.

"That oughtta get your blood movin' and your toes tappin'! Are you as excited about spring as I am, pardners? It seems like we've been buried in snow forever. But today on my way to work I actually saw a robin, and kids playing outside without coats on, and a few lovers walking through Holiday Park holding hands. I love it, and so do the friendly folks at Tyrone Chevrolet."

The microwave dinged. Jason removed the lasagna and sat down at the kitchen table. After a long day of calving, he was tired and so hungry his belly button was sayin' howdy to his backbone, but something was missing that would have made this meal a feast. And that something was reading advertising copy and making a new car sound irresistible.

Well, really, he was only hearing a tape, but Mel still wasn't where he wanted her to be. Hell, he'd be happy eating a peanut-butter-and-jelly sandwich for supper if Mel were here with him. And he hated peanut butter.

Jezebel rattled her supper dish with one paw and looked up at him expectantly, adding an indignant whine when he didn't start moving fast enough to suit her.

"I'm gettin' it, Jez. Be patient."

Sighing, he got up and opened a can of Alpo. As always, it was a major challenge trying to keep Jezebel out of the way long enough to spoon the food into her dish.

"Whoa, Jez. Hold on a minute, will ya? Now mind your manners."

He shook his head at Jezebel and returned to his own meal. No sense letting Carolyn's great lasagna go to waste just because he was lonesome for Melody. The past six weeks had been quite a revelation.

Who would have believed old love-'em-and-leave-'em Wakefield would completely lose his heart to a little slip of a gal? Not him, that was for sure.

But he had.

And who would have believed old steady-as-a-rock Wakefield would be feeling as emotionally strung out as a teenager, up in the clouds when he was with Mel and lower than a snake's belly in a wagon rut when he wasn't? Not him.

But he was.

And who in his right mind would have believed that sweet little slip of a gal, who had the softest heart in Laramie County and enough love and empathy in her to mend the hurts of her family and half her friends—not to mention the students who lingered after class for the daily ego boost she never failed to deliver—would have a will of iron that would try even a grandma's patience and have old man-of-the-world Wakefield so tied up in knots and confusion he barely knew what day of the week it was? Not him.

But she'd done all that to him and more.

She made wild, uninhibited love with him that made him consider the possibility of cardiac arrest, and slow, tender love with him that rocked his soul and made him tremble. Her eyes always lighted up when she first saw him, and her smile always made him feel welcome. She demonstrated her love for him in a thousand thoughtful little ways nobody else had ever done for him. But she had never once said she loved him.

He would have bet the ranch and his political career that Melody Jane Hunter was a one-man woman, the kind of woman who wouldn't be satisfied with an affair, no matter how passionate or exciting that affair might be. But she refused to discuss the future with him. She refused gently, of course; Mel didn't know how to be mean. But she refused as stubbornly as a damn jackass all the same.

He'd never loved anyone, never needed anyone, never wanted anyone as much as he loved, needed and wanted Melody Jane Hunter. And he'd never wanted to strangle anyone as much, either! The woman was downright unreasonable!

Finished with the lasagna, Jason carried his plate to the sink, rinsed it and stuck it in the dishwasher. He didn't really want the apple. He picked it up and stuck it in his pocket for Lucky out of habit, and he'd reached the back door before he rocked back on his heels, realizing what he had done.

Lucky had taken a turn for the worse on the first of March and had looked and sounded so miserable that even he could no longer justify prolonging her suffering. Mel had been there for him as no one had been when his mom and his dad had died. She had held him, encouraged him to reminisce and allowed him to grieve, and had never once made him feel silly for making such a fuss over an animal. It still hurt whenever he thought of Lucky, but he could handle it with Mel's loving support.

He knelt down and gave Jezebel a goodbye belly scratch and eyed the phone as he straightened up to head back out and relieve Harlan for a supper break. He wanted to call Mel, just to hear her voice instead of Wendy's, but he'd promised himself he wouldn't. It wouldn't do for her to know how much she had the upper hand with him.

"Now here's a good one for all you...lovers, from the Bellamy Brothers."

Jason let out a snort of irritation, reached over to the counter and snapped off the radio. That was another thing she had him all confused about. He still got a kick out of Wendy Wyoming; she had such a delightful wit, such an earthy bluntness about her that it was hard to dislike her. But he was starting to do just that.

He'd always thought he was a modern, liberated man. He believed women had a right to a career and should be allowed to follow their dreams just as men did. He also knew Melody was finding a lot of satisfaction in her radio show, and he wouldn't have denied her that opportunity for anything.

But dammit all, when she said lines like the one she'd just delivered she raised his blood pressure and stirred up his hormones, and he couldn't help thinking about the hundreds of other guys out there listening to her and having the same fantasies about her that he did. And he didn't like it, not one damn bit. His only consolation was that all those other guys didn't know who Wendy Wyoming really was. Nonetheless, he felt jealous and possessive and small-minded and chauvinistic all at the same time.

He was also beginning to resent the time she spent away from him to do her show. Their respective schedules were so crazy, it was hard to find time to be together. He admitted his attitude was both childish and selfish, but that didn't change the way he felt.

Jason stepped outside, shoved his hands deep into his pockets and scuffed the toes of his boots through the grass as he ambled back out to the pasture. What would it take, he wondered, to get that infernal woman's brain off school and Wendy Wyoming and onto him and marriage? He'd done everything he could think of to change her mind.

He'd surprised her with flowers and candy on Valentine's Day and one of those funny balloon bouquets on St. Patrick's Day. They had gone shopping in Denver and Fort Collins, and then out to dinner and dancing before driving home. They'd gone hiking and horseback riding, to parties and movies. They'd even gone bowling when he would have enjoyed staying home and watching TV, because he hadn't wanted her to think being married to him would be boring.

They had laughed together, cried together, made love when they'd wanted to and sometimes just cuddled, argued and made up, worked and played. But he knew that if he proposed to her again, Melody would refuse. She was worried about something, holding something back, gradually withdrawing from him; he could feel it. And as he approached Harlan, who was hunkered down beside a laboring cow, Jason muttered the age-old question generations of men, no doubt starting with Adam, have asked themselves.

"What the hell does that woman want?"

"That's it for tonight, pardners. I hope you enjoyed the show as much as I did. I'll be back with you next Monday night. In the meantime, have a great weekend, and don't forget to pass on a little...love. This is Wendy Wyoming saying good-night."

Melody switched off her microphone and laid her headphones aside. Resting her elbows on the shelf in front of the control panel, she rubbed her eyes beneath her glasses, probably smearing her eye shadow and mascara. She was too tired to care. She stretched her arms over her head, hoping to get some of the kinks out of her neck and shoulders, then rewound the tape and finished shutting down the control booth.

After she picked up her purse and her latest batch of fan letters and switched off the lights, Melody paused for a moment, remembering the day David had brought her a pizza and talked her into doing the show. She'd been so thrilled then, so eager to make exciting changes in her life. Well, she had made changes. And those changes had certainly spiced up her life.

The problem was, Melody thought, smiling wryly at the glamorous life-style she had envisioned for herself, she barely had time to sleep anymore. Between teaching, Wendy Wyoming and Jason, there simply weren't enough hours in the day. And, as the old saying went, it was going to get worse before it got better.

Now that the weather was finally warming up, her students were showing the symptoms of spring fever. And since this was their last year in junior high school, her ninth-graders would try to start slacking off long before the end of the school year. The only way to combat this problem was to give them more exciting, more demanding classes, which meant more preparation time and paper grading for her. And that didn't include the extra end-of-the-year paperwork, such as final exams and report cards and inventory sheets to fill out and on and on.

Melody shook her head, then walked out of the building. The cool, fresh air outdoors somewhat revived her, and she slowed her pace as she crossed the parking lot. The streetlights had come on. She could hear laughter and horns honking, no doubt from the high school kids cruising Lincolnway, and for a moment she envied them.

Oh, she knew adolescence was a painful time for a lot of kids, and she really wouldn't want to go back and live through those awkward years again. But the idea that the most important problem in life was whether or not the pimple on your chin would heal before a big dance or whether the boy you'd had a crush on for weeks would ask you out appealed to her.

Sighing, she got into her Mustang and drove home. Though it wasn't even nine o'clock yet, she put on a nightgown and bathrobe, turned on the television for a little mindless entertainment and plopped herself down on the sofa. She had gotten so used to being with Jason every evening while the legislature had been in session and up until his calving season had started that it seemed strange that he wouldn't be coming over tonight.

She understood why he had to be out at the ranch now. And, while she missed him, she was also secretly and a little guiltily glad to have an evening to herself. She had always enjoyed quiet evenings at home, but she'd had darn few since Jason had asked her to marry him. He just didn't seem comfortable unless he was out doing something. And she was becoming exhausted trying to keep up with him.

So what could she do about it? She couldn't give up her teaching job or cheat the kids; her professional pride couldn't stand that. She wouldn't give up any of her time with Jason; it was too precious to her to even consider it. That left Wendy Wyoming.

"Ah, yes," Melody muttered. "Good old Wendy."

She supposed she could give up being Wendy. The extra money was nice but not necessary. And though she enjoyed doing the show and receiving fan mail and all, teaching would always be her real vocation. Or, since she spent so much time listening to other people's problems, maybe she should go back to school and get a master's degree in counseling.

But Jason had never paid much attention to her until she'd started being Wendy Wyoming. If she stopped doing the show she would probably go back to being plain old Melody Hunter, and then what would happen to her relationship with Jason? Wouldn't he find the real Melody about as exciting as a snail race?

Melody sighed, then left the sofa and turned off the TV, cutting off Angela Channing and Lance Comson in the middle of an argument. They would just have to get on with their fighting and machinations without her. She picked up the newspaper she hadn't had time to read, then tossed it back on the coffee table. She was tired enough to sleep without reading for once. And she'd better get as much rest as she could while Jason was still tied up with his cattle.

Melody woke up at six-thirty the next morning, refreshed and eager to start the day. If she hurried she could finish her schoolwork and drive out to the ranch to spend the rest of the weekend with Jason. She showered, dried her hair and dressed, then put on a pot of coffee, opened the drapes in the living room and went to bring in the morning paper.

Jason was just parking the Blazer when she opened the front door. Her heart leaped at the sight of him. She smiled and waved, but he didn't wave back. Instead, he slammed the Blazer's door and stormed up the sidewalk, a scowl darkening his face and what looked like a rolled-up newspaper in his right hand.

Her smile fading, Melody watched as he ascended the front steps. "This is a surprise. I thought I was supposed to drive out to the Lazy W this afternoon," she said.

He stepped inside, his tone as grim as his expression. "We've gotta talk."

"All right."

Melody gulped. Something was wrong, terribly wrong. Jason always kissed her in greeting. But with his jaw clenched, his eyes blazing and his knuckles white from gripping the newspaper, he looked as if he'd much rather throttle her than kiss her. She closed the door and led the way to the kitchen.

She felt his eyes burning into a spot between her shoulder blades as she walked and a huge lump growing in her throat. Was this it? The end of their affair? They'd been dating for almost six weeks, so it was about time. She didn't want to be right, but she couldn't think of anything else that would have turned Jason into this furious, forbidding stranger.

She walked over to the counter and took down two mugs. But before she could pour him a cup of coffee, Jason smacked the newspaper down on the table. "I suppose you saw yesterday's paper?"

Though her stomach was in knots, Melody replied calmly, "No, I didn't have time yesterday. What's wrong, Jason?"

"I didn't get to it, either, so I read it this morning while I ate breakfast." He spread the paper out, turned to the entertainment section and jabbed at an article in the lower right-hand corner of the front page with his index finger. "Take a look."

Melody edged in front of him and, balancing her weight on her left palm, leaned over the table. She couldn't help smiling at the headline: Who is Wendy Wyoming? The rest of the article was brief and to the point.

> For the last two months, Cheyenne residents have been entertained by a new, seductive radio personality. On Monday, Wednesday and Friday nights, Wendy Wyoming broadcasts four hours of country music and sexy patter from FM station KBOY.
>
> Wendy's listeners are naturally curious about the sultry-sounding disc jocky, but when questioned about her true identity, station manager David Hunter refused to comment. However, the *Wyoming Star* will not be denied.
>
> If you know someone who could be Wendy Wyoming, type or print your guess on a postcard and mail it to: Wendy Wyoming Contest, P.O. Box 975 Cheyenne, WY, 82001. Our staff will tabulate and publish the results one month from today.
>
> If anyone can produce concrete evidence of an accu-

rate guess, he or she will win a dinner for two at a restaurant of his or her choice from the *Wyoming Star*

Forgetting Jason's surly attitude, Melody laughed with delight when she finished reading the article. Her fan mail had given her ego a healthy boost, but this contest was a public affirmation of her talent. And she loved it!

For a moment she wished she could call the newspaper office and tell them the truth. If she weren't a school teacher, she might just do it. But Wyoming was hardly a bastion of liberal thought; her life would be much easier if her identity remained a secret.

She turned back to Jason then and was startled to see his eyebrows drawn together, his lips compressed into a tight, straight line. She took a step backward when he jammed his fists on his hips, towering over her in a dominating stance. Tipping her head slightly to one side, she asked again, "What's wrong, Jason?"

He pointed at the paper. "That article is what's wrong. Don't you see what it means?"

"I think it's funny. And a bit flattering," she answered, more heatedly this time, her tone matching his. "But I don't think I'm seeing the same thing you are. Why don't you spell it out for me?"

"It means," he said slowly and distinctly, in a tone that made Melody grit her teeth, "You'll have to stop doing your show."

Melody's chin lifted and her hands clamped on her waist. "Stop doing my show? Are you out of your mind? David will be thrilled with the ratings this contest will generate."

"I don't care if David is tickled plumb silly. I'm worried about you."

"Worried? Why on earth would you be worried?"

"Somebody's gonna find out, Mel."

"Oh, phooey. You laughed so hard you cried when I tried to tell you I was Wendy Wyoming. And if nobody's guessed in three months, why would anyone figure it out now?"

"You've changed some since then, Mel. You're more confident and assertive now, more...uh, well, sexy than you used to be."

"Why didn't that sound like a compliment?"

He sighed, then lowered his voice. "Look, honey, I didn't mean it to come out quite that way. You've always been attractive and all—"

"Thanks a bunch, Jason."

He continued as if she hadn't interrupted him. "But since you started being Wendy Wyoming, it's like you're more aware of your own sexuality or something."

She crossed her arms over her chest. "Really? What am I doing differently now?"

"Well, you give off signals to men you never did before."

"That sounds interesting. What kind of signals?"

"Would you knock off the sarcasm, Mel?" he asked, raking the fingers of his left hand through his hair in frustration.

"I'm sorry, Jason," she answered, not sounding one bit sorry. "I'm just trying to understand."

"Oh, hell, I don't think I can explain it right. But take my word for it, somebody will guess you're Wendy Wyoming."

"So what? They'd have a hard time proving it. I've worked at the station off and on since I was in high school. And I can tape my shows at different times so that I'm never there when Wendy is on the air."

"But you're a teacher in a public school. You'll have parents screaming for your head if you're exposed. And the school board will probably give it to them. You have to quit, Mel."

It was one thing for Jason to be concerned about her welfare. It was something else entirely for him to stomp into her apartment and start telling her what to do. Though she had worried about her teaching career herself, and had even thought about giving Wendy up, Melody squared her shoulders and raised her chin even higher. "I can't quit, Jason. It wouldn't be fair to David."

"Dave would understand."

"He might. But I like doing the show."

"If you won't do it for yourself, Mel, do it for me."

"Why would you want me to quit? You've liked Wendy from the start."

"We'd have more time to be together, for one thing."

"And?" she prompted when he looked away.

"Well, I'm not sure I like all the changes you've made. You were fine just the way you were before."

Melody snorted in disbelief. "You never even noticed me before I started being Wendy. And I resent it when you try to boss me around."

"I'm not bossing you around."

"Oh, yes, you are. And it makes me wonder what else you'll tell me to give up if it inconveniences you."

"Aw, Mel, be reasonable. That's not the problem."

"What is the problem, then?"

Jason sighed and looked away. He crossed his arms over his chest, then faced her again and admitted grudgingly, "I don't like other guys hearing you talk like that."

"Of all the old-fashioned, chauvinistic—" Melody fumed. She took a deep calming breath, then said, "Let me get this straight. You want me to be sexy for you, but the rest of the time you want me to be prim and proper? Jason, that's ridiculous."

"What's so ridiculous about it? I can feel jealous just like anyone else."

Her expression softened. "You're jealous? Oh, Jason, that really is ridiculous."

"No, it's not. If everyone in this town finds out you're Wendy Wyoming, you'll have so many guys sniffing around I won't even be able to get close."

"Oh, I'd love to see that."

"Yeah, I'll bet. That's probably why you won't marry me."

"That's not fair."

"Maybe not, but we've been goin' out together and making love for quite a while now, and you haven't committed yourself at all as far as I can see. How do I know you won't dump me for someone else?"

It was her turn to look away. "I wouldn't do that. And we're not ready for a commitment."

"I am. We're so good, so right together, I'll be damned if I can understand why you're hesitating. But that's another issue. First I want your promise to quit doing the show."

"I can't promise that."

"You mean you won't."

"All right, I won't."

"Okay. Fine. Have it your way." He pivoted on the heel of one boot and stalked back into the living room.

Melody hurried to catch up with him. "Jason, don't leave like this."

He opened the front door, paused and looked back at her over his shoulder. "Changed your mind?"

"No. But at least stay and talk this out."

"I don't have time. I've got so many cows dropping calves I shouldn't have come at all. But I thought you might care enough about my feelings to quit doing the show. Guess I was wrong."

He left then, before Melody could get out another word. And when she did get one out, it was brief and explicit. That big lug! How could he possibly say she didn't care about his feelings? That was really a low blow. It was also emotional blackmail, and she wasn't about to give in to it. If she did, he would always have the upper hand in their relationship. If they still had a relationship.

That thought rocked her back on her heels. She wrapped her arms around her waist and shivered, wondering if ending their affair had been Jason's intention all along. Despite what he'd said about her not making a commitment, it seemed to Melody that he'd been looking for a fight from the minute he'd entered her apartment.

But maybe it was for the best to end it this way. They would make a quick, clean break now, and each of them would be spared having to tell the other it was over. She had received more in the last six weeks with Jason than she'd expected. Nobody could ever take away her memories of making love with him, of hearing him say he loved her and wanted to marry her. So it was only a matter of time until this deep, raging pain and disappointment wore off and she could get on with her life, right? Right!

She gulped, lifted her chin and squared her shoulders, but all the positive thinking in the world could not hold back the scalding torrent of tears pouring down her face. She cursed and reached for a tissue, then ran into her bedroom, threw herself across the bed and wept into her pillow until she had no more tears left. And when the tempest had passed, Melody knew that she had never felt so empty, so completely alone, in her entire life.

"You're a damned fool, Wakefield," Jason told his reflection in the rearview mirror as he drove out of town. Melody was right. His demand hadn't been fair; he'd known it all along. And he should have known better than to storm into her apartment and start telling her what to do without even kissing her hello.

He should have held onto his patience, sat down with her and discussed the matter calmly and quietly with her as a rational, reasonable adult. But dammit all, when he'd seen that article in the paper he'd felt threatened and chock-full of jealousy, and anything but rational and reasonable. Why couldn't she understand that?

He owed her an apology, but he didn't feel much like giving her one right now. His emotions were still too raw, his temper still too close to the surface, for him to have any confidence that he could apologize and mean it. He smacked the steering wheel with one fist and shook his head.

Since he had avoided commitments with women all his adult life, there was a certain amount of poetic justice in his having finally fallen in love with a woman who wouldn't admit she loved him or make a commitment to him. But he sincerely hoped he had never made another human being feel the bone-deep, gut-ripping pain he was now feeling.

And just what the hell should he do next? What *could* he do? Melody hadn't responded to his romantic overtures, and he'd really knocked himself out to show her a good time.

He saw the sign announcing his exit off the interstate just in time to signal and stomp on the brakes to slow down enough to make it. Good Lord, he'd been going eighty miles an hour and hadn't even realized it! He'd been damn lucky he hadn't passed a patrolman.

But once he was headed down the gravel road to the ranch, his mind turned right back to the question he hadn't answered and left the driving to automatic reflexes again.

What was he going to do about Melody? There weren't many alternatives. The only one that made sense to him was to simply leave her alone for a while. If he didn't phone her or see her for a week, maybe she would miss him and be happy to accept his apology.

He groaned and rubbed one hand wearily down over his face. Not see Mel for a whole week? He was so damned addicted to her it would feel like an eternity. But unless he could think of something else, he'd just have to live through it.

Melody parked in front of her apartment at four-fifteen the following Thursday afternoon and tiredly hauled herself up the steps. She pulled a couple of envelopes out of her mailbox and let herself inside, then dropped her satchel next to the front door and collapsed on the sofa. After closing her eyes, she laid her head back against the lumpy cushions and inhaled a couple of deep breaths in a futile attempt to relax.

She had expected life without Jason to be miserable, but Lord, not this miserable. She was impatient with her kids at school, and both of the Wendy Wyoming shows she had taped so far this week stank. She couldn't sleep, couldn't eat, and even after five days of silence on Jason's part, her heart still leaped with hope every time her phone or her doorbell rang.

And if it wouldn't have cost every last scrap of her self-esteem, she would have phoned Jason and promised to give up Wendy Wyoming or do anything else he wanted if he would only say he loved her again. She was an idiot, a pathetic, weak-willed, sniveling idiot— No, she was in love. One minute she felt like following David's example and drowning her broken heart in a bottle of wine, and the next minute she wanted to punch Jason's lights out. But she couldn't bring herself to do either.

Moaning, she forced herself to sit up straighter, opened her eyes and looked down at the envelopes she still held in her right hand. The top one was a credit-card bill; her recent shopping sprees for new clothes to impress Jason with were no doubt catching up with her. Not needing one more blessed thing to depress her, she tossed it aside.

Expecting more of the same, she glanced at the second envelope and started to toss it on top of the first one, then did a double take at the return address. A Denver return address. With shaking figners, she ripped open the envelope and quickly scanned the letter.

Then she read it again, more carefully this time. When she had finished, Melody glanced at her watch, stood up and walked slowly to the telephone. She hesitated a moment, then gritted her teeth, picked up the receiver and dialed.

"This is Melody Hunter in Cheyenne. I'd like to speak to Mr. Harvey Whitman, please. Yes, I'll hold. Hello, Mr. Whitman. I'm calling about your invitation to come for an interview. Yes, I can take a personal leave day. Two weeks from tomorrow at eleven o'clock will be fine. I'll see you then. Goodbye."

Chapter Eleven

Melody left KBOY in a hurry after taping her show on Friday evening, thinking of nothing but a hot shower and bed. But when she reached her car she blinked to make sure she was seeing correctly, and her mouth fell open in astonishment. Sitting on the hood was an enormous bouquet of red roses with a white handkerchief tied to a stick hanging out of one side of the arrangement.

She reached for them instinctively. Then, realizing someone must have put the flowers there, she looked up. Off to her right she heard a car door open, saw a dome light go on in a big, squared-off vehicle and, a moment later, recognized Jason stepping out.

Melody swallowed hard. She hadn't dared to hope the flowers were from him, but there he was, wearing a dark suit and a white shirt, striding confidently across the parking lot toward her. But why would he give her roses? Did he want to continue their relationship after all? Or was he trying to end their affair on a more pleasant note?

He stopped in front of her. "Hi."

"Hi yourself."

He gestured at the flowers. "Like 'em?"

"They're beautiful, Jason." Then she lifted one corner of the handkerchief and asked, "But what's this for?"

Jason picked up the roses, plucked out the stick and handkerchief and handed her the bouquet. Then he removed his Stetson and held it in front of him with his right hand while he stroked the brim with his left.

"I, uh, thought I might need a white flag after the way I acted last Saturday. I was a jerk, and I'm sorry, Mel. I promise I'll never walk out on you like that again."

Almost giddy with relief, she couldn't resist closing her eyes and deeply inhaling the flowers' fragrance. When she looked up again, her gaze met Jason's, and her heart speeded up—just as it always did whenever he was around. He looked as if he hadn't slept any better than she had over the past week. But he looked so good to her... Damn, she was never going to get over him! She dropped her eyes to the roses again.

Still fiddling with his hat, he shifted his weight to the opposite foot. "Am I forgiven, then?"

"Of course."

"Good. Will you have dinner with me tonight?"

Melody hesitated. Jason's apology and nervous behavior touched her deeply. There was nothing she wanted more at this moment than to kiss and make up. But she had suffered a thoroughly rotten week because of him, and she didn't feel up to any more conflict at the moment.

"I don't know, Jason."

"I wanted to call and apologize a thousand times this week, but I just couldn't do it over the phone. And I thought maybe it'd do us some good to spend a little time apart," he said quickly, reaching out a hand to gently stroke her cheek. "But I've missed you, and I want to spend some time together. I promise it'll be a nice, relaxing meal. No hassles, no fights. Okay?"

She shouldn't agree to this. She really shouldn't. But she couldn't refuse him anything when he touched her and looked at her with such love and tenderness in his eyes. She had already done the practical thing in agreeing to an interview with Mr. Whitman. What could one more evening or another month of evenings with Jason hurt?

"All right." She glanced down at the simple skirt and blouse she'd worn to school that morning, then looked at Jason's suit. "But I can't go anywhere too fancy."

"No problem. Mind if we take my car?" he asked, eyeing her Mustang doubtfully. "I'm not sure I'll fit in that thing."

"That's fine."

He escorted her to the Blazer, holding the flowers for her while she climbed aboard and handing them back when she was comfortably settled. He shut the door for her, hurried around to the driver's side and turned left onto Lincolnway a moment later.

"Where are we going?" Melody asked as they passed the downtown area.

"It's a surprise."

She shook her head and smiled at him. "If we keep going west, it has to be either the Hitching Post or Little America."

"You'll see."

She settled back and relaxed, watching the Friday-night traffic, until Jason passed the Hitching Post and took the entrance ramp to I-80 near Little America. When they passed that, too, her head swiveled to the left and she demanded, "Jason, where are we going?"

"To the ranch."

"I only agreed to dinner."

"I know. Carolyn's spent most of the day cooking it." He glanced at her before turning his eyes back to the road. "I want to be alone with you, Mel. I'll bring you back to town later if you want me to."

She groaned silently and looked away, uncertain whether she was miffed by his high-handed tactics or not. She really shouldn't be so easy on him after the week he'd put her through. But he *had* apologized, and it was silly to spoil the evening by holding a grudge—especially when she already knew he wouldn't be taking her back to town later if she had anything to say about it. She wanted him too much to pretend otherwise. Still, it rankled her that he'd taken it for granted she wouldn't have another date.

"Pretty darn sure of yourself, Wakefield," she observed tartly.

"Not at all, Hunter," he replied. "Just mighty hopeful."

When they arrived at the Lazy W, Jason hustled her into the house, a contagious air of suppressed excitement about him. Once inside, he crossed the living room to the fireplace and touched a match to a carefully stacked pile of kindling. Melody followed, carrying her roses and appreciatively sniffing the tantalizing aromas coming from the kitchen.

Dusting off his hands, he walked over to her and said, "Dinner should be ready in a few minutes. I'll put these in water for you if you want to go freshen up."

As if on cue, her stomach growled. Melody laughed and handed him the boquet. "Sounds good to me."

He bent and dropped a quick kiss on her mouth, then headed in the direction of the kitchen, calling over his shoulder, "Meet me in the dining room in five minutes."

When she left the bathroom at the appointed time and walked back through the living room, Melody noted that Jason had gone to a lot of trouble for this dinner. His house had always been neat and clean on the occasions she'd visited him at the ranch, but tonight it was immaculate. The drapes were closed, the lights were dimmed, and soft, dreamy music coming from the stereo created a romantic atmosphere.

And when she entered the dining room, Melody smiled and shook her head over the elegant table draped in a burgundy linen tablecloth. Sparkling crystal, china and silver caught and reflected light from a slender pair of white candles burning in silver candlesticks. A single red rose, no doubt from her bouquet, standing in a delicate cut-glass bud vase served as a centerpiece.

Jason entered the room from the kitchen then, carrying a bottle of wine in an ice bucket. Doing a passable imitation of a snooty headwaiter, he seated Melody at the table, filled her wineglass and disappeared back into the kitchen, carefully shutting the swinging door behind him. Melody smiled and sipped the wine and chuckled over a hissed argument between Jason and Carolyn that was obviously not meant for her ears but carried quite clearly into the dining room anyway.

She jumped when the swinging door crashed open and again Jason strode through, his face flushed with indignation until he saw her startled expression. He paused in midstride for an instant. Then, after shooting a rebellious look over his shoulder at the kitchen, he put on a smile, served Melody a shrimp cocktail and sat down across from her to eat his own.

In between clearing away their dirty dishes and bringing out the next course, Jason did his best to be a charming and entertaining dinner companion. And Melody *was* charmed. She felt like a queen as he waited on her, serving a crisp salad, mouth-watering beef Stroganoff on a bed of fluffy white rice, steamed vegetables and, finally, a fat wedge of cherry cheesecake.

Afterward, as they sat side by side in the living room and sipped coffee, Melody rested her head against Jason's shoulder with a sigh of pleasure. He shifted, raising his arm to the back of the sofa to accommodate her more comfortably. Melody heard the back door close and said, "Remind me to compliment Carolyn on a wonderful dinner the next time I see her."

"Don't bother," Jason grumbled good-naturedly. "She's conceited and bossy enough in the kitchen now. You should have heard her ordering me around out there!"

"She must have been giving you the right orders, cowboy. That was the nicest dinner I've had in a long time."

"You think so?"

"Definitely."

"Must have been the company."

"That didn't hurt, either."

They watched the fire together in quiet contentment while they finished their coffee. Then Jason set their cups aside, stood up and added another log to the fire. The look in his eyes when he came back to join her on the sofa again was familiar to her now. She welcomed it and him with an inviting smile.

He went down on one knee in front of her and, taking her hands in his, coaxed her onto the plush carpeting beside him. When she straightened her legs and rested her back against the sofa, he turned and stretched out perpendicular to her, resting his head in her lap. She toyed with his thick, shining hair as they talked, catching each other up on the past week's events.

He captured her hand and kissed her palm. She leaned down and kissed the tip of his nose, then glanced around the room, asking, "Where's Jezebel, Jason?"

"I sent her home with Carolyn."

She fluttered one hand over her heart as if she were truly shocked. "Why, Mr. Wakefield! Does that mean we're all alone now?"

His eyes dancing with laughter, Jason raised up and turned to face her, supporting himself with one hand while he twirled the tip of his mustache with the other. "It does indeed, Miss Hunter." He stepped out of character then, admitting with a laugh, "I couldn't risk another one of her jealous fits when I'd planned to seduce you, could I?"

Tipping her head slightly to one side, she gave him a sultry smile. "Are you seducing me?"

"I'm sure trying like hell. Is it working?"

"What do you think?"

He leaned closer. "I think it's working. Want me to take you home?"

"Uh-uh."

"Wanna fool around?"

"Uh-huh."

"Good. Me too."

Nose to nose, they smiled at each other. Jason removed her glasses and set them on the coffee table. Then he crooked one finger beneath her chin and kissed her. It was a sweet, tender touching of lips to lips. They pulled apart and smiled again. But when their mouths came together a second time, tenderness fled before a sudden onslaught of passion that took them both by surprise.

Melody put her arms around Jason's neck, clinging tightly as he eased her over onto her side and followed her down to lie beside her. She opened her mouth to receive his tongue, feeling a desperate hunger to see and touch and taste all of him all at once. Impatient with the barriers of clothing between them, she stripped off his tie and went to work on his shirt buttons, popping one off in her haste.

He concentrated on the buttons on her blouse, and after a few moments of heated kisses and tangled arms and legs, they were free of their clothing. Shaking with excitement, she felt his hands move over her, stroking, fondling, pleasuring. She returned the favor as best she could.

But it wasn't enough. It would never be enough. When it came to loving Jason, she was hopelessly addicted. And if there were ever a cure for such an addiction, she would refuse to take it.

She wrapped herself around him, exulting in the sensation of naked flesh against naked flesh, and strung a chain of stinging little love bites along his neck. He groaned and crushed her to him. Then, breathing as if he'd just run five miles, he raised himself up on one elbow. "Sweetheart, we've got to slow down."

Hooking one hand around the back of his neck as if to pull him back down to her, she whimpered, "I don't want to."

Smoothing the riotous curls away from her face, he resisted her tugging. "We'll be more comfortable in bed."

Since he wouldn't come to her, she reached up and caressed his chest and then moved down his side with her free hand, deliberately seeking out all the pleasure spots she'd found on his body over the last six weeks. "I don't want to wait that long, Jason."

His breathing came in rough, ragged gasps. She felt his heart thumping against his rib cage and his skin twitching and rippling when she accidentally grazed a ticklish spot.

And when she raised up and kissed him in the crevice where his neck and shoulder met, he shivered.

"I meant this to be a perfect night for you, Mel, but—Oh, hell. I don't want to wait, either."

He let her pull him down and then plundered her mouth with long, intoxicating kisses. Their mutual need was so urgent, so intense, there was no time for subtle niceties. She opened herself to his marauding fingertips, and when he'd satisfied himself that she was ready, she guided him into her, arching to meet him on the very first stroke.

As she rode the waves of pleasure higher and higher, her fingernails dug deeper and deeper into his shoulders, as if she could anchor herself to the safety of earth in a galaxy gone crazy. He praised her, encouraged her, begged and demanded her total surrender. And when she gave it with a shuddering, joyful cry, he joined her in a powerful climax.

His arms buckled, and he collapsed on top of her, gasping for oxygen. Still feeling as if she'd left the planet, Melody ran her fingers over his sweat-slicked back in long, languid strokes. Jason rolled off her and onto his side. When she turned and faced him, he opened one eye and smiled at the dazed yet ecstatic expression on her face.

Mel loved him. She had to, to make such love with him. He'd never experienced anything like this before, and he knew he never would again with anyone else. If he only had the energy, he'd get up and pound his chest and yell like Tarzan. But, for the moment, she'd wiped him out, and he settled for kissing her forehead instead.

She snuggled closer in response and murmured, "Wow. When you seduce somebody, Wakefield, you don't fool around, do you?"

"You ain't seen nothin' yet, Hunter."

"Is it safe to open my eyes now?"

"Any time, darlin'. I've been wondering why you haven't opened 'em."

"I'm scared of heights."

"Why, Mel. That's the nicest thing you've ever said to me."

She opened her eyes, grinned at him and traced his mustache with her forefinger. "Poor Jason."

He captured her hand and splayed it across his chest. "Honey, right now I feel like the richest man in the world. But do you think we could get up off this floor?"

"I guess so. But you have to move first."

Jason sat up, wincing slightly at the stinging in his shoulders. Melody sat up, too, gasped when she saw the evenly spaced red crescents on his smooth skin, then bit her lower lip in remorse. She touched the fiery marks, unable to believe she'd gouged him that way.

"Oh, Jason, I'm sorry."

He glanced at his left shoulder and shrugged off her concern. "No problem. You've probably got a few bruises yourself. We both got a little carried away."

He got to his feet, grabbed his shirt and stood up. As he leaned down to pick up the rest of his clothes, he spotted the button that had popped off his shirt lying in front of the bookcase. Melody followed his line of sight and flushed as she remembered her feverish haste to strip off his clothes.

Chuckling, Jason gave her a hand up and, pulling her close to his side, teased her in a silly falsetto voice. "You're such an animal, Mel! Try to be more gentle with me next time."

She glared up at him, then burst out laughing at the prissy look on his face. He tossed his shirt back on the floor, scooped her up high in his arms and carried her down the hallway to his bedroom. He set her on her feet beside the bed, gave her a long, lingering kiss and whispered, "Last one in the Jacuzzi's a rotten egg."

He won, of course. It took a full five seconds for his challenge to sink into Melody's brain after that scorching kiss. But she didn't mind losing, especially since Jason was already ensconced in the tub, ready to assist her in climbing in. She sat down beside him, leaned back, closed her eyes and let the hot bubbling water work its magic.

After a few minutes, her muscles felt like melted wax. Jason lifted her onto his lap and gently urged her to lie back, tucking her head under his chin. Then his hands began to move over her in sweet caresses from her knees up to her thighs, from her hips to her waist and on up to her breasts. Her head lolled to one side, and he accepted the silent invitation, kissing her neck and shoulders.

Somehow they dried off and made it to the bed before she was lost in a world of sensation with Jason, oblivious to everything but his touch and his voice as he made slow, achingly beautiful love to her again and again, until exhaustion claimed them both and they slept.

The smell of coffee and cooked bacon woke Melody the next morning. She sniffed, opened one eye and saw a blurry Jason waving a blurry plate in front of her face. She wrinkled her nose at him and squinted. He chuckled and obligingly handed her her glasses.

"Good morning, sunshine."

"Good morning," she answered, stifling a yawn.

He looked disgustingly chipper, clean-shaven and dressed in jeans, boots and a long-sleeved blue Western shirt. He plumped the pillows for her and she sat up, pulling the sheet and blankets over her breasts. When she leaned back and looked up at him, he kissed her good-morning, then set a loaded tray across her legs.

She patted his cheek and said, "Hey, first you wait on me at dinner, and now breakfast in bed? You'll spoil me." Then she looked in dismay at the mounds of bacon, scrambled eggs and toast. "I can't eat all that."

He sat facing her on the edge of the bed, handed her a fork and picked up a second fork and pointed it at her. "I'd love to spoil you. And you'd better not eat all of that. It's my breakfast, too. Now eat, woman. We've got things to do."

With much help from Jason, Melody ate every bite. Considering that Jason had cooked it, the food wasn't half-bad. But what she enjoyed the most were the orange-juice-flavored kisses, the coffee-flavored ones and the jelly-flavored ones, not to mention the kisses that tasted of bacon and eggs.

Though she shamelessly tried to coax Jason back into bed with her after they'd finished eating, he laughingly yanked the covers away and pushed her into the shower. When she came out of the bathroom wrapped in one of his huge towels he was waiting for her, holding a grocery sack in one hand. He held it out to her and said, "I, uh, borrowed a key to your apartment from David and picked up some clothes and stuff for you."

She raised an eyebrow at him but accepted the paper bag with a wry smile. "I see. So you really did plan to seduce me last night."

He shoved his hands into his pockets and studied the floor for a moment. "Well, yeah, I did."

"Then I think it was very thoughtful of you to get some of my stuff for me. What are we going to do today?"

"I thought we could ride up into the mountains. There's something I want you to see."

"That sounds interesting."

"It will be," he promised. Then he ruffled her wet hair with one hand and gave her a playful swat on the bottom with the other as he headed for the door. "I'll saddle the horses while you're getting dressed. Come on out to the corral when you're ready."

"I will."

Melody watched him walk away, her chest feeling tight as her heart overflowed with love for him. He could be so stubborn and irritating, and so tender and sweet. But mostly he was just plain nice to be around.

She tossed the towel onto the bed and opened the sack, chuckling to find that Jason had packed her sexiest fire-engine-red underwear, along with a ratty old pair of jeans and a sweatshirt that too many washings had faded into a rather putrid shade of green. And, bless his heart, he'd packed her brush and comb, toothbrush and hair drier, as well.

Eager to join him outside, she hurriedly dressed and dried her hair, made the bed and raced to the back porch, where she yanked on the boots Jason had insisted on buying for her before he had taken her riding the first time. Jezebel struggled through the doggy door and greeted Melody with the usual gyrations. After she'd petted and visited with the dog for a minute, Melody pulled on the jacket Jason had packed for her and left the house.

It was a glorious spring morning. Though the air was cool, the sun was shining, and for once there was very little wind. Spotting Jason, she waved and ran down the back steps, then hurried across the barnyard to join him.

By the time she reached the corral, Jason had already saddled his mount, a big black gelding named Smokey, and was tightening the cinch on a bay mare named Diana. Not wanting to startle the horses, Melody slowed down as she approached the split-rail fence. Diana bobbed her head and snorted in greeting, and Melody obligingly patted her neck and scratched behind her ears, then had to do the same for Smokey.

Jason smiled indulgently at the silly words she crooned to the horses and reached for a pair of saddlebags draped over the fence. Smokey shifted restlessly as Jason attached them to the back of his saddle but calmed down at his master's quiet command. Then Jason led the animals through the corral gate, helped Melody mount Diana and swung himself up onto the gelding's back.

They rode west, into a pasture Jason called the nursery. While he consulted with Harlan Peters about the herd, Melody spent an enjoyable half hour watching the frisky white-faced calves and laughing at their antics. When Jason had finished his business, they headed north into the foothills.

Melody tipped her face up to the sun and took in a deep breath of the pristine, pine-scented air. She relaxed in the saddle and wondered why horseback riding had never been touted as a stress-reduction exercise. Who could feel tense out in the fresh air and sunshine, talking to Jason and rocking along with Diana's smooth, easy walk?

The trail rose gradually at first and then more steeply as the foothills became mountains, and the sun climbed to the apex of its trip across the blue sky. The pines grew taller and closer together. Their voices took on a hushed quality to match the whispering breeze through the trees. They saw chipmunks and rabbits and heard the rustling of other forest animals in the undergrowth.

When the path narrowed and curved up higher to the right, Jason and Smokey took the lead. Diana's gait was no longer smooth and easy; it hadn't been for over an hour, in fact. Melody's backside and thighs were yelling for relief, and she called to Jason, "What were you planning to show me, cowboy? The Continental Divide?"

Jason laughed and called back, "Gettin' tired?"

"Not me. But my fanny sure is."

"It's not much farther."

Diana snorted, and Melody sighed in sympathy. Not much farther to Jason bore little relation to her definition of the phrase. But to her surprise the trail leveled off five minutes later, and Jason urged Smokey onto a wide, grass-covered bluff and reined in. Diana followed Smokey, and a moment later Melody's breath caught in her chest.

The earth dropped away only a foot or two ahead, exposing a vast panorama of snow-capped mountains in the distance and a lush valley below. Jason dismounted and Melody followed suit, barely able to tear her eyes away from the view long enough to watch what she was doing. He led the horses to a small creek at the south end of the bluff, made certain they had plenty of grass and removed the saddlebags, slinging them over his left shoulder.

Then he returned to Melody. Standing behind her, he wrapped his arms around her midriff and smiled when she automatically leaned back against him. They might have stood there for minutes or hours; neither knew and neither cared. It was enough to be together, absorbing the beauty and watching a pair of hawks floating in lazy circles overhead. Finally, with a heartfelt sigh, Melody broke the silence.

"This is a beautiful place, Jason."

"I used to ride Lucky up here a lot when I was a kid. I've never shared it with anyone else," he answered quietly.

"It looks like a wonderful place to sit and dream."

"It is. I'd pack myself a lunch and spend whole afternoons planning what I'd do with the ranch when I was grown up. See it down there? Off to your left?"

"It looks so tiny."

"But it's not, Mel. It's plenty big enough for a family."

She shot him a sharp glance over her shoulder. Jason casually released her and stepped back a couple of paces before sitting down on the grass with his legs crossed in front of him. Then he opened the saddle bags and started lifting out Tupperware dishes and laying them on a large flat rock, calling to Melody, "Come on over here and see what Carolyn made us for lunch."

It had been hours since breakfast. At the mention of food, Melody discovered she was ravenously hungry. She sat down on the other side of Jason's makeshift table, and in a few minutes they were wolfing down thick roast-beef sandwiches, homemade dill pickles, carrot sticks, deviled eggs, and giant chocolate-chip cookies for dessert.

When they'd finished eating and had cleaned up the remains of their picnic, Jason leaned back on his hands, booted feet crossed in front of him. With a sober, intense expression on his face he studied Melody as she wandered to the edge of the cliff for another look at the view. Sensing a change in the atmosphere, she glanced back at him, her eyebrows raised questioningly.

"I brought you up here for a reason," he said quietly.

She stood very still for an instant, then came back and sat down beside him, propping her elbows on raised knees. "Besides showing me the view, you mean?"

He nodded. "Nobody will bother us here. We've got to talk, Mel. I can't go on like this anymore."

"Like what?"

"Like we're just good friends who happen to be lovers."

"That's what we are, Jason."

"But that's not all we are, is it?"

She looked away, feigning a sudden interest in watching the horses eat grass. Then she said softly, "It's been such a perfect weekend so far, Jason. Don't spoil it."

"Spoil it?" He leaned forward, his eyes boring into her. "How can talking about our relationship spoil it, Mel?" When she didn't answer or look at him, he said, "Dammit, Melody, you're not going to do this to me again."

Her head whipped around at the accusing tone in his voice. Her chin lifted. "Do what to you again?"

"You know what! I've been trying to get you to talk about our future for weeks. And every time I've tried to bring it up you've dodged the issue better than any politician I've ever seen." He paused to take a breath, his eyes practically shooting sparks now. "I acted like a jealous idiot last weekend and made an ass out of myself. And I finally figured out I did it because I'm not satisfied having an affair with you."

"We could always end it," she retorted, then turned away again so he wouldn't see how much she dreaded that possibility.

He heard the catch in her voice, saw the rigid set to her shoulders and the defiant angle of her chin. She looked small and brave but defenseless. His heart softened momentarily, as did his voice. "I don't want that, Mel. I hope you don't, either."

She turned confused brown eyes on him. "Then what do you want?"

He lifted a hand and caressed her cheek, as he said earnestly, "I want to talk about us, darlin', like two rational, reasonable adults. I want to tell you how I feel, and I want to know how you feel about me. I'm already in so deep with you, I need some reassurance that you care about me. That's what last night and our ride up here today have been all about. Surely you knew that."

His eyes were so green, they seemed to see right through her body to her roiling emotions. She wanted to look away, but couldn't. He was right. She had been putting him off, because she knew how this conversation must end. But she couldn't avoid it any longer. It was time for the showdown. She cleared her throat and nodded. "All right."

Jason withdrew his hand and scooted back, as if to give her some needed space. Then he smiled at her; it was a gentle, open smile that promised, *It won't be so bad. You'll see.* But all he said was, "Want me to go first?"

"Please."

"Well, first off, I want to apologize again for trying to make you promise to give up your show. I was way out of line, and I want you to know it won't happen again. As far as I'm concerned, you can be Wendy Wyoming or Bozo the Clown."

"It's okay, Jason."

"No, it's not. After I'd cooled off, I got to thinking back over that talk we had out at Little Bear. You know, the one where you told me what you wanted in a marriage? You said you wanted an equal partnership."

She started to speak, but he held up one hand to indicate he wasn't finished. "You and Dave are about the only people who've ever stood up to me, and, believe it or not, I value that. I know I didn't treat you as an equal partner. And since I'm sort of naturally bossy and I've never had a partner before, I'm not sure I know how to treat one. But I'd sure love to learn if you're willing to teach me."

Melody had to blink hard to keep her eyes from misting over. She'd been so afraid of being hurt by Jason that she hadn't considered the possibility that she might hurt him. But it was obvious that she had. Self-doubt and humility did not fit the Jason Wakefield she knew and loved.

She met his steady gaze head-on. "Everything's happened so fast, and so much has changed that I'm not even sure who I am or what I want anymore."

"I can understand that. I guess it has happened pretty fast, but it seems like years to me. Maybe I was just waiting for you to grow up all this time and I didn't realize it. But once I stopped thinking of you as a little sister I knew I loved you."

"I don't know what to say, Jason," she confessed.

"Why don't you start with how you feel about me?" he suggested. "And for God's sake, Mel, don't be kind. Just tell me the truth. Do you love me at all?"

"Of course I do. In fact—" She gulped. Oh, Lord, could she really tell him that? Should she? But what was the point in prevaricating? They'd never get anywhere if she wasn't as honest with him as he'd been with her.

A smile crept across his face. He leaned toward her, an eager, boyish expression replacing the somber one of a moment ago. "In fact what?"

"I, uh, well..."

"Come on, sweetheart, spit it out. It can't be all that bad."

Feeling her cheeks flush crimson, she said bluntly, "You're the man I told Alan about the night of our last family dinner."

His mouth fell open in surprise. Then it was his turn to gulp. "The one you've loved for years?"

She nodded, perversely glad to see him at a disadvantage for once.

"The guy you thought was out of your league was me?"

She nodded again, unable to squelch a smile. "You even offered to punch his lights out and said I was too damn good for him."

He shook his head and stared at her as if she'd just announced that the world was flat after all. Then he threw back his head and laughed. It was a boisterous, joyful sound that echoed off the mountain and brought both horses' heads up from their peaceful munching.

Melody watched him, remembering another time he'd laughed like this and practically ripped the heart right out of her. His laughter had started it all, cutting her so deeply that she'd been forced to reexamine her life and make some long-overdue changes. But this time she couldn't resist joining in. When he finally brought himself back under control, she added, "There's more, if you're interested."

He wiped his eyes with the back of his hand and said, "Oh, I'm interested, all right. I'm just not sure I can take any more. Do you have any idea how jealous I've been of that guy? I thought he was Vic Grant and you just wouldn't admit it."

"Oh, Jason, you didn't!"

"I sure as hell did. I don't know how I could have been so blind when it came to you. I knew you had a crush on me when you were a kid—"

"Oh, no!"

Chuckling, he reached over and peeled her hands away from her face. "Hey, don't be embarrassed. I thought it was cute. But I honestly thought you'd gotten over that by the time you hit junior high."

She shook her head at him and said in a voice so soft that he had to lean closer to hear it, "I never got over it, Jason. What I told you about my engagement to Vic was true, but I broke it off specifically because of my feelings for you."

The laughter in his eyes faded at that confession. He looked deeply into her eyes and saw remembered pain. He tipped her chin up with an index finger and kissed her gently. Then he whispered, "I'm sorry, Mel. I didn't know."

She pulled away, suddenly glaring at him. "Don't you feel sorry for me, Jason Wakefield. I can stand anything but your pity."

He reared back as if she'd slapped him. "Pity? Shoot, I don't pity you, Mel. I'm just sad it took me so long to wake up and really see you. And I've learned what it's like to wonder if someone you love loves you back. It's no fun."

"No, it's no fun at all."

They fell quiet for a moment, as if each were regrouping and getting ready for the next round. Then Jason said, "There's something I really don't understand now."

"What's that?"

"I told you I loved you, and I meant it. If you loved me, why didn't you accept my proposal?"

"It was too soon, and—"

"All right, I'll give you that. I was too impatient." He yanked a blade of grass out of the ground and twirled it around his right index finger before continuing. "But it's not too soon now, and I still don't think you'd marry me. I want to know why."

She sighed. "Do you really want to go into all that?"

"Yes, dammit, I do."

"Well, for one thing, you ignored me for so long, I've never been sure why you started dating me."

"That's simple enough. When I finally realized you'd grown up, I got the hots for you. What else?"

"I was worried about other women, of course." His eyebrows drew together, and a muscle hardened and stood out on the side of his jaw. Seeing that, she hastened to finish. "I mean, after knowing you for so long and knowing the kind of women you always dated, I, uh... well, I just couldn't believe you were all that serious about me."

Impatience entered his voice. "I can understand your feeling that way at first, but I hope you know me well enough by now to know that's not a problem. What else bothered you? Give me the whole damn list."

"Okay," she replied in the same gritty tone he had used, her chin lifting another defiant notch in response to his anger. She spread the fingers on her right hand, ticking off her concerns with the index finger of her left. "I thought maybe you were lonely rambling around in that big house and you thought I could solve that problem for you. I thought maybe you were dating me as a way to get to Wendy Wyoming. And I doubted we could get along in the long run, because our life-styles are so different."

"How are they different?"

"You like big parties, and I hate them. You like going out every night, and I like staying home with a good book. You like politics and excitement, and I—well, I'm not all that wild about either. We're just too different."

"Whoa there a minute. Maybe I got carried away trying to court you in style, but believe me, I don't want or need to go out every night. I like staying home with a good book sometimes, too. And as for the politics, I'm sure we can work out any problems that crop up if we try hard enough."

"But what if you decide to run for Congress or governor?" she protested. "I don't know if I could handle all the social functions, and—"

"Sweetheart," he interrupted in a soothing tone, "I've come to believe you can do anything you put your mind to. But you don't have to worry about getting railroaded. Any decisions to run for higher office will have to be agreeable to both of us. Now, what else is bothering you?"

"There's only one more thing."

"Let's have it."

"I heard what that old fellow at the governor's party said about your having a better chance to win a congressional seat if you were married, and—"

Jason bolted upright, spat out a string of short, explicit curses and threw down the piece of grass he'd just mangled. Melody seriously considered making a run for the horses or throwing herself off the cliff—either alternative looked more promising in terms of survival than staying here with Jason. Then he looked away and inhaled deeply several times in a visible effort to control his temper. And then he laughed. It was a bitter, hurting sound that had the same effect on Melody as having one of her students scrape his fingernails down a chalkboard.

His laughter died abruptly. His eyes tore into her. He shook his head and said in a grim, hostile tone, "Let me get this straight. You heard what that old geezer said, and then you thought I proposed to you to help my political career. Is that right?"

She gulped and nodded, then added, "You'd never shared your goals with me before, and I knew you were ambitious—"

"Lord, I've never been so insulted in my whole life!"

"I didn't insult you."

"You sure as hell did! If you think I'm that shallow, no wonder you don't want to marry me."

"Jason, don't look at me like that. I never thought you were shallow, I just—"

"Thought I was shallow."

"I did not."

"Then why did you keep all these doubts to yourself? Why didn't you ever ask me about any of them? For God's sake, am I that hard to talk to?"

The disgust in his voice when he asked the last question ignited Melody's temper. "Yes, for me, sometimes you are. I've had you on a pedestal for years. You've always been older and wiser, you've treated me like a kid, and you were Jason Wakefield, the man of the hour. Whether it was in football or basketball or politics, you've always been a star. And I've always been quiet, mousy little Melody Hunter!"

"Mel—"

"No, dammit! You're the one who wanted all this honesty, and by God you're going to listen to it. I loved you desperately, but I had to tell myself you were out of my league for years, Jason. Maybe you think that's stupid, but that's how it's always felt to me."

"I never meant to make you feel that way."

"I know you didn't," she said, softening her voice. "You didn't have to. Other people did it for you. They can't wait to talk to you, but they act as if I'm invisible. And it's not just you. The same thing happens when I'm with David and Barbara and my parents. Don't you see, Jason? Whether you realized it or not, you were always out of my reach, and I always had to protect myself from being hurt. That's why I've questioned your motives for getting involved with me."

She looked at him then, her heart in her eyes, her palms turned up in a plea for understanding. After a moment, he answered, "All right. I think I understand how you felt. But I think some of that's changing for you because you've changed. I saw a lot of people eager to talk to you at the governor's party."

"Maybe."

He yanked up another blade of grass and chewed one end thoughtfully for a moment. Then he said, "Now that you've explained all these doubts you've had about me, I'd like to know why you made love with me."

She shrugged helplessly. "I loved you, Jason. I decided that if there was any chance at all that you could learn to love me, I couldn't pass it up."

"But you never really believed we had a future together."

"Oh, I wanted to. But it seemed such wishful thinking...."

"How were you planning to protect yourself from getting hurt this time? You must have thought up something."

Jason's voice had gotten progressively quieter over the last few minutes. Melody knew that meant trouble. Worse trouble than if he were still yelling at her. But she'd come this far in telling him the truth. She wasn't about to back down now. Glancing away, she admitted, "I, uh, applied for a teaching job in Denver for next year."

"You what?"

"I applied for a job in Denver. I have an interview in two weeks."

"Oh, that's great. That's just dandy! You never even gave me a chance. Talk about a double standard! I was supposed to see that you'd grown up and changed since you were ten, but you weren't willing to consider the fact that maybe I'd grown up and changed some since then, too. You still see me as some adolescent kid with his hormones all screwed up. You never had any faith in me at all."

She reached out and tentatively touched his forearm. Its muscles bulged out above a clenched fist. "Now, Jason—"

He jerked his arm away. "Don't try to placate me, Mel. I'm so damn mad I could paddle your backside."

"That attitude doesn't exactly encourage honesty."

"Tough!"

She started to get up, but his hand clamped onto her shoulder like an eagle's talons grasping a victim for dinner. "We're not finished yet."

"I am."

"Well, I'm not." He looked away, sighed and loosened his grip on her shoulder. Then he turned back to her, a weary yet hopeful light in his eyes. He raised his hand from her shoulder and brushed his fingertips gently over her flushed cheek, coaxing her to meet his eyes.

When she did, he said softly, "I don't want to fight with you, Mel. I love you, and I know you love me. We can work all this stuff out, I know we can. All either one of us needs is to know that the other is committed. Marriage would give us that."

"Jason, I don't know."

"What's to know? You love me, and I love you. Let's get married and raise enough kids to make that house down there look puny. And when we're old and decrepit, then we can worry about all this other stuff."

"I don't think we're ready yet."

"Why not? You still don't trust me?"

"No, it's not that. I want to say yes, but I'm scared. Couldn't we take a little more time before we decide?"

"How much time?"

"Three or four months, maybe?"

"No way. That's what Liz did to David, and I'm not putting up with it. You'll just worry yourself into an ulcer and end up talking yourself out of marrying me. I want an answer now, Melody. Will you marry me or not?"

"Dammit, Jason, I'm not Liz! I've got two careers going at once now, and I just need a little more time—"

"Now, Mel."

"How about a month?"

"Now."

"That's not fair, Jason. I can't say yes now. I'm just not ready."

He stood up. Looking down at her, his green eyes cold enough to make a Popsicle shiver, he said, "I guess you've made your decision, then."

Blinking back acid tears, she climbed to her feet and murmured around the lump in her throat, "I guess I have."

It was a hell of a long ride back to the ranch, and an even longer drive into Cheyenne. When Jason parked in front of her apartment, he said, "We could still salvage this relationship if you want to, but I'm not gonna wait long. I really don't think your problem is with my past, Melody. It's with your own. Let me know if you change your mind."

Melody nodded, opened the door and climbed out, leaving the roses he'd insisted she bring along on the seat. Then she watched Jason drive away and knew he wouldn't be back this time. It was finally over for good.

Chapter Twelve

The news spread all over Cheyenne in a matter of days, anding the gossips a juicy morsel and giving renewed hope o a host of single young women. There had been plenty of xcitement when David Hunter had started turning up at the Roadway Inn without his fiancée. But now, so the story vent, Jason Wakefield was back on the market, as well. Ie'd finally dumped Melody Hunter and was chasing redeads again. And the women of Cheyenne welcomed their wo favorite bachelors back with delight.

Though she heard all about David's and Jason's romanic exploits from well-meaning—and a few not-so-wellneaning—friends, Melody held her head high. She refused o make any comments about her past relationship with ason and got through April and May by burying herself in vork. She was doing four Wendy Wyoming shows a week ow and had even gone so far as to assign a surprise term paper for her kids at school so she'd have more papers to read and correct.

She told herself that Jason's behavior completely vindicated the decision she had made that last awful day they had spent together. He had barely waited a week to start dating again. If she had married him, he wouldn't have been faithful to her. She was sure of it.

Unfortunately, working herself to the point of exhaustion and feeling vindicated provided scant comfort for the gaping hole he'd left in her life. She accepted invitations for dates she would rather have passed up because she didn't want Jason to think she was pining for him—if he even bothered to think of her at all these days. But no matter how many activities she crammed into her schedule, she still had too much time to think about Jason.

Her family didn't help matters, either. Despite her efforts to explain her feelings, David blamed her for ending the relationship with Jason and rarely spoke to her unless it was about her show. Her parents were more tactful, but they couldn't hide their disappointment. And Barbara insisted that Melody ought to be checking out psychiatrists.

Still, there were a few bright spots for Melody during this bleak time. When the *Wyoming Star* published the results of their contest to guess Wendy Wyoming's identity, she received fifty-five votes. No one had been able to prove anything, but it gave her ego a welcome boost to know at least that many people had considered her a possible candidate.

Her interview with Mr. Whitman provided another source of satisfaction. He had asked some pretty tough questions during the hour and a half she'd spent with him. She hadn't heard from him yet, but he had seemed so pleased with her answers that she felt confident enough of being hired that she hadn't signed the contract the Cheyenne school district had offered her.

Not wanting to lose one of his best teachers, her principal had warned Melody that she might very well find herself in an unemployment line in the fall. Melody honestly didn't care. Whether she found another teaching job or not, she had to leave Cheyenne. There were too many reminders of Jason here for her to find any peace.

All in all, Melody felt she had handled breaking up with Jason fairly well until school got out on the third of June. Without the distracting, time-consuming work provided by her teaching job, the summer stretched before her like two hundred miles of bad road in a blizzard. Though the prospect of keeping busy enough to keep her mind off how much she missed Jason was daunting, Melody gritted her teeth and determinedly plunged into a new whirlwind of activity.

She spent the first day of summer vacation cleaning out closets, taking clothes she didn't want anymore to the Goodwill Industries store, trading in her used paperbacks for some new reading material and cashing in all the cartons of pop bottles she'd been ignoring since January. The second day she walked to her parents' house, mowed the lawn for her father and attacked the weeds in the flower beds with such a vengeance that her mother confiscated the gardening tools before she started hacking up the flowering plants, as well.

The third day she washed all the windows and scrubbed all the woodwork in her apartment, then rented a carpet-cleaning machine, even though the ugly red carpeting her landlord had provided already looked as good as it was ever going to look. On the fourth day she searched the help-wanted ads in the newspaper but didn't find anything even remotely interesting. Then she tried to get into one of her "new" paperbacks but gave up after the third novel in a row failed to catch her interest and spent the rest of the day at the city swimming pool instead.

Suffering from a crimson sunburn on the fifth day, Melody succumbed to depression and lay on her sofa in an old T-shirt and a disreputable pair of shorts, watching game shows and soap operas until she felt like taking a baseball bat to the television. The only thing that prevented her from collapsing into a puddle of tears and self-pity was a phone call at one-thirty.

"Hi, Melody. Enjoying vacation?" Debbie Adams said cheerfully when Melody answered the phone.

"Sure," Melody lied.

"Good. Listen, I'm planning to take a couple of summer school courses in Laramie, and I'm looking for someone to carpool with. Are you interested?"

Melody straightened up. Summer school would be a perfect distraction. She could start on her master's degree program. Why hadn't she thought of it herself? "I sure am, Debbie. When's registration?"

"Next Tuesday. I've got a catalog and have already picked out my classes. Want me to drop it by?"

"I'd love it."

"Is now a good time? I've got a dental appointment, so I can't stay to visit. But you're right on my way."

"Fine. See you in a few minutes, Debbie."

Her painful sunburn forgotten for the moment, Melody hung up the phone, let out a loud whoop and danced around the room in jubilation. Debbie delivered the catalog as promised. Fortified with a glass of iced tea, Melody carried the booklet outside, sat on the back steps and quickly scanned the College of Education's offerings.

Since many teachers attended UW's summer school, there was plenty to choose from. Better yet, the classes Melody was most interested in taking were held at compatible times with the ones Debbie had marked. She lifted her glass of tea in a salute to the University of Wyoming and Debbie.

Thanks to them, she just might get through this blasted vacation after all. And there was something else she wanted to do this summer. Unfortunately, for that she would need David's permission.

She went inside, changed clothes in record time and drove over to KBOY. David was in his office, the phone receiver tucked between his ear and shoulder as he signed a letter. He glanced up when she entered the room, holding up one finger to indicate that he would be with her shortly. Melody seated herself in a blue armchair across from David's desk and waited for him to finish his conversation.

He hung up the phone a few minutes later. "What can I do for you, Melody?" he asked in a brusque tone that informed her in no uncertain terms that he hadn't forgiven her yet.

"You can quit being so judgmental, for starters," she retorted.

"Look, I've got too much work stacked up here to get into that with you, so if that's all you wanted—"

She cut him off. "No, that's not all I wanted. I want to try doing my show live for a while so I can take requests for songs from the audience."

David sat back in his chair and crossed his arms over his chest. Then he asked, "Why?"

"I've been getting some mail about it. And I think I've had enough practice now that I can handle it."

"You'll be taking a bigger chance somebody will find out you're Wendy Wyoming. The other disc jockeys will have to know."

"That's not such a problem anymore. I won't be teaching here next year."

He raised an eyebrow at that. "Oh? What are you going to do?"

"I don't know for sure yet."

"Want to work for the station full-time?"

She shook her head. "I don't think so. But if my other plans don't work out, I'll let you know."

"What other plans?"

"Never mind, David. Now will you let me do the show live or not?"

He leaned forward and propped his elbows on the desk. "It's funny you decided to come here today. The music director's mad at you."

"Me? What for?"

"He says you haven't been following the playlist."

"Oh, for pity's sake."

"I checked into it, Melody. He's right. You're playing too many heartbreak songs. Do you realize, in the last month, you've played 'You Done Stomped on My Heart and Mashed That Sucker Flat' eight times? And you've played 'Your Cheatin' Heart' at least ten times. It's all here in your log."

"So? I like those songs. They're classics."

"'Your Cheatin' Heart,' maybe. But the other one sure as hell isn't. The point is, you're letting your personal problems come through on the air. And it's not very professional behavior."

Melody looked away, sighed, then faced David again. "I'm sorry. It won't happen again. May I do my show live?"

"I don't see why not. Why don't you start next Monday?"

"Fine." She started to rise. "I'll let you get back to work, then."

"Wait a minute." David waited until she sat down again. "I've been trying to work out the vacation schedules. Would you like to do five shows a week instead of four? It'll save me hiring someone else."

"All right. Could I have Saturday or Sunday? I'm taking summer school classes, so I'd like to have at least one weeknight free."

"You can have both if you want."

"Thanks, David."

She stood and walked to the door, then looked back over her shoulder when he said quietly, "Mel? I'm sorry I've been so mean to you."

She turned to face him, leaning against the door for support. "It's all right."

"No, it's not." He shrugged. "It's just that your situation with Jason was too similar to mine with Liz."

Her expression and voice softened. "You still miss her, don't you?"

"Yeah. I still miss her. But I hear she's practically engaged to someone else now."

"I'm sorry, David."

"I'll get over it one way or another. How are you getting along without Jason?"

"As well as can be expected."

"He still misses you. A lot."

"He has a funny way of showing it."

"Don't be so hard on him, sis. These babes he's taking out now don't mean a thing to him. He's just working on his hurt."

"I've got to go, David. I'll see you later."

"Bye, Mel."

All the way home, she replayed David's remarks about Jason in her mind. Was David right? Did Jason really miss her as much as she missed him? Was he still angry with her? She could always call him and find out. But she'd already survived the worst of the pain of breaking up with Jason. Maybe. Only a masochist would go back for another round.

* * *

Cursing himself for his own stupidity, Jason switched on the Blazer's radio. Wendy Wyoming would come on any minute. It didn't matter how many times he promised himself he'd never listen to her again. If he was anywhere near a radio when her show started, he couldn't resist tuning in KBOY. It wasn't much of a link to Melody, but it was all he had. And though hearing her voice still hurt like hell, he couldn't stop himself.

"Howdy, pardners! Welcome to the Wendy Wyoming show here on KBOY, FM 97. We're at the top of the hour on a balmy June fifteenth. Let's start out with Janie Fricke's latest release."

He scowled at the radio. He'd better drive into Cheyenne again tonight. The bar scene wasn't all that interesting or exciting to him anymore. But if he stayed home he'd just sit there with Jezebel, listen to Melody and tear himself apart. At least at the Roadway he could avoid radios, and there was always a chance he'd meet somebody who could make him forget Melody. Maybe.

This kind of pain was no stranger. He'd felt it when his mother had died, when he'd realized his stepmothers couldn't care less about him and when he'd had to have Lucky put down. He'd felt lost, alone, abandoned. But losing Melody had taught him about an entirely new classification of pain; it was a hell of a lot worse than anything he'd ever experienced before.

He had expected it to be bad at first, and then, gradually, to get better. But now, two months later, the hurt was still fresh and razor-sharp as it had been that last day he'd let Melody off in front of her apartment. Some days it was even worse.

Up until the end of April he had hoped and prayed Mel would come to her senses and at least phone him. But she hadn't. And the word he'd gotten on the grapevine wasn't at all encouraging. If the stories he had heard about her were true—and he had no reason to doubt them—she wasn't exactly pining away for him.

Jason pulled into the Roadway Inn's crowded lot, slammed the gearshift lever into Park and turned off the radio. Tempted to turn around and drive right back to the ranch, he stayed in the driver's seat for a moment, drumming his fingertips on the steering wheel while he watched two women in tank tops and tight jeans coax a third woman out of the back seat of a red Dodge Omni. He could see part of the third woman's face and guessed from her expression that she didn't want to be here any more than he did. He got a better look at her when she climbed out of the car.

She was pretty enough, he noted, though not as flashy as her companions. She had short, light brown hair and a slender figure, and her summer blouse and jeans looked neat and comfortable rather than sexy. Before he'd fallen in love with Melody he wouldn't have given her a second glance. He'd have gone after her friend with the well-endowed chest and the long red hair.

But he wasn't getting anywhere chasing buxom redheads, and he knew it. He just plain wasn't interested anymore. Maybe he should ask this woman to dance. Two months of loneliness was more than enough. She wasn't Melody, but he had to start somewhere, didn't he?

They were walking toward his Blazer now, on their way into the bar. They passed under a street lamp, and in the brief moment of illumination he felt a flicker of recognition for the woman he'd been studying. He heard soft feminine laughter through his open window, and then the redhead said impatiently, "Susan, don't be an idiot! You'll have a great time tonight if you'll just relax a little."

Susan? She wasn't Susan Wolcott, was she? That bashful, studious little sophomore who used to work in the library when he was a senior at Central High? The one who blushed and stammered whenever she had to wait on him or any of the other senior boys? He'd enjoyed teasing her back then, but he hadn't thought of her in years.

Well, shoot, he thought as he stepped out of the Blazer, locked it up and shoved his keys into his pocket. *Now I'll just have to go in there and see if I'm right*. It was not an altogether unpleasant prospect. Maybe he was going to survive after all.

Every year during the last full week of July, Cheyenne, Wyoming goes crazy. All the motels, hotels and restaurants are crowded, the streets are clogged with thousands of tourists and traffic that would make a southern Californian panic, the bars do a record business and the atmosphere contains enough enthusiasm and excitement to rival Mardi Gras. The cause of this annual madness is called Cheyenne Frontier Days, a cherished tradition that started with Cheyenne's first public rodeo on September 23, 1897.

The entire staff of Hunter Communications worked overtime during Frontier Days, covering the parades and chuck-wagon breakfasts; the night arena shows featuring some of the biggest names in country music, the melodrama performances, the carnival, the ceremonial dances performed by the Oglala Sioux; and, of course, the daily rodeo, proudly and justifiably nicknamed "The Daddy of 'Em All."

Though a few Cheyenne residents complained about the invasion of their otherwise peaceful community, Melody had always looked forward to Frontier Days, particularly the rodeos. Since her summer school classes had ended David assigned her to work at the arena, interviewing the odeo contestants and clowns, the Oglala Sioux, Miss 'rontier and Miss Rodeo U.S.A., members of the Frontier)ays Committee—in short, anyone who might have an in-eresting perception of the events for KBOY's audience.

Any other year, Melody would have been thrilled with her ssignment. But this time she couldn't work up much en-usiasm for the hoopla going on around her. She felt ner-ous and exposed to be doing live interviews without the rotective shield Wendy Wyoming provided on her regular iows.

Still, she pushed her personal feelings aside and threw erself into the job, talking all day and sometimes far into ie evening. And as the days passed she became so genu-iely interested in what her subjects had to say that she)axed some great interviews out of even the most reticent odeo cowboys.

She was proud of her efforts, but found it difficult to al-ays be "up" for the audience. By the time the champion-iip rodeo on the last day rolled around, Melody had had iough. Since she'd already interviewed everyone she could iink of, she bought herself a ticket and found her seat in e stands.

Other people began filling the seats around her. It was tting close to the one-o'clock starting time when she rec-gnized a familiar beige Stetson moving through the crowd ie tier of seats below, slightly off to her left. Her breath ught in her chest; her heart thundered against her ribs. She aned forward, drinking in the sight of Jason the way a ant soaks up rain after a long dry spell.

She had seen him from a distance a few times during the mmer, but never this close. He looked so handsome to-y in crisp new jeans and a bright red Western shirt. Maybe e should try to speak to him. If they couldn't be lovers, e would at least like to be friends.

He sat down, looked up at the woman and two little bo wearing cowboy hats and boots who'd been walking b hind him and gestured toward two empty seats to his rig and one on his left. One of the little boys jumped into t chair on Jason's left, the woman took the first seat on h right and the other little boy plunked himself down besi his mother.

When she realized he wasn't alone, Melody sat back in h seat, sighed in resignation and focused her attention on t action taking place on the floor of the arena. She resisted th temptation to look at him again until the opening cerem nies were finished.

Then, as if pulled by some malevolent unseen force, s couldn't prevent herself from studying Jason and t woman sitting beside him. She had heard that Jason h stopped chasing redheads and started dating a divorc named Susan Miller, who had been Susan Walcott back high school. Melody vaguely remembered her as an uppe classman but had never known her very well.

Bile rose up in Melody's throat as she took in the pictu the four people made. They looked like...like a family. T little boy on Jason's left jumped up and stood on his se pointing toward the thrashing Brahma bull in the middle the arena floor with unabashed excitement. Jason smil and hauled the boy onto his lap. It looked as if he were e plaining the finer points of rodeo to his fascinated you listener.

The rest of the afternoon was the worst kind of tortu Melody could have imagined. She wanted to leave, but h pride or maybe some latent masochistic tendencies s hadn't known she possessed wouldn't allow it. She repe edly tried to watch the rodeo, especially her two favor events, the wild horse race and the chuck-wagon races. B her eyes inexorably returned to Jason, Susan and the bo

All four of them were having a wonderful time. Jason bought treats and pop, helped Susan wipe up the inevitable spills and took the boys, presumably, to the rest room like a veteran father. When they returned, Melody watched Susan's face light up and Jason's smiling response and felt a pang of jealousy and regret so strong it nearly suffocated her.

Susan Miller was no raving beauty. She was pretty in a wholesome kind of way, but she wasn't Jason's "type" any more than Melody was. And yet Jason was here with Susan, looking happier and more relaxed than Melody had ever seen him.

Obvously he really had changed; she couldn't doubt that he was ready to settle down after observing him this afternoon. And one thing Melody had learned about herself during the unbearably long summer vacation was that she had changed, as well.

The other disc jockeys at KBOY hadn't appeared to be the least bit surprised to learn she was Wendy Wyoming. Meeting new people in her classes in Laramie this summer had been easier than it ever had been before. Doing her show live and talking to the listeners who called in requests had taught her she could think fast under pressure, certainly well enough to handle almost any social situation. And doing so many interviews this past week as Melody Hunter had taught her she didn't need Wendy Wyoming to run interference for her.

Wendy was part of her personality, all right. But she only came out when Melody stopped worrying about how others perceived her and quit trying to measure up to some impossible standard of comparison she'd invented to rationalize her feelings of inferiority to the other members of her family. Wendy had a sense of humor and a compassion for others that were every bit as meaningful and useful

as her mother's writing ability, her father's business sens
or David's and Barbara's outgoing personalities and physi
cal attractiveness. And while her teaching career didn't mak
headlines, it was darned important work, Melody realized

She no longer feared that if she stopped doing the sho
she would go back to being plain little Melody Hunter. Sh
liked people, and they liked her back; and her feelings o
inadequacy had gradually faded away. After testing he
abilities and finding them more than sufficient, there was n
way she could return to her old, insulated life-style again.

She wasn't like Liz, not really. Liz had never lived awa
from home, never held a job outside her family's busines
Liz was a lovely person, but it wasn't exactly surprising t
Melody that she'd felt too threatened by David's reput
tion and former girlfriends to make their relationship work
Her sheltered background provided a reasonable explan
tion for their broken engagement.

"So what's your excuse, Hunter?" Melody whispere
with a searing pang of regret as her eyes were drawn back t
Jason and Susan again.

Barbara had tried to tell her, David had, Alan had, eve
Jason had tried to tell her she had plenty of good thing
going for her, but she hadn't been ready to listen. Oh, she'
thought about what they'd said, but she hadn't really b
lieved them. Instead, she had fallen back into her old ha
its, clung to adolescent hurts and doubts and hidden behin
them in an attempt to avoid the adult hurt she feared sh
would suffer if Jason ultimately rejected her.

But it wasn't Jason who had rejected her love. It wasn
Jason who had been afraid to make a commitment. It wasn
Jason who had broken off their affair, not really. She'
done it all herself.

And she, Melody Jane Hunter, could have been the woman sharing the fun and excitement of Frontier Days, maybe even a lifetime with Jason Wakefield, if she hadn't been such a damnably insecure fool and thrown him away!

Chapter Thirteen

The next day, the first of August, an aching, bone-dee
misery moved in and became Melody's constant compan
ion. With summer school and Frontier Days over and mos
of her friends gone or involved in relationships of their own
she was at loose ends again. And except for a brief phon
call in which Mr. Whitman had apologized for the delay an
assured her that she was still being considered for a posi
tion, she still hadn't heard from the Denver school district
Worst of all, she was constantly haunted by mental picture
of Jason and Susan Miller, and of Jason and those ador
able little boys.

The memories of her own brief time with Jason, memo
ries she had pursued so foolishly and then tried to sup
press with work, manufactured or real, broke free now. The
assaulted her without the least provocation. And afte
shoving those memories aside for weeks, she was too ex
hausted emotionally to fight back. Rather than inflict he

wretchedness on anyone else, Melody kept to herself, rarely leaving her apartment other than to go for long, solitary walks or to do her show.

Playing Wendy Wyoming wasn't half the fun it had been back in January—not even a quarter of the fun, if the truth were told. Whenever she was Wendy, she thought of Jason. And whenever she thought of Jason, she hurt all over. And she was sick of sounding like a sex kitten. The only part of the show she really enjoyed now was talking to the members of the audience when she took requests.

She was in limbo, waiting for something—a job in Denver, word of Jason's engagement to Susan Miller, she didn't know what, exactly. She would have quit the show and left Cheyenne, but the feeling of having unfinished business was too strong to ignore. So, aching inside, she became Wendy Wyoming five nights out of seven and continued to wait.

Two weeks later, when Melody feared her mental health couldn't take much more strain, Mr. Whitman finally phoned with the news that a contract would be in the mail in a couple of days. Could she get settled in Denver and be ready to teach by the twenty-seventh of August? Melody assured him she could, hung up and heaved a sigh of relief mingled with a hefty dose of pain.

Now it really was going to be over—completely over, this time. She should be ecstatic over Harvey Whitman's phone call. She didn't want to be in Cheyenne to hear of Jason's engagement. She didn't want to continue the Wendy Wyoming show, either. She would have a fresh start and a new job. And that was exactly what she needed. Wasn't it?

So why the hell was she crying? she wondered, furiously wiping away the tears with the back of her hands. It was too late for tears, dammit! She'd already cried gallons of them over Jason Wakefield. It was time to quit torturing herself with maybes and if onlys and get on with her life. Nobody pined away and died over a lost love anymore. This god-awful pain had to stop someday. Didn't it?

When she was able to regain control of her emotions, Melody marched into the bathroom and splashed cold water on her face. Trying to conceal her bloodshot eyes and puffy eyelids, she used eye drops and applied plenty of makeup. Then she changed her clothes and drove over to KBOY to work her regular shift.

To her surprise, David was waiting for her when she stepped out of the control booth four interminable hours later. He studied her intently for a few moments, noting how thin and tired she looked, the barely perceptible quivering of her chin, the silent misery in her eyes. Then, without saying a word, he opened his arms to her.

Uttering an inarticulate little cry, she threw herself against him and sobbed her heart out, just as she had when she'd been five and had gashed her knee and her big brother had been ten and had known how to put on Band-Aids. But he didn't have any Band-Aids for what hurt her now. Nobody did.

Murmuring comforting words, he sheltered her with his arms and stroked her hair and gradually led her into his office. He shut the door and seated her in the blue armchair, handing her his handkerchief before stepping back out in the hall, where he fed money into the pop machine.

Melody was honking her nose into his mascara-streaked handkerchief when he returned to the office. He handed her a can and perched on top of his desk facing her, then drank half of his Coke in one long gulp. Melody sniffled, sipped her root beer and gave him a watery smile.

"Thanks, David."

He shrugged and sent her a sympathetic smile. "What are brothers for? Want to tell me about it?"

She shook her head. "I don't think I can without bawling again." She took another sip, then wiped her nose again before asking, "Why were you waiting for me?"

"Nothing important, sis. It can wait."

His gentle voice and expression nearly shattered her tenuous control. She sighed, impatient with her weakness. "No, tell me now. Maybe it'll help to get my mind off...other things."

David crumpled his now-empty Coke can and shot a basket in the trash can with it before turning back to her. "All right. Our beloved music director is after your head again. He claims you've dug out every damn sad cowboy song ever written and you're going to bum out the entire city if you don't shape up."

Melody laughed. It was a thin, sickly excuse for a laugh, but a laugh nonetheless. Then she admitted, "He's right, David. I'm sorry."

"Hey, I understand. Don't worry about it."

"I won't. And you won't have to much longer, either."

"Mel—"

"No. really. Let me explain." She sniffled, gulped, then continued. "You see, I was planning to tell you I had to quit in the next day or so anyway. I, uh, found out today that I've got a teaching job in Denver. I'll have to go down there pretty soon to find a place to live anyway. So I'll finish out this week, and that'll be it. I'm sorry I can't give you more notice."

He shook his head at her. "Aw, sis, I know you're hurting, but you've never run away from trouble before. Don't start now. It won't solve anything."

"I have to, David. I'll never get over Jason if I'm always afraid I'll run into him. And Cheyenne's so small I will run into him now and again. Besides, there's no reason for me to stay. My old job's already been filled, and I'm wrecking Wendy's show...."

"Have you already signed the contract?" he asked anxiously. When she shook her head, he urged, "Then talk to Jason first."

"It's too late!" Tears rained from her eyes again. She dabbed angrily at them with David's handkerchief and went on. "I s-saw him with S-susan M-miller at Frontier D-days, and I r-realized I b-blew it. But it's t-too damn l-late. He's going to m-marry her, David. And I don't w-want to be here to see it!"

"Aw, sis..." David leaned forward, grabbed one of her wrists above its clenched fist and pulled her to her feet between his spread knees. He patted her back while she soaked his shirtfront again, then held her at arm's length and gave her a hard shake.

"Dammit, Mel! It's not too late if you don't let it be. I don't know, maybe Jason *is* thinking about marrying Susan, but he doesn't love her."

"How do you know? I saw them together and—"

"Then you saw how much Susan is like you."

"Do you need your eyes checked? She doesn't look like me at all."

"Well, maybe not all that much physically," he admitted before continuing in a tone filled with conviction, "but believe me, sis, he's attracted to Susan because he sees some of the same things in her he loves in you."

"Like what?"

"Well, she's kind of quiet and she's got a nice sense of humor. And she's warm and loving, like you are. Trust me. I know what I'm talking about."

Melody stepped back, crossed her arms over her chest and turned away. "I wish I could believe it, David, but I said and did some really stupid things. Jason doesn't want anything more to do with me."

"Will you at least think about it?"

She gave a bitter laugh. "I'm sure I will. That's about all I've been doing ever since Frontier Days."

"Well, before you sign that contract, think about it extra hard. Okay?"

Melody nodded. "I'd better go home now. And I promise I'll only play happy songs for the rest of the week. Even if it kills me."

Chuckling, he slid off the desk and walked over to her. He ruffled her hair with a big hand, then hugged her against his side as they left the building. "Come on, Squirt. I'll drive you home. I'll help you get your car back tomorrow."

"David?"

"What?"

"Did I ever tell you you're the best brother in the whole world?"

"No, I can't remember hearing that from you before. Think I should get it in writing?"

"It couldn't hurt. Remind me tomorrow."

"Good night, pal." Jason kissed Eric's soft, freckled cheek and shut his eyes against the bittersweet emotion brought on by the boy's sturdy little arms squeezing his neck in a fierce hug. He went through the same routine with Timmy, then followed Susan out of the bedroom, through the living room and on into her small kitchen. She poured them each a glass of iced tea and led the way to the front porch swing.

Jason sat beside her, stretched his right arm along the back of the swing and set it in motion with the heel of one boot. Susan exhaled a soft, contented sigh and gazed up at the evening sky, a dreamy look in her eyes. He looked at her, then glanced away when his stubborn heart refused to flip over as it always had whenever he'd been this close to Melody.

Impatient with himself for even thinking Melody's name, Jason interrupted the smooth rocking motion of the swing, shifting his weight until he had turned more toward Susan. She shot him a questioning look. He smiled an apology and offered his shoulder as a pillow. Susan accepted the invitation and started them moving again with her bare foot.

The neighborhood was quiet for a Saturday night. Hoping it would relax him, Jason inhaled a deep breath and slowly let it out. The air was filled with the scent of flowers and freshly mown grass and Susan's apricot shampoo. The crickets offered a constant serenade, punctuated every once in a while by the sound of cars passing a couple of blocks north on Pershing Boulevard.

But he couldn't relax. He knew what was wrong—he was in the right place, but with the wrong woman. He respected Susan, enjoyed her company and the company of her rambunctious little boys. He even wanted her sexually, though he hadn't consummated that part of their relationship yet. It just didn't seem fair to make love to Susan when he couldn't keep his mind off Melody for more than an hour at a time.

Susan closed her eyes and rubbed her cheek against his shoulder like a cat requesting a petting. He obliged, stroking her soft, shiny hair. Her eyes still shut, Susan smiled and snuggled closer. Jason felt a hard lump form in his throat and silently cursed Melody for the hold she still had on him.

What if he never forgot her? Was he doomed to spend the rest of his life alone? Dammit, Susan was a warm, loving, intelligent woman. So why couldn't he love her? Why pine for someone who obviously didn't want anything more to do with him when Susan and her boys needed him?

As if she sensed the turmoil inside him, Susan pulled away slightly and looked up at him. Apparently whatever she saw in his face in the dim light of the porch lamp disturbed her, for she braced one foot on the floor and stopped the swing.

"What's wrong, Jason?"

He gave her a reassuring smile and shook his head. "Nothing. I was just doing some thinking."

"About what?"

"About us." He glanced away before adding hesitantly, "I was thinking, maybe—"

Shaking her head, Susan laid two fingers across his mouth and silenced him. Speaking softly but firmly, she said, "Be honest with me, Jason. You were thinking about Melody Hunter again, weren't you?"

He took her hand from his mouth and laced their fingers together, resting them on his thigh. "I'm sorry, Susan, I—"

She jerked away and went to stand by the porch railing, her back to him. The proud, stiff set to her shoulders cut through him, communicating how much he'd hurt her more clearly than tears and recriminations could have. He sighed and ran his fingers through his hair in frustration, and Susan turned to face him, leaning back against the railing, bracing her hands on either side of her hips.

Looking him straight in the eye, she said bluntly, "I can't handle this anymore."

"Susan, don't," he protested, rising to his feet. "We're good friends. In a while, maybe—"

Bitterness crept into her voice. "I want more than friendship from you, Jason. You know that. And I want more than maybe. I've tried to be patient, but I can't see that you're any closer to getting over her than you were two months ago."

"Dammit, I've tried to get over her."

Her expression softened to a sad smile. "I know you have. The problem is, I'm falling in love with you faster than you're falling out of love with her. If I learned anything from my divorce, it's that the next time I get seriously involved with a man we're going to love each other so much there won't be any doubts. For either of us."

"Then give me a chance, Susan. Give me a little more time," Jason argued, moving toward her.

She shook her head, halting him in his tracks. "What good will that do me? I'll just learn to love you more, and if you don't get over her it'll hurt me more to lose you later. She's still right here in Cheyenne. You never know when you'll run into her. I can't handle it, Jason. I don't think we should see each other anymore."

He put his hands on her shoulders. "You don't mean that."

She looked up at him, genuine regret in her eyes. "Yes, I do mean it. I knew we were getting to this point, but I kept hoping it wouldn't—" Her voice cracked. Blinking back tears, she swallowed, then continued. "You're a dear, sweet man. The best friend I've had in a long time, but I want you to leave."

"What about the boys?" he asked, his voice coming out gruffer than he'd intended.

Susan's chin rose to a determined angle, one that reminded him of Mel when she got her back up.

"They're part of the reason we have to stop seeing each other. I might gamble on you if I only had myself to think of, but they're getting too attached to you, too, and I can't risk having them feel rejected again by a man they care about."

There was no mistaking the implacability of her expression. With another woman he might have persisted. But Susan had had a rough time building a new life after her divorce. She didn't spell it out, but he knew she was asking him not to upset her hard-won equilibrium any more than he already had. He owed her that much.

Jason bent to kiss her goodbye, unable to forgo holding her close against him for a moment. Lord, he was going to miss her. Not the way he missed Melody, though. Susan didn't resist, but she didn't respond, either. When he raised his head, she gave him a misty smile.

"So long, friend," she whispered.

"You'll call if you ever need me?"

"You betcha."

They both knew she wouldn't. Susan Wolcott Miller was a fiercely independent person, determined to make her own way in the world. He turned and stared down the front steps. When he was halfway to his Blazer, she called to him.

"Jason?"

He turned back to face her. "What?"

"Call her. You still love her. And after getting to know you, I can't believe she doesn't love you back."

"I'll think about it."

"You do that. And dammit, Wakefield, invite me to the wedding. Maybe by then I'll be able to wish you happiness and mean it."

Susan whirled away and rushed into the house, banging the screen door behind her. Feeling like a heel for hurting her and deeply shaken by her insights into his feelings for Melody, Jason drove home and tried David's cure for a broken heart. Of course, it didn't work. But, as David had claimed, it seemed like a helluva good idea at the time.

"Hey there, pardners, this is Wendy Wyoming, bringing you the very best in country music from KBOY, FM 97."

Stretched out full length on the sofa, Jason shut his eyes and rubbed his temples. He was over the worst of his hangover now, but a faint headache lingered. Jezebel waddled over and plopped her head onto his stomach. His attention focused on Melody's voice, he absently petted the dog's head.

He hadn't listened to her show in quite a while, not since he'd started dating Susan, in fact. But it seemed as if the compulsion to hear her was stronger than ever. And if his brain hadn't still been a little fogged up with alcohol he'd have sworn her voice had changed in a subtle way.

"I hope you had a great Saturday today, August fifteenth. I'll be opening up the request line in a little while, but let's start out with Loretta Lynn's latest hit."

His brow wrinkled in confusion. Request line? When had she started that? And there *was* something different about her voice. Oh, she still sounded sassy and sexy as all get-out. But, dammit, she sounded less like Wendy Wyoming and more like Melody. Didn't she care if everyone knew she was Wendy Wyoming, for God's sake?

He sat up, dislodging Jezebel's snout. If he'd been paying any attention, he would have seen Jezebel give him a dirty look before waddling back to the kitchen. But Jason's total attention was focused on the sound system.

Impatient for Loretta to finish her song, he got up and paced around the room. He cursed when Melody started up a Conway Twitty song at the tail end of Loretta's, and he continued pacing. When the second record finally ended, the infernal woman played three commercials in a row, unwittingly trying his patience, a commodity he was dangerously short of this evening.

She made a brief introduction for the next song, then started the record, and Jason was forced back to pacing his living room again. Maybe she wasn't doing it unwittingly, he thought darkly. Hell, she probably knew exactly what she was doing to him. And if she didn't, she ought to. He was sick and tired of tearing himself apart over her—

He flung himself back down on the sofa and yanked a throw pillow over his face. He was going nuts, completely nuts, even paranoid. But the second her voice filtered through the pillow he slung it over the back of the sofa and listened as if what was left of his sanity depended on it.

"...something to tell you, pardners. Our music director mentioned in passing the other day that I've been playin' too many heartbreak songs, and I had to admit he was right. But there's a reason I've been playin' those sad songs."

Jason heard suppressed tears in her voice and started to groan; though Mel wasn't much of a crier, he'd never been able to stand her tears, not even when she'd been ten. But he shut up fast when she continued.

"You see, pardners, it's time for me to move on. I can't tell you how much I've enjoyed spending time with you during the last seven and a half months. Your warm response to my show has meant a lot to me, but like the guy in the song about Ol' Paint, I'm leavin' Cheyenne."

Jason bolted upright, the sudden movement starting a dull roaring in his ears. No! She couldn't leave! Dammit, he wouldn't let her! But her voice, touched with a trace of melancholy, went on relentlessly.

"I hope you'll keep listening to KBOY. I know the other folks here at the station will be sure to keep providing you with the best country music in Wyoming. I'm gonna open up the request line now. If there's some special song you'd like to hear, let me know at 555-KBOY. But let's keep those requests upbeat, all right? You wouldn't want that nasty old music director snarlin' at poor Wendy, now would you? I'll play a new hit from the Judds while I'm waitin' to hear from you."

Jason was stunned for a moment. Then, nearly beside himself with anger, frustration and a sickening, nameless dread, he raced into the kitchen, grabbed the wall phone and started dialing, his fingers shaking so badly that he dropped the receiver and had to start over again. Of course, by the time he finished redialing, Wendy's line was busy.

He knocked over the slender portable radio he kept in the kitchen in his haste to turn it on. Letting out a string of violent curses, he slammed the receiver back onto the phone base, righted the radio and snapped on the power and yanked a chair across the room next to the phone. Then balancing the chair on its back legs, he forced himself to calm down and start dialing methodically.

Sooner or later he'd get through to Melody or Wendy or whatever the hell she wanted to call herself. He wasn't sure what he'd say when he did. But, by God, he'd think of something when the time came!

"Hi, pardner. This is Wendy Wyoming. What can I play for you?"

"Wendy, sweetheart, you can't leave us! You're the best dang deejay west of the Mississippi."

"Aw, it's nice of you to say that. What's your name?"

"George, ma'am."

"What would you like to hear, George? Tell me quick now. I've got other calls coming in, hon."

"Uh, well, shucks, how 'bout 'Cryin' My Heart Out over You'?"

"By Ricky Skaggs?"

"Yeah. That's the one."

"Sure thing. Thanks for callin', George."

Melody hung up the phone, located the requested record, cued it and switched the mike back on, talking over the

extro at the end of the record that was nearly finished play-
ng.

"Wasn't that pretty? We're at the bottom of the hour now
at FM 97. This next song is for George. Here's Ricky Skaggs
with 'Cryin My Heart Out over You.'"

Melody hurriedly switched off the mike as the phone began ringing again. She eyed it balefully, wishing she'd never
tarted the request line. It was hard saying goodbye to the
eople of Cheyenne. Harder than she'd ever thought it
would be. Oh, well, she only had another hour and a half to
go. She let out a sigh and adjusted her headphones so she
ould answer the telephone and still hear the record.

"Hi, pardner. This is Wendy Wyoming. What can I play
or you?"

"Hello, Mel."

Her blood curdled. She nearly dropped the phone, but
hen her fingers automatically tightened around the re-
eiver until her ring bit into her flesh. Though she'd never
eard him sound quite this way before, there was no mis-
aking Jason's voice. Finally, she stammered, "What c-can
p-play for you?"

"I'd like to hear 'Are You Lonesome Tonight?' by Elvis
'resley." His voice dropped to a rough tiger's purr. "You
now what, Mel? I am."

"You am? I mean, you are?"

"I sure am. I'm darn lonesome tonight."

"I, uh, I'm sorry to hear that."

"Are you?"

"I— Oh, damn, I've gotta go. The record's ending."

So rattled she couldn't think of anything else to do, Mel-
dy shoved a cartridge with a public service announcement
or a local church bazaar on it into the tape deck and
witched off the ringer on the telephone, which had started
nging again the split second she'd hung up on Jason. Her

mind raced while she grabbed two more commercials to play after the public service announcement, anything to preven the dreaded dead air.

Jason's voice had sounded so strange—not like he wa drunk or anything, just . . . well, deadly intense. He'd bee trying to tell her something, she was sure of it. But what That he was lonesome for her? Or for Susan? Why the hel would he call her now, after all these weeks without a singl word? Was he just bugging her—trying to make her crazie than she already was? Or was he looking for a sign from he that she still loved him? Oh, damn the man!

The second commercial was ending. Melody inhaled deep breath and started to give the time and temperature but something was wrong with her lungs. She was talking but she couldn't breathe out. Her heart was pounding vio lently. Oh, hell! Now she had mike fright! It was a goo thing this was her last show. She'd be laughed out of th station if she ever showed up here again!

She slammed another commercial into the tape deck an switched off the mike while the air whooshed out of he lungs. She reached into the record bin, and, without both ering to read the label, grabbed the first record her han touched and cued it. When the commercial ended, sh started the record without trying to announce it and couldn' help chuckling when it turned out to be Kris Kristofferso singing "Why Me, Lord?"

Her sense of balance and perspective returned while Kri sang. She located the record Jason had requested and cue it on the second turntable, and when Kristofferson's voic started to fade she said smoothly, "Sorry for all those com mercials back there, folks. You're keepin' this telephone s darn busy, you kinda got ahead of me. But keep on callin if you've got a song you'd like to hear. I'll be glad to play it This one is for a pardner named Jason."

Despite what she'd just said, Melody left the phone turned off, cued the next record and leaned back on her stool, listening to Elvis singing. A deep calm settled over her as she listened to the lyrics. It didn't matter what Jason had intended when he'd called in. She knew what she was going to do.

She had received the contract from Denver in this afternoon's mail. She hadn't signed it yet, but once she put her signature on it and mailed it off she would be committed to at least nine months away from Cheyenne. What did she have to lose? Her dignity? Her pride? Her heart? She'd already lost all of them.

Elvis finished the song. Melody switched on the mike and leaned close, her elbows propped on the counter in front of her. Then, using her most seductive voice, she said, "Yeah, pardners, I'm lonesome tonight. I'm lonesome for a big, handsome cowboy. A blonde one, with sexy hazel eyes and a gorgeous mustache. Why, if I could get my hands on him—and believe me, pardners, he knows who he is—well, I'd love him until he was plumb tuckered out."

"Hot damn!"

Jezebel's head jerked up at her master's ear-shattering yell. She whined when he threw back his head and laughed, and when he tipped his chair back too far and crashed to the floor, she struggled to her feet and waddled over to lick his face in canine concern.

He laughed harder and hugged her. He even kissed her back—on the top of her head, of course. Picking up his wild elation, she wagged her tail, clicked her toenails on the tiles in joy and slurped him across the mouth.

He wiped his lips with the back of his hand, hugged her again, picked himself up off the floor and blew a kiss at the radio. She whined and cocked her head to one side at this bizarre behavior, then hurried after him as he tore through the house to his bedroom. More weird behavior followed but he seemed happy enough.

She curled up beside his recliner and sighed. Then, her chin resting on her paws, she watched him disappear into the bathroom. He shaved, then stepped into the shower and started singing at the top of his voice, a sound that made her howl. That shut him up, but a few minutes later he bounded back into the bedroom, whistling off key.

He rubbed something under his arms, slapped some smelly stuff on his face, then grabbed some underwear out of the dresser, tossed it into the air with one hand and caught it with the other. Jezebel sneezed in disgust, struggled back to her feet and left the room. Enough was enough

She had finally returned to her favorite spot in th kitchen, tromped down the imaginary grass to her satisfaction and settled into a comfortable position when she heard the sound of his boots coming closer. Blowing out a tire sigh, she dutifully raised her head. What did he think sh was? A puppy?

He appeared a moment later, still whistling, wearing happy smile she hadn't seen lately. He grabbed his keys of their hook by the door, righted the chair he'd knocked over leaned down and patted her head and said with a wicke smile, "Don't wait up for me, Jez. I'm plannin' to ge plumb tuckered out."

When he left, Jezebel heard him chuckling all the way ou to the Blazer. Then she heard the engine start up and grad ually fade away. She plunked her head back down an closed her eyes, wagging her tail at the familiar woman' voice still coming from the black box on the counter.

"We're at the top of the hour now, pardners. This KBOY, Cheyenne, FM 97. Stay tuned for the news."

"That's it for tonight, pardners. Hope you enjoyed the how as much as I did. Steve Harmon is up next. Take care ow. And remember, it never hurts to pass on a lite...love. This is Wendy Wyoming, signing off from BOY, Cheyenne."

Melody played the station's theme song, took off the eadphones and handed them to Steve. Then she collected er purse and coffee cup, took one last glance around the ontrol booth and quietly stepped out into the hallway. The oles of her sneakers made funny little squeaking sounds on ie tiled floor in the otherwise silent building. It seemed odd ie had never noticed that before.

When she reached the front door she hesitated for a moient, feeling unwilling to leave the security and fun she'd ound at KBOY over the last seven and a half months. So uch had happened to change her life since she'd started the Vendy Wyoming show. Wendy had taught her a lot about erself and about other people. But now it was time to move n.

She sighed, then squared her shoulders, lifted her chin id pushed the door open. Without another backward ance, she marched down the sidewalk and across the ghted parking lot. When she arrived at her car and reached it to unlock the door, a huge, dark shape came out of the iadows toward her. Melody opened her mouth to scream, it no sound came out.

The dark shape moved closer and said, "Hello, Melly."

"Jason?" she croaked, her vocal chords still too startled do more.

He stepped into the light, took off his hat and ran the igers of one hand through his hair. "Yeah. I didn't mean scare you."

"It's all right."

Lord, she'd rehearsed so many things to say to him if sh ever got the chance, but at the moment her mind was a bi zero. She only felt capable of standing here and staring a him, absorbing all the little details of his appearance she ha missed so much. She raised her eyes to his face and re ceived a lopsided smile that told her he was feeling as awk ward as she was. That deep, wonderful calm she' experienced in the control room when she'd played Jason request returned.

He broadened his stance and held his hat at waist level. "I need to talk to you, Mel. Will you come have a cup of co fee with me?"

"Yes."

He gave her that endearing smile again. "You're gonr make it easy on me for a change?"

"Yes."

"Good. Where would you like to go?"

"My apartment."

He raised an eyebrow at that, but all he said was, "A right. I'll meet you there."

She broke all posted speed limits on the way home. Jaso arrived only a second behind her. They walked up the sid walk and entered the apartment in silence. Jason tossed h Stetson onto the coffee table, then followed Melody into tl kitchen. She started the coffee maker and turned to fa him.

He held out a chair for her at the table. She took i watching as he sat down across from her. They studied ea other for a long, breathless moment. Then Jason aske "Are you really leaving Cheyenne?"

She shrugged. "I've been offered a teaching job, and gave up my job here."

"Have you signed the contract?"

"Not yet."

His expression softened; his voice came out just above a whisper. "I've missed you, Mel."

"I've missed you, too."

"You didn't act like it."

"Neither did you."

"Did you mean what you said on the air tonight?"

"I did if you meant you were lonesome for me."

"I did."

"Good. I was afraid you might be lonesome for Susan Miller."

"We broke it off last night."

She raised an eyebrow at that. "You're on the rebound?"

"Hell, no. Susan told me to call you because she knew I wasn't over you. She asked to be invited to our wedding."

"I'm beginning to like Susan Miller a lot."

"We were good friends. That's all, Mel."

"Good. Now I can really learn to like her. I hated her guts, you know."

"You were jealous, huh?"

"Extremely."

"So was I."

"You didn't need to be."

"Neither did you. Why didn't you call me?"

"I thought it was too late. You were right about my problem being with my own past instead of yours, but I didn't understand what you meant for a long time."

She got up and poured two mugs of coffee and carried them back to the table before continuing. "I didn't have enough confidence in myself to accept what you were telling me, that you really did love me." She looked him straight in the eye then and said, "I was trying to make you prove you loved me, but nobody can do that. I'm sorry I put you through that, Jason."

"What made you realize that?"

She spoke slowly, thoughtfully. "It was a combination of things. I guess I finally stopped comparing myself to other people, like you and David and Barbara. I, uh, realized that I had plenty to offer just being myself, and I didn't have to be an extrovert to be happy. There are lots of quiet people who live happy, productive lives, and I don't have to compete with anyone but myself."

He gulped. His voice came out low and husky. "I'm so glad you learned that, honey. You really are special. And I made plenty of mistakes, too. When God passed out patience, I must have been standing in the wrong line."

She reached across the table and laid her hand on top of his. "That's not true, Jason. I think you're an amazingly patient person."

"I was so afraid of losing you, and then I turned right around and drove you away."

"You know, I think we both let our pasts get in our way."

"What do you mean?"

"I mean maybe it would have been easier if we'd been strangers."

"Go on," he encouraged when she hesitated. "I think you're on to something."

"Well, it's just that since I'd known you for so long, I kept expecting you to act in certain ways. If I hadn't known you before, I would have asked more questions about what you were thinking and feeling, instead of assuming I knew what was going on inside of you."

"Yeah, you're right. I had a lot of preconceived ideas about you, too. I sure never understood why you didn't believe me when I said I loved you. It hurt a lot that you could doubt me. I figured you knew me well enough to know my feelings for you were different than anything I'd experienced before. I guess we should have done a better job of checking things out with each other."

They fell silent then, sipping their coffee while they each digested what had been said. After a moment Melody stood, intending to refill their mugs. But Jason reached out and grasped her wrist and tugged until she came around to his side of the table to stand in front of him. He put his hands on her waist and locked her gaze with his.

"Don't go, Mel."

"To get coffee?"

"No. Don't go to Denver."

"Why not?" she asked, smiling a little at the shameless way she was fishing for the words she wanted him to say. He didn't disappoint her.

"Don't go because I love you. I still want to marry you, but I'll wait as long as you want."

She draped her forearms over his shoulders, leaned down until they were nose to nose and said in Wendy's voice, "Who said I wanted to wait, cowboy?"

He blinked, and then a smile spread slowly across his lips. "You don't want to wait?"

"I've always thought August was as good a month for a wedding as June."

"Your mother and Barbara will kill us if we don't have a big, fancy wedding."

"Do you want a big, fancy wedding?"

He kissed her briefly, then pulled back a little and said seriously, "Well, I don't want to wait any longer than necessary, but yeah, I'd like a nice wedding. It'll save me from climbing every tall building in town and yelling how much I love you."

Laughing, she collapsed onto his lap, her arms still around his neck. "You're crazy, Wakefield. It's one of the reasons I love you."

He went very still. Then his arms closed tightly around her. He shut his eyes and bowed his head, resting his cheek against the top of her head.

"Jason? What is it?"

"Say it again."

"I love you?"

He swallowed hard. "Yeah. Say it again, Mel. I've waited a hell of a long time to hear it."

She turned slightly and clasped a hand on either side of his head, and when he opened his eyes she said with complete conviction, "I love you, Jason Wakefield. I always have, I always will, and I'll marry you any time, any place you say. I love you."

He kissed her then, long and lovingly, sealing the vow she had made to him. They were both trembling and short of breath when the kiss ended, but neither could stop smiling. She laid her head on his chest, cherishing this special moment of oneness. He stroked her hair and rubbed her back as if to reassure himself that this was not merely another dream.

Then he said, "I want you to be happy, honey. Is there any way you can get your job back here in Cheyenne?"

"I don't think so. But I'll worry about that later."

"Maybe you can work at KBOY."

She shook her head. "No, Wendy Wyoming died a natural, peaceful death tonight. But I've been thinking about something else lately."

"What's that?"

"I'd like to get my master's degree in counseling. I could use it in the school system or on the radio if I wanted to do that."

"You mean on one of those call-in shows? Like Dr. Ruth?"

She chuckled, then said, "Why not? There are lots of possibilities. I could even open a private practice."

"Can you get all the classes you need in Laramie?"

"I'm sure I can."

"Then go for it, honey."

"What about your political career?"

"What about it? If it upsets you, I can give it up, Mel."

She elbowed him in the ribs. "No, silly. I don't want you to do that. I'm not afraid of it anymore, but I'd like to know what your plans are."

He gave her a quick squeeze. "Oh, well, to tell you the truth, my mind isn't exactly on politics at the moment."

Wickedly smiling her agreement to his shift in mood, she said, "Okay. We can talk about it . . . later."

Still holding her in his arms, he stood up and gazed down at her, passion flaring in his eyes. She pulled his head down for a heated kiss, and when it had ended he carried her into the bedroom. He set her down beside the bed and they hurriedly shed their clothing, stopping often to kiss and caress.

Then they climbed into bed together. Jason propped himself up on one elbow and reacquainted his free hand with the delights of her body. After a moment, he said softly, "You know, I'm gonna miss Wendy Wyoming."

"Oh yeah? Why's that?"

"She brought us together twice. It's a shame she had to die."

Melody drew circles on his broad chest with her palms, then clasped her hands behind his neck. "Oh, you never know about Wendy. She's bound to turn up again from time to time."

"You think so?" he asked, trailing kisses down the side of her neck.

She purred, "Oh, yeah, pardner. You keep on doing that and she'll be back. I can personally guarantee it."

* * * * *